The Queen of Xana

The Queen of Xana

FRED PILCHER

ISBN 10: 0-692-98896-3
ISBN 13: 978-0-692-98896-1
ISBN 978-0-692-07785-6 (ebook)

Contents

Prologue

This is a fictional work of political allegory sympathetic to the common people ahead of the fabulously wealthy. It is enlivened by elements of fantasy and occasional sexual activities.

Call me Traveler. I journey to seldom-visited corners of the world to immerse myself in ancestral cultures which are still alive and vibrant, before they become homogenized into our modern world with its instantaneous communication. I heard in one remote land a most remarkable story that had been meticulously preserved from ancient times, about one Queen Agatha. She had conquered an evil sorcerer and, striving thereafter to achieve prosperity for all her people, was much loved by them. All that is said about her has been handed down by word of mouth for many generations. I could find no written record. Whether Queen Agatha is a real historical character, a beautiful legend, or perhaps a real person whose story was embellished through centuries of retelling, I cannot say. But her story is a vital part of these peoples' cultural heritage. Different versions have evolved among the many storytellers. Here I have attempted to collect details of Queen Agatha's life that are found in several sources, in order to write them down in a single coherent story. Where two versions are both widely told, with details of her life different, I have presented both.

From time to time, where the stories may be incomplete or unclear, I have found it helpful to offer my own commentary. These explanatory passages are set out in distinct typography, like this preface.

No detailed description survives of Agatha's physical appearance. The sources are vague and often contradictory. At least in her younger decades, everybody considered her to be the most beautiful woman in the world, in both face and figure. Likely she was slightly shorter and more slender than the average woman in her land, but not greatly so. The hair on her head was either black or dark red, superbly arranged, and wavy. Her eyes were probably blue.

One term that all accounts use to describe her is 'naked.' Whether this meant that she was considered naked because she declined the accoutrements of wealth and wore plain dresses, clean and neat but unadorned, or that she wore no clothes at all, is not resolved. There is also general agreement that the people, including the queen, called their country not just Xana or the monarchy of Xana but rather the land of Xana.

Nowadays, we find the world's wealth increasingly concentrated in the possession of an ever smaller number of people, and people in ever increasing numbers find their routes to advancement blocked. Queen Agatha also grew up in such a society. She resolved to correct the imbalance by empowering the commoners rather than taking wealth from the privileged few. I believe the methods Queen Agatha used many centuries ago to distribute wealth and prosperity to everyone will also work in our age. Some readers may disagree. The consequent discussion and argumentation will enlighten all who participate.

Chapter 1

L ong ago in the faraway and mystical land of Xana, an auspicious royal birth occurred. Queen Julia gave birth to a healthy daughter, ensuring that the royal line would continue as monarchs of Xana. The midwives had completed all the birthing and clean-up tasks, and left Queen Julia alone with her baby in the small birthing room. Its only furnishings were a bed, a cushioned chair on which the queen rested, a table with some infant needs, and a torch on the wall opposite the chair. Clutching her suckling newborn to her breast, Queen Julia declared, "My sweet baby Agatha, you are all I have left. Your father, my dear Prince Consort Marcel, died five months ago with many other soldiers, in a great battle to protect you and our country. But, despite huge losses, our army repulsed the barbarians, and our land is safe for you to grow up in."

Queen Julia sensed that another person had entered the royal chamber undetected. She looked up to see standing before her an old woman, slightly plump, with white hair, a gray cloak, an almost unwrinkled face, and a sweet manner. "As you love your child," the old woman purred, "I grant her the gifts of wisdom and compassion. She can become the greatest monarch Xana has ever known."

"Who may you be to grant such gifts?" the queen demanded.

"I am Agatha's fairy godmother," the old woman replied. "But you must also do your part. Nurture her. Give her strength of character. Without this, wisdom and compassion alone are not sufficient to overcome the many challenges that will be thrown against her."

Queen Julia looked down at the tiny bundle now sleeping in her arms. When the mother again looked up, Agatha's fairy godmother had vanished.

Remembering the fairy godmother's pronouncement, Queen Julia summoned dignitaries both from her own land and visiting from afar. At her command, they assembled in the grand palace ballroom. Holding the infant Agatha cradled in her arm, the queen decreed, "I vow to all of you, I vow to the world: I will teach Agatha, the only child I will ever have, to be a great queen."

By the time Agatha was two years old, Queen Julia was taking her to all the great palace gatherings. She had taught the girl to curtsy to the many distinguished guests. At the age of three, Agatha was treating all of them with the utmost courtesy and giving everybody kind compliments. She had already learned that with such gracious behavior she could get people to do everything for her. Until her fifteenth year, Agatha's only duties were to attend to her education, look pretty, and behave properly at palace functions. Her first-year teacher was both kind and inspiring—a stroke of good fortune. She gave Agatha a love for learning, which provided the young girl with all the motivation she needed to continue her education. Agatha considered any book about the world outside the palace to be a doorway to enchantment. It has been suggested that between the ages of ten and fifteen Agatha read a complete book every day in the huge palace library, in addition to her teacher's regular assignments. This may be an exaggeration, but Agatha quickly learned how to select the books that provided the most useful information, summarize their contents, and store them forever in her mind.

Even when Agatha was a small child, the governing aristocrats and visiting foreign dignitaries at state receptions and banquets congratulated Queen Julia on her daughter's beauty, courteous and tactful behavior, and exemplary manners. Everyone marveled at how all of these qualities improved as Agatha grew up. By Agatha's eighteenth year, Queen Julia had seen how well her daughter charmed—even dazzled—the assembled guests. And so she put the princess in charge of palace entertainment. Agatha earned the trust and love of the commoners who served as cooks, servers, and cleaners. She greatly boosted their joy and efficiency in their work. Agatha considered this to be important preparation for the time when she would become queen.

Looking pretty and behaving properly were part of Agatha's basic nature. What others called duties, she considered pleasures, and Agatha's life up to age ten was an unending round of joy. At that age, she began to venture beyond the palace and the center of the capital city, and to read about the larger world. She was distressed to learn that people who lived beyond the palace did not share in the wealth and grandeur she had known all her life. As she saw more people living in wretched poverty, her anger grew at the wasteful extravagance in the palace. She became frustrated that she could not reduce the waste. She often dreamed about correcting this imbalance, and as she grew older she devised one scheme after another to achieve her dream. Many of her early schemes were wildly impractical, but they became more reasoned as she accumulated knowledge and experience.

By the time she was about fifteen years old, she spent most of the time not taken up by official palace obligations among the simple, honest people of her land. Beyond the elegant buildings near the palace, the houses were small, often poorly built. The paved and well-drained streets at the city's center degenerated farther away into dirt paths that stayed muddy long after rains ended. The people's clothes were often shabby, usually mended instead of replaced as they wore out. With every daily visit, Agatha was jolted again by their poverty, such a distressing contrast from the riches she knew in the palace. But she found the common people of the land to be friendly, and she greatly admired their handicrafts.

One day Agatha was walking through one of the town's impoverished sections when she heard shouting. In front of a tiny, tumbledown house, an elegantly dressed man demanded, "You owe me one thousand livres. Pay me, right now."

"I don't have one thousand livres," pleaded a man in a dirty brown shirt and breeches. "I have to sell my saddle before I can pay you."

The contrast between creditor and debtor could not have been greater. The creditor was short, stout, and bent over. The debtor stood tall and straight, displaying a dignity that even the most extreme poverty could not remove.

"Next week it's one thousand one hundred livres. I don't like to wait," the moneylender shouted.

Agatha recognized the moneylender as Furmal Glender. Of all the people who frequented the palace, Agatha considered him one of the meanest and most ill-tempered. She rushed right between the two combatants and pushed them apart. "Break it up," she demanded. "Now tell me what this is all about."

"You stay out of this, Princess," Glender retorted. "It's not your business."

"I just made it my business," Agatha declared. Turning to the debtor, she said, "Please tell me the real story."

"I am Alberto Sanichez, a maker of saddles. Not four months ago, I had to borrow five hundred livres to buy the leather, bolts, and everything else I need to make the saddle. The best price I can find for my saddle is one thousand two hundred livres. Now I have to pay most of it back to this moneylender. And then I'll need another loan. No matter how hard I work, I cannot get ahead. I can barely feed my wife and my son, Ricardo."

Glender raged on. "All right, Princess. You give me one thousand livres and I'll go."

"Where is the loan paper?" Agatha asked. "I insist that you sign it as proof of repayment."

"Always supporting the beggars," Glender grumbled. But he pulled out the loan paper, marked with an X by the apparently illiterate Alberto. Agatha pulled one thousand livres in gold from a small purse. Glender took it with a scowl. He signed the document and stomped away, muttering, "Well, I got my thousand livres. That's all that matters."

"Thank you, thank you, thank you," Alberto said. "Won't you please come in and let me show you the saddle?"

"I would love to," Agatha responded.

The main room's furnishings were plain but clean and neat. Agatha gazed past an old stove, a wooden cabinet, a table and a few chairs, and ragged curtains covering a single glass window. The saddle in a corner seized her attention. "Why, it's beautiful!" she exclaimed.

"I put a lot of loving care in making it," Alberto said.

"You keep your house so clean and neat." Agatha added, noticing a boy standing in the shadows. "And your son is a charming boy. Come to me, Ricardo."

Agatha held out her arms to the lad, who ran to her and climbed into her lap. He held a simple object in each hand. "This stick is a pretend horse," Ricardo told Agatha. "And this stone is a pretend saddle. Watch me saddle up my horse and take a ride." He put the stone on top of the stick, and put another stone on top of the first to represent the rider, and moved them all around.

"Could you please fetch me a horse, so we can ride side by side?" Agatha asked.

Ricardo leaped down, looked quickly around the dirt floor, and found another stick and stone for Agatha. She stood and picked up a second stone to represent herself riding her horse. The two of them raced their sticks round and round the room.

Even as she played with Ricardo, Agatha spoke to his father. "How much money do you need to buy all the materials and have enough left over to feed your family until your saddle is completed and ready for sale?"

"One thousand livres."

"I will give you one thousand livres to make another saddle. Please sell it for a good price. Then keep all the money so that from now on you can buy everything you need without ever again going into debt. Please, I do not want you to pay any of it back to me."

"Another one thousand livres? Do you really mean this is a gift? When I sell my next saddle, can I keep all the money I receive from the sale?" Alberto fell silent for a moment as he considered this astonishing news. "I'll never have to borrow money again! Oh, my dear princess, I can never thank you enough. I am overcome with joy at your generosity. Never in my life have I imagined such an opportunity."

"It is my gift," Agatha affirmed. "Every person should be able to keep the fruits of his labor."

As she was leaving, the son asked the father, "Is she really a princess? She's so much fun."

"And so very kind and generous," Alberto said. "Everything in our life is changed. I will forever be devoted to Agatha and her ideals."

But the next poor artisan she visited, a maker of candles, distressed Agatha greatly. As the princess entered, the man's wife clutched his arm. Their house, though clean, had very poor furnishings. And while the husband's clothes were shabby, the wife wore a new dress decorated with flowers of all colors.

"Five hundred livres!" he exclaimed excitedly. To his wife, he said, "Now I can buy you the fancy blue dress you always wanted. We can take a trip."

"Then you will have no money left over to buy the wax and cotton for your candles," Agatha chided him.

"We can always go back to the moneylender," he replied.

"And be as poor as ever," Agatha replied sternly. "Don't you understand? If you don't have to keep repaying the moneylender at such a usurious interest rate, you will soon have enough money of your own to buy both the dress for your wife and your wax and cotton."

"I don't understand," he replied.

"I am so looking forward to the dress," the wife exclaimed. "And this may be the only chance we'll ever have to travel."

Hand in hand, clutching the money that had just been bestowed on them, husband and wife rushed out of the house toward a clothing shop. That left Agatha at their front door, thoroughly disgusted.

"I saw their extravagance the instant I entered their house," she was heard to complain to herself. "Even people who can't afford it can be extravagant. Five hundred livres wasted. No use chasing them down and asking them to give it back. That's one bitter lesson to learn. Henceforth I'll give money only to people I'm confident will use it to create more wealth."

Two years after her first visit to Alberto Sanichez, Princess Agatha returned to his home. She was impressed to see both father and son wearing much finer clothes. The house had been freshly painted outside; inside, she noticed new furniture and decorations.

Ricardo, now grown six inches taller than when she had first seen him, came running to her. "Look at my horse," he proclaimed enthusiastically. Made of leather and about eight inches high, it was beautifully crafted. "My father has taught me leather working. See? He gave me two scraps from one of his saddles, and I made a horse for you, too." Ricardo fetched a second leather horse, identical to the first.

"Beautiful work," the princess said. "You will become a master craftsman just like your father."

Ricardo then produced a ragged boy doll and an even more ragged girl doll. "This is me," he said, placing the boy doll on a leather horse. "And this is you," placing the girl doll on the other horse. The doll looked more like a street urchin than a princess, but Agatha was delighted. "We ride together again," she proclaimed. As they pushed their horses side by side, Agatha made her horse rear up on his hind legs and make a whinnying sound. She made her horse jump over furniture and the other horse. And she turned him around and made him run backwards beside Ricardo's horse. Ricardo laughed with all his might.

But all the time Princess Agatha was playing with Ricardo, she was listening to his father. "Thank you, thank you," he said, "for paying off the moneylender. I have never again visited his vile shop. After I sold several saddles, I was able to give five hundred livres to John Siever. He is a boot maker and the most honest, upright man I ever knew. I made him promise he would never take out another loan."

"Wonderful!" the princess exclaimed. "I am delighted. I see you also had enough to buy new clothes and new furnishings for your house."

"My deepest thanks, my generous princess," Alberto continued. "I will never be poor again. And neither will my good friend John Siever."

After taking her leave from Alberto and Ricardo, Agatha visited John Siever for the first time. Though he instantly recognized her, she gave him the courtesy of introducing herself.

John immediately bowed deeply to the princess. With a trembling voice he replied, "I can never thank you and Alberto Sanichez enough." He continued, "I can begin making gifts myself. Your gift to Alberto has vitalized my life as much as his. I have a dream, that these small gifts to virtuous people can lift one family at a time out of the moneylenders' clutches and into comfort."

"It is more than my dream; it is my mission," the princess replied. "I am most grateful for your help to achieve this mission."

Princess Agatha was ever sensitive to the needs of these humble commoners. She would always be helpful to those in need. Others among the wealthy showed only contempt and scorn for the meager circumstances of the vast numbers of poor people. Agatha, for her part, admired the quality of their crafts and the cleanliness and neatness of their homes and simple furnishings. She gave them sincere praise. She encouraged those in despair. She played with their children. This delighted the parents, who saw how much their children enjoyed their frolics with the royal princess. From the vast royal treasury, she made small gifts to hardworking craftsmen who lacked the money they needed to make their wares. These gifts let them keep for themselves the modest wealth their labor brought them, instead of having to hand most of it to the lenders. She saw that each gift was paltry compared with the riches in the treasury, but that each tiny sum was a great boon to a humble artisan. Even as a young maiden, Agatha had grown skillful in assessing human character. After the hard lesson in the spendthrift candle maker's house, she resolved to give only to those who would put her gifts to useful work, building prosperity for themselves and their families. Her empathy alone boosted her people's spirits. Artisans, laborers, and merchants who had been blessed by her visits spread stories of her kindness throughout the land. For these many caring acts, Princess Agatha was beloved by the common people.

Agatha's grooming and demeanor were impeccable, but when in her people's sight, she displayed none of wealth's usual trappings, particularly costly jewelry and clothing. In most versions of the legend, she went about in a simple cotton peasant's dress, its colors faded, rejecting the lavish ornaments and brilliant dyes of the nobility. Her dress was said to be sleeveless, like those peasant women usually wore to free their arms for the routine drudgery of their household tasks. In other versions, Agatha wore no clothes at all. This display, both modest and blatant, was meant to show her rejection of the extravagance of the wealthy. She was naked among the common people and in the palace alike. By either account, Agatha truly was equally beautiful on the outside and the inside.

———

*A*ll that is told in the many stories indicates that ancient Xana was a gender-neutral society. Women and men enjoyed equal rights and privileges. Male abuse of women was virtually unknown. Philandering may have been frequent, but it was always between fully consenting adults, never involving coercion. It was acceptable for women to enter such traditional male occupations as construction, repairs, and manual crafts. Husbands assisted their wives in household tasks and child rearing, and wives often provided some assistance to their husbands in their craft shops or other work.

Ancient Xana was also an age-neutral society in which people of all ages were treated with respect. Children were privy to discussions of family affairs, required to assist with household chores and, as they grew up, in their parents' livelihoods. As in many ancient societies, children cared for their aged parents in their homes. Neither venerated nor discarded, the elderly lived in dignity. As long as they were able, they continued to work at their earlier occupations, though at a slower pace. If no longer able, their children selected simple but useful tasks at home to provide them with a sense of self worth. Their knowledge of *family history and the wisdom acquired from a lifetime of experience were valued by family and neighbors alike.*

———

The carefree life Princess Agatha had enjoyed as a small child seemed less idyllic as she grew up. Seeing with her own eyes how most of Xana's people lived without comfort made her appreciate the luxuries, great and small, she knew in the palace. But daily she grew more angry at the waste and frivolity of the palace routine. As much as she could while maintaining the dignity and decorum expected of the heiress to the throne, she turned away from the palace and its excesses to extend her love and devotion to the commoners, her people.

Agatha dreamed of a time that she would be able to make great changes, help more people find some comfort in their lives, and of the happy land she wished Xana to become.

And then the day arrived that Queen Julia would reveal a great secret. In the privacy of her bedchamber, she told her daughter how the fairy godmother had promised that Agatha would be the greatest monarch Xana had ever known. But the queen admonished her to tell no one else. In a flash, Agatha knew how she would use her promised greatness.

In the years before she came of age, she sat beside Queen Julia at the council meetings, learning how the kingdom's decisions were made and carried out. She began to perceive how her government might provide the means she could use to achieve her dream for her people. But at these times, great frustration would come to Agatha. Her early suggestions to improve the common people's lives were always met with nay-saying from Queen Julia or from one of her councilors.

On one occasion, Agatha had said, "I propose that we establish a system of making grants of royal funds to our craftsmen. This will unleash their creativity and support their production. The wealth they will create will benefit everyone."

An aristocratic councilor instantly snapped, "Can't do it."

Another declared, "Too radical."

Furmal Glender, whom Agatha especially despised, complained, "As if Agatha hasn't interfered too much already in my lending business. This will disrupt it completely. Tell Agatha to leave me and my business alone."

"It's called competition," Queen Julia advised Glender. "I would fail to fulfill my vow to make Agatha a great queen if she did not become better at business than you are."

Nevertheless, the council quickly and unanimously rejected Agatha's proposal.

In frustration and despair, Agatha opened her mouth, about to scream. But before she uttered a sound, she checked herself. She took a succession of slow, deep breaths until the first flash of passion subsided and she had collected her thoughts. And thus she learned a habit of behavior that served her well the rest of her days. The governing aristocrats' disdain for the commoners she could not change. Yet, when at last she became queen, her wishes would immediately become the law of the land. But she would find other circumstances beyond her control even as queen. No matter how dire her country's circumstances, she knew she must show that she could remain calm and confident, always inspiring confidence in her people.

As the princess bided her time and held her tongue, a senior council member implored of Queen Julia, "Can't we remove Agatha from the council? She wastes our time with notions that cannot be achieved."

Queen Julia replied, "Agatha is my only child. She is heiress to my throne. She must learn how to govern—and learn the limits of governing. With experience in this chamber, her youthful ideals will mature into an understanding of reality."

After the council meeting adjourned, Queen Julia scolded her daughter. "I do not like your spending so much time with the rabble, but I will not forbid it. Learning how to keep them under control, and profiting from business with them, is part of your education."

"Mother, they are not rabble," Princess Agatha protested. "They are honorable and creative people. They will return to our country many times the wealth we give to support them."

"No doubt a few of them make useful things."

Angrily, Princess Agatha interrupted. "All of them will if we give them the chance!"

Queen Julia put on the face of authority and lectured her daughter. "I and all of our ancestors have kept the land of Xana peaceful by maintaining strict control from above. You must know that a small group of enlightened governing people are the strength of our country. You will not be fully enlightened until you understand our duty to preserve the aristocracy's privileged position."

Agatha snorted, "Humph," and stormed out of the room.

Queen Julia truly desired prosperity for the land of Xana, but she lacked imagination enough to see beyond her circumstances. She was a product of the aristocracy. She sincerely entrusted the welfare, and the wealth, of her land to the people she knew best. And as she truly knew only the aristocracy, so she chose aristocrats as her advisers.

Princess Agatha, on the other hand, identified herself with the ordinary people. Bitterly disappointed again and again as her ideas were rejected, Agatha renewed her faith by returning to her people, the commoners. Her encouraging words, plus the small but carefully directed help she could offer, made their lives happier. Between her duties in the palace and her sojourns outside its walls, in a few short months Princess Agatha learned all the means of governing.

———

Princess Agatha loved to visit the wharves where the fishing folk brought their catch every afternoon. She talked their own homely language, and the fishermen and women in turn cooked her the most delicious fresh fish, for which she paid generously. "Better than the food in the palace," she told them. "Too bad there are so many state dinners I really must attend. I'd rather be dining with you."

One afternoon she heard a shouting match between a fisherman and a buyer bidding for his catch. "Hernando Franklin," the buyer roared, "I don't like your complaints. Everybody else accepts my bid, and no more. And you will, too."

Princess Agatha walked straight between them and commanded, "Settle down. Now tell me what this is all about."

Hernando Franklin explained, "Yesterday, Sebastian Malloy offered five livres for twenty pounds of fish. Today only four livres."

"That's the way it is," Sebastian asserted. "You take what I offer or your fish can rot on the dock and you get nothing."

"Stop cheating Hernando," the princess rebuked Sebastian.

"What are you going to do about it, Princess Agatha?" He uttered the last two words in a contemptuous tone. "You've really hurt some of my best friends' money-lending business, but you can't hurt *my* business. Go ahead. Offer twenty livres if you want. How are you going to carry all those fish to the market stalls, Princess?"

Several of the fishing folk had gathered to listen, and some of them wheeled up a large cart. "We'll pull them to market ourselves."

"Oh, no, you won't," Sebastian Malloy chortled. Several burly men stepped forward, each of whom grasped and roughly restrained one of the fishermen. "Princess Agatha, heiress to the throne," he continued derisively, "I have to let you do whatever you want. But not anyone else. Go ahead, pull the loaded cart all by yourself. I won't get in your way."

Princess Agatha tugged on the cart, but it was too heavy for her to move even one inch.

"You could carry one fish at a time to the stalls and give it away for all I care."

Princess Agatha knew that would take forever. She seethed with anger. The onlookers, seeing the rage in her face, stood and watched, curious how the princess would respond. Had this occurred a few months sooner, she might have thrown a very public tantrum. Instead, she fought to control herself, standing almost motionless for several minutes, taking slow, deep breaths.

Eventually she placed her hands on Hernando's shoulder. "I'm sorry, there is nothing I can do," she admitted. "Some year, I promise, I will end this cheating forever."

"Ha, ha, ha," Sebastian sneered. "Brave talk, no action. Will you go crying to Mama?"

Yet on this day, Princess Agatha already had sufficient strength of character to disregard Sebastian's insolence.

The next day Princess Agatha visited the fish market stalls in the city. "What?" she gasped. "He raised his price for twenty pounds of fish from twenty livres to twenty-five? That's not business. It's cruelty."

"What could I do?" the stall owner moaned. "It was pay his price or have nothing to sell."

———

At Agatha's birth, the fairy godmother instructed Queen Julia to nurture her daughter and give her strength of character. I suggest that the teenaged Princess Agatha gained her strength of character by defying her mother's political and economic system. Successful on a limited scale against the loan sharks, she failed completely to circumvent the middlemen in the marketplace. She would need all the strength she could muster when even greater and completely unexpected challenges arrived. As they would, very soon.

———

One day, Queen Julia told her daughter, "It is time for you to understand why our country cannot afford all the things you desire. I am introducing you to Hector Ramirez. He has no ambition whatsoever to acquire wealth for himself, and he lives very modestly. He is interested only in numbers. As my inspector of financial records, his job is to find mistakes in arithmetic and allocation of funds. He does not set policy, but he knows everything about our treasury. You will find him to be friendly and helpful. I have selected him to teach you the subject."

Hector's origin was uncertain. He may have been a minor aristocrat, or he may have been a commoner raised to high office by an aristocrat who recognized his genius at numbers and finance.

"My gracious princess," Hector told Agatha, "I am honored to be asked to explain our realm's finances. It is critical that we balance our budget and assure ourselves sufficient income to pay the many expenses of governing. If we allow ourselves to go into debt, the added burden of paying interest on the debt will prevent us from keeping our land safe and secure."

Perhaps carelessly, Agatha blurted out, "I understand. I have seen how the lenders take away all the profits our artisans earn from selling their creations."

"Dreadful, the interest rates they charge to poor people," Hector said, "knowing full well they cannot bear the cost. How much worse it would be if such a fate befell our whole country."

Agatha felt an emotional thrill. "Hector, you are the first person I've ever met inside the ruling inner circles who perceives the common people's wretched poverty."

Hector ignored her remark and went on. He delivered his speech like just another tutor's lecture—but what wisdom flowed from it. "Our first responsibility is to pay, equip, and train our soldiers well," he declared. "For many generations, our army has been the foundation of support for Xana's kings and queens. The expense is enormous, but it keeps secure your mother's position as queen of the land of Xana." He fixed Agatha with a steady gaze. "And your future position as her successor."

The young princess interrupted, showing the astute understanding she had already gained of her country's affairs. Now it was her turn to lecture the royal treasurer. "The army beckoned young men of every station who sought adventure and excitement. More important, it opened a road to advancement for commoners with ambition. The army treated the common people equally with volunteers from the aristocracy. Anyone who volunteered to serve five years or more—and did so capably for their first two years—was taught to read and write. They learned mostly military history and tactics, just as soldiers need. Soldiers of humble families could live much better in the army or the navy than they ever had before. Promotion came to those of ability, not of high social rank. The poorest street sweeper's son could aspire to become the army's commanding general. Some of them did. Every day of every soldier's service, they were reminded that they owed loyalty to the monarch. And in return they absorbed the unwritten understanding that the crown will pay and equip the army well. For generations, the army has remained faithful to the crown. Discontented young men were lured into the army, where they learned loyalty and discipline. And that is the reason the poor commoners have never risen in rebellion."

Hector nodded at these enthusiastic words. "I never thought of it that way before," he said. "But it makes good sense." He continued, "The army is just the first of the realm's obligations. Also, we have roads to keep in order, ships to build, a navy to sustain, and the proper rewards for high officials in the government and the palace. Many other things require funds, as well. In the months ahead, I will ask you to share with me the everyday keeping of accounts. You will learn by actual practice where our money comes from, and where we distribute it. It won't be quite like your tutors' assignments. It is training for your job. It will be work, hard work, for you. Are you ready?"

"Yes!" Agatha replied with a flourish. "This knowledge will be indispensable to me when the year arrives that I become queen. A responsible queen."

Hector continued as if she hadn't spoken, and as blandly as ever. "No one likes to pay taxes, and so many people have nothing from which to pay taxes. Our merchants' trade with foreigners brings some of the crown's wealth. If only we could get more income from trade, we could take less tax from our people and still provide for Xana's needs."

Agatha said very quietly, as if to assure herself she was really hearing this, "The other members of my mother's council want nothing except more money for themselves. Here is an honorable man who places our country's welfare above his own gain."

Then, without even thinking about it, Agatha spoke aloud. "I have read much of the world's history and have been especially impressed by a faraway island kingdom. There, an honest nobleman was outlawed by a usurper king and his lackeys. This noble outlaw robbed the rich and gave to the poor. I wonder if that is a good idea."

Hardly had she finished speaking when she recognized she had made a dreadful mistake. If Queen Julia or any of her other advisers heard her make such a subversive statement, unspeakable fury would descend upon her. Her mother might even find a way to disinherit her from succeeding to the throne. Might she, princess or not, even be outlawed herself?

Hector Ramirez's reaction told her he thought it was not a good idea. Rather than arguing with his princess or chastising her, he asked a simple question. "If we took all the wealth of the crown and the aristocracy and divided it equally among all of our people, how much would each receive? As a princess, you are privy to all the property evaluations and census numbers for the entire land of Xana. I can provide some guidance, but you will have to search the records yourself and calculate these sums to find the answer to your question."

Princess Agatha required several months to complete this task, when she could spare time from her duties as Hector's apprentice in accounting for the treasury's day-to-day transactions. She found that not even the vast wealth of the royal treasury and the aristocrats combined could alleviate the poverty of so many people.

"Only eighty-seven livres per person," Agatha complained to Hector. "Not enough to improve anyone's life enough to notice. I would never have believed you if you had just told me. Finding out for myself has been a revelation."

"As I had intended," Hector replied with his usual nonchalance.

Even during her time in the treasury, Agatha was no drudge. She did not spend all her time poring over accounts and records. Every day she spent a few hours among the commoners, giving them support and hope. One day, she visited the bazaar and spoke with its owner, Benjamin Hartly.

"What lovely products," Agatha exclaimed. "You seem to have everything. And the fruits and vegetables look delicious. But how can the people afford them?"

"It's a sort of balancing act," Benjamin replied. "For the more costly goods I need to charge richer people all the market can bear. That lets me keep prices of cheaper and necessary items within reach of poor people. But I still make a healthy profit.

I give most of that to my dear wife, Sylvia, for her charity to the genuinely destitute."

"So you and Sylvia really care about our great masses of people?"

"You would be shocked at how miserably poor some people are," Benjamin said, "most of them victims of circumstances beyond their control."

"Shocked, yes, saddened, yes," Princess Agatha replied. "But I've seen them, too, with my own eyes."

"My assistants, Francis, here, and Beowulf, can manage the bazaar capably—for a time—in my absence. Let me introduce you to Sylvia. She is a gem, possessed of both compassion and superb talents at organizing. I'm sure you'll like her."

Benjamin escorted Agatha into their small but handsome home.

"Sylvia, darling, this beautiful young lady is none other than Princess Agatha."

Sylvia replied, "All over the city the people are calling you an angel of kindness and compassion. I am so pleased to meet you at last. Welcome to our humble home."

Though the house was small, Agatha complimented her enthusiastically on its furnishings and appointments. "And your dresses: how stylish! I am sure you could afford more, but these seem to be your only luxuries."

"I love beautiful things," Sylvia replied. "But we must not be extravagant or it will interfere with our mission to the poor."

As she spoke, an emaciated man in rags appeared in the doorway. "Please, my lady. My wife and daughter haven't had anything to eat for two days. Can't you please help us?"

"Can you do a job for me?"

"Oh, yes, yes. Just feed my family," the man said, "and I'll do anything."

"Go to Manuel's, two blocks that way." Sylvia came to the door and pointed. "Then turn right for two more blocks. You can really help me by delivering to the palace's back door several loads of Manuel's bricks."

"Oh, thank you, thank you," replied the man. He scurried off to attend to his assigned errand.

"My darling Sylvia's genius is at managing people," continued Benjamin. "She can always find a place in her group where people can help others."

Another man sidled up to the door. "I'm hungry. Please, can you give me some food?"

"Yes, we can help. I have several loads of secondhand clothes that I want you to bring here; then we'll give them to people who have nothing decent to wear."

The man grimaced. "That sounds like a lot of hard work."

"Of course it is. I can't do it all myself. Help yourself by helping others."

"Awww," he groaned.

Silvia drew herself up and gave the man a peremptory wave. "I have no sympathy for loafers," she declared. "Goodbye."

With no answer for that, the man slunk away.

Benjamin wrapped his arms lovingly around his wife. She returned the gesture. "Isn't Sylvia a gem?" Benjamin stated this more as fact than question.

"You two really do love each other," Agatha said.

"We certainly do," Sylvia replied. "We are a wonderful team, each a complement to the other. Benjamin brings in the money.

I distribute it, carefully, where it will do the most good for the most needy. We are absolutely faithful to each other." She gave her husband a fond look. "So much better than philandering around like so many people we know."

Agatha paused to consider that.

"I've read all about marital infidelity in the history books," she said. "Lying together is necessary to have children. All evidence says carnal lust is very strong, and it corrupts. Just like the lust for money and power. I have read about events in history where wanton copulation destroyed whole kingdoms."

Sylvia replied, "We can see all around us how vexing is the search for new partners, how its rewards usually are not as imagined, and how sorrow follows. But for me and Benjamin, fidelity every night is beautiful. It relaxes us after the day's troubles. We both know what each other likes, and how to satisfy each other. And then we go to sleep in each other's arms."

"I would never lie with anyone except Sylvia," Benjamin declared.

Agatha was astounded. "This, ah, fidelity to each other isn't found in our books, either history or literature. Your devotion to each other, and to the land's poorest people, has opened a whole new world for me." The princess pondered this a moment. "I wish," she declared, "for you to serve on the queen's council of advisers. She must hear other voices than those of the selfish old aristocrats."

"Please, no," Sylvia replied. "That would call attention to our charity. And those same aristocrats would make it more difficult for us to serve so many people whose need is great. But Princess," she continued, "I need not hold any office to advise you in person. And when the day comes that you become queen, I will be proud to serve on your council."

"More than an adviser," the young princess replied. "For the first time in my life I have found in you a worthy model to emulate."

———

To understand the next scene, I should explain that Xana's people did not have the hang-ups about sex and nudity that prevail in most of our modern world. They considered sexual expression and the human body, especially a woman's body, to be wholesome and beautiful. While sexual intercourse was properly conducted in privacy, after passing puberty, many women, especially among the aristocrats, wore nothing but their jewelry and perhaps sandals when walking outdoors. Public nudity was, however, entirely voluntary. Some of the less beautiful young women, and some few others, chose not to follow this practice.

Reverence for the female body by both men and women was strongly entwined in Xana's culture and history. Several sources agree that nearly all of the land's young women, aristocrats and commoners alike, made great effort to care for their bodies and faces. Visitors from abroad agreed: Xana's women were exceptionally beautiful. Central to their culture was the concept that a woman's beauty on the outside symbolized her beauty on the inside: pure of heart and noble of deed. The most noble and revered of all a woman's deeds was to use her body to make a new life. Everyone in Xana knew, of course, that a man's seed was also needed to start that life. It was into her body that the man must immerse a part of himself, and that coupling brought fabulous pleasure to both man and woman. The nurturing in the womb was the great gift that the woman alone could give.

In one of Xana's grandest traditions, upon coming of age, young ladies of great wealth would be presented naked before dignitaries in the palace's grand ballroom. They were granted the same honor and respect as are women in our society in their formal dresses. To be sure, many of Xana's aristocratic young ladies were probably greedy and materialistic, jealous of anyone they perceived to be ahead of themselves; in short, not at all beautiful inside. But in social gatherings, all behaved with the grace and politeness they had been taught. Among the commoners, the practice of female public nudity was much less frequent. Even so, some of the more ambitious daughters of city merchants or prosperous farmers would display their naked beauty in hopes of winning a husband with greater wealth.

It must be emphasized, however, that by presenting herself naked, a woman was not issuing a sexual invitation. Men, especially aristocrats, courted women of their own class by treating them with great courtesy and kindness. Xana's people knew a special set of signals to use as sexual overtures, but these were not used carelessly. A woman would not give such signals to a suitor until she was confident of his kindness and his devotion to her.

Thus, the suggestion in the legends that Queen Agatha may have presented herself naked before her people is not as preposterous as it may seem to us so many centuries later. Queen Agatha would have been equally honored as monarch and revered by her people whether or not she wore clothes. Where all the stories agree is that she truly was beautiful both inside and outside. After a careful comparison of the legend's different versions, I consider it less likely, though not impossible, that Agatha did present herself naked in public. If she did appear naked, I believe it to have been a rejection of the expense of extravagant clothing. Where appropriate, I will present Agatha both as clothed and as naked. I leave to you, dear reader, as you form mental images of the scenes about which you read, to decide whether to picture a clothed or a naked queen.

———

A grand party was prepared for Princess Agatha's twentieth birthday, at which she would be officially proclaimed heiress to the throne. On this day, Queen Julia had invited all the aristocrats of the land, foreign ambassadors, and even kings and queens from other lands to her huge royal palace's grand ballroom. The ballroom was decorated in a dramatic fashion that reflected the state of the realm. The walls were hung with colorful paintings and tapestries. Some showed armored soldiers in epic battle scenes. Others presented ladies, many of them naked and being courted by gaudily dressed dandies, in sensuous outdoor scenes or against elegant indoor backgrounds. Dramatic statues of beautiful naked ladies and battle-ready soldiers added depth to the grandeur. The contrast between the prevailing peace within the realm and the violence needed every few decades to preserve Xana's peace was dramatized in art and sculpture.

Queen Julia possessed a regal dignity that would have commanded respect even without the rich purple gown she wore. She presided from the center of a grand table in the shape of a horseshoe, around which were seated one hundred high-ranking men and women in equal numbers. All those attending were dressed with the greatest elegance and draped with costly jewelry. Jewelry may have been all that some of the more beautiful younger women wore.

As arranged, Princess Agatha herself sat inconspicuously at one side of the room, awaiting the queen's formal announcement before she would take her place as heiress beside the monarch. Although the festivity was in her honor, the princess fumed at the senseless extravagance. A dignified celebration could have been held, she knew, without wasting enough money to give a hundred poor craftsmen the means to carry out their business, free of the moneylenders' clutches.

No one paid attention to a tall, slim figure, in a yellow robe and a conical hat decorated with large black stars, standing in the middle of the room. A few noticed a menacing scowl on his face. But all eyes turned to him when he bellowed, "I am Magi and my sorcery is all powerful." Whether he materialized out of thin air or used sorcery so a simpler entrance went unnoticed, none can say. He extended his arms toward Queen Julia. From his fingers shot a ball of fire the size of a clenched fist. It flew straight toward Queen Julia and hurled her body—instantly lifeless—to the floor. All the domestic and foreign nobles gasped in horror. Soldiers stationed at the room's entrances drew their swords and rushed toward Magi. The sorcerer whirled around, arms extended, and the soldiers fell flat on their backs, unconscious. With none left to threaten him, he proceeded to cast spells, causing the fine jewelry and furs to fly off the aristocrats and onto his own person.

Chaos gripped the room. Some guests screamed; some ran aimlessly; some tried to hide under the tablecloths. A few of the more resolute headed toward one of the doors on each of the room's four sides.

Magi's attention was diverted as he gathered from the tables every rare vase and priceless drinking cup that had been arranged for the meal. Several alert courtiers hustled Princess Agatha out of the room. The princess, shocked and confused, let herself be led. She felt rather than understood the need to flee to safety, and ran with the courtiers through the maze of palace corridors. What she was certain of, however, was that a monstrous evil had been let loose and would inflict immense suffering upon her people.

Her mother had not interfered in her "business" of granting money to talented craftsmen and craftswomen. The princess had freed an ever increasing number from financial bondage to the lenders. Now the royal treasury she had drawn upon was being stolen by Magi. When this sorcerer had depleted the palace's riches, Agatha knew he would rob the very people she had helped. All her achievements were being lost.

And so, having now taken the wealth of the aristocrats as Agatha had feared, Magi went forth from the palace. In the weeks to come, he pillaged and plundered food and valuables from all the people of the land. His evil spread disease and famine.

Princess Agatha had been hidden in a dingy, distant room, in the hope that Magi could not find her there. That she herself was likely safe gave her no solace. Whether or not her mother had been killed, she felt a solemn duty to protect her people. But the catastrophe that had befallen her land had left her feeling helpless—and hopeless. How could she protect anybody from the powerful sorcery she had witnessed?

Into the secret hiding place came her fairy godmother. "I cannot alone undo what Magi has done, but I can protect you," the kindly old lady declared. "Magi can do you no harm. To you alone I can give the power to overcome him.

"Magi has also destroyed the kingdom of Wan," the godmother explained. "The crown prince of Wan, Olaf, survives. Olaf will come to you, but he cannot identify himself to you. If he does, all is lost for both the land of Xana and Wan. You must choose him correctly on your first try from among all the many young men who aspire to become your prince. This you must do using only your intuition and your ability to read people. You will not get a second chance. When you make love to Olaf, Magi will be destroyed and his evil banished from the world. If you make love to anyone else before Olaf, Magi's evil spell will last forever."

Agatha remembered the stories her mother had told her, stories of the blessings she had received at birth. She would need all the greatness her fairy godmother had promised and all her understanding of human character to protect her people. That would be her mission until she could find Olaf, and then she would rebuild whatever remained of her realm. Her fairy godmother's pronouncement had given her a spark of hope. She resolved to meet the challenge head on. She would lead her people through all the agony Magi inflicted and defeat him. Then she would finally fulfill her vision of prosperity for even the humblest of her people.

Agatha ran back through the palace corridors. All of the costly furnishings and decorations had disappeared, looted by Magi. Only a few trinkets remained, scattered in disarray. The palace was also empty of people. It looked as if it had been deserted for many years. At last, Agatha reached the grand ballroom to find all the table settings, statues, and tapestries removed, with only a few cheap utensils remaining on the tables. And she found her mother lying alone on the floor in an otherwise deserted room. Until now, she had hoped Queen Julia had only been knocked unconscious. Finding her body cold and clammy, with no pulse or breath, Agatha knew her mother was truly dead.

Agatha burst into tears. "Why," she sobbed, "couldn't you have lived another few years? I know we could have reconciled and ruled the land of Xana side by side. We could have brought prosperity to everyone." Agatha wept again. Then she promised, "I will give you a dignified royal funeral and burial."

But she would need help from the palace staff. She started searching the building for anyone who might have stayed behind. At last she found a kitchen custodian named Hebert hiding in a closet. "Queen Julia has been murdered," she declared. "I need you to help me bury her."

Agatha saw the look of shock on his face. After several seconds, he bowed deeply. "You are now my queen. I am your obedient servant, Queen Agatha."

"I am not worthy of being called queen while the sorcerer Magi is ravaging our people. I promise you—I promise myself—that I will find my prince. United, we will send Magi forever away from our land of Xana. But our first duty is to bury Queen Julia. Please help me find some more people to carry her coffin."

Eventually they found two more men, palace menials. Agatha led the three servants to the room bearing the gilded coffin that had long ago been prepared for Queen Julia. Magi had stripped it of its silver and gold ornamentation, but the coffin itself was still secure. The four of them carried the coffin to the grand ballroom and gently laid the queen's body inside.

Funeral services were short and simple in the culture of Xana. Agatha repeated the brief ritual she had memorized years earlier. "We thank you for sharing your life with us. We thank you for your passing through and for enriching our lives as you passed. We now commend you to the Great Unknown. May you travel into your unknown with courage and kindness." Agatha then closed the coffin lid.

Agatha was strong. She and the three male commoners became the pallbearers—Agatha herself on the front right corner—who carried the coffin to the royal cemetery. Shovel in hand, she dug as hard as the others for two hours, laid the coffin into the pit, and spent another hour covering the coffin with dirt and then smoothing the ground. She knew her royal duty on this occasion was to bury the queen, to lay her mother to rest, but all the time her thoughts were on the commoners outside. The burial now complete, with the dignity a queen required, Agatha hurried out of the palace. She feared she would find great suffering, and prepared to comfort her people as much as her strength would allow.

Chapter 2

In the kingdom of Wan, Prince Olaf sat idly on his murdered father's throne. The prince was of only medium height, though somewhat taller than Princess Agatha. He had a broad, powerfully muscled chest and narrow waist. His jet-black hair was immaculately combed, his eyes were soft brown, and his clean-shaven face had a robust look of authority that, sadly, his mannerisms did not match. His surroundings also did not match his position. All the elegant furniture and wall decorations that had once graced his throne room, even the cushions on his great chair, had been looted by Magi. Into this dispiriting setting came several of his closest companions. Angry, one of them demanded, "You have the finest education in the kingdom. You know not only our history, but also all the world's history. Yet you sit here and do nothing while the sorcerer plunders and pillages our people, violates our women, and brings disease and famine to all of us."

"What can I do?" Olaf lamented. "I never read anything about events in history like what is happening here, nor did my father tell me what I should do when this happens. We're all powerless."

"You never had any interest in ruling a country, nor do you care about people." The companion, made bold by disaster, went on to tell his prince to his face what everybody knew, to tell him what nobody before had dared to say: "You care only for your own selfish pleasures."

"To pursue the manly arts of horsemanship, hunting, jousting, swordsmanship, and archery is noble for a prince," Olaf retorted. "Not one of you can defeat me with a sword, and I can hit more distant targets with my arrows than any of you."

"You cannot defeat Magi with a sword, nor kill him with all your arrows."

"I know all that, and I'm sorry."

"He's sorry," someone chided. "He's sorry only for himself."

"Unlike most of you," Olaf said, stung by their harsh words, "I have not embraced the negative manly arts of drinking, gambling, and womanizing. I remain pure for my true love, whenever and wherever I might find her." His voice now barely a whimper, he concluded, "What would you have me do?"

"He doesn't know. He's not fit to rule."

"Don't you castigate your ruler," Olaf snapped. But again he pleaded, "What would you have me do?"

"Go to the oracle," someone suggested.

"No one's gone to the oracle for five hundred years," Olaf said.

"You don't have any better suggestion?"

Olaf acquiesced. "Very well, then. We shall visit the oracle."

Soon Olaf and his companions were mounted. For one long day they rode into the countryside, traveling thirty miles before they reached a small stone pavilion. Here lived the oracle, behind pillars more massive than needed to hold up the roof. Before the front door lay a large stone terrace surrounded by meticulously trimmed trees. The oracle herself, wrinkled and bent over, leaning on a cane, hobbled slowly toward her visitors. Her withered form said otherwise, but she might have been Agatha's fairy godmother in disguise.

Fixing the prince with her gaze, the oracle decreed, "Olaf, Crown Prince of Wan, follow Magi when he travels to the land of Xana. There you will see the noble Princess Agatha locked in a desperate struggle. She fights to protect her people from ravages even worse than you have seen in Wan. But you must not make yourself known to her, or all is lost for goodness in our world. Behave like a man worthy to be called a prince, and she will know you. Your love for one another will conquer the evil of Magi and restore her land and yours."

Selfishness still ruled Olaf's heart. He asked, "My true love? A princess?"

"The oracle says you must behave as one 'worthy to be called a prince,'" one of his companions admonished him. "What have you ever done for anyone but yourself? Nothing that a princess would admire."

All his companions heard and saw how Olaf had been humiliated within the oracle's hearing.

"Yours only if you behave in a manner worthy of a true prince," the oracle declared. With a thump of her cane on the flagstones, she shuffled back inside her dwelling.

———

Though nothing in Prince Olaf's training had prepared him for this crisis, he understood his mission: he must make himself known to Princess Agatha without revealing his true name or station. Almost immediately after he stepped ashore in Xana, a wretched-looking boy came to him, crying out, "I'm so hungry. Do you have any food?"

Olaf hesitated. The boy continued, "Please."

Olaf reached into his rucksack and gave the boy some food. The boy replied with a polite "Thank you." Other boys, seeing this, flocked to him, also begging for food. Olaf, in what may have been his life's first kind act, gave them all his food. He turned his bag and his pockets inside out to show them they were empty.

Olaf searched through the city, wondering how he was to find Princess Agatha. Could he even recognize her? Everywhere he saw unhappy people. From the shadow of the palace to the desolate market square, he went up one lane and down another alley. Hours later, his feet sore and his stomach growling, he came to a back street even poorer than those he had already traversed. There he spied a young woman of great beauty. The more he watched, the more he saw that her spirit also set her apart from everyone else. He fell in love with her at first sight. Desperately, Olaf hoped this was Princess Agatha, about whom the oracle had spoken. She was giving a drink of water to an older woman whose face glowed red with fever. She held a wet rag to the sick woman's forehead. A man nearby handed her some oddly shaped leaves and said, "Princess Agatha, here are the Leaves of Healing." The princess—for indeed she was the princess—placed the leaves in the sick woman's mouth and offered her more water. With a sweet voice, she encouraged the woman. "Here. Chew on these leaves. They're good medicine for fever. They will make you feel better."

Having heard the man call her by name, now Olaf was sure. Henceforth, he was hopelessly smitten with a terrible craving for the princess. He admired both her beauty and the almost super-human strength and compassion she showed in devoting herself to easing her people's suffering. At the next instant, a vision came to Olaf. It might have been sent by the oracle, or by Agatha's fairy godmother. Or it could have been something conjured from his mind's deepest recesses. "Admire her only from a distance. If you reveal yourself to her, you and she will both die instantly. Let your princess identify you by your acts." Prince Olaf at last truly accepted that he, too, must spend his days caring for Agatha's people.

Many of Agatha's people understood the story of the fairy god-mother's prophecy, at least in part. This arose from Agatha's state-ment to Hebert, "I promise you—I promise myself—that I will find my prince. United, we will send Magi forever away from our land of Xana." A well-to-do farmer named Elias came to the prin-cess, inflamed with desire to experience her body's sweetness, with or without her consent. By so doing, he hoped to acquire wealth and prestige and become her prince. His lustful look and manner infuriated Agatha. She put her hands on her hips and glared at the impertinent farmer. Ashamed of Agatha's anger, he wilted. "I confess," he pleaded. "I sought your special favors."

Agatha demanded, "Promise you will never again try to de-base me and that hereafter you will work with me to relieve our people's suffering."

"I promise," Elias stammered. Despite his presumption, he knew well what Agatha had done, and understood what she had asked of him. After a pause, he pledged to change his ways. "I shall provide food from my own farm and other farms," he said. "I shall keep accounts and expect to be paid for all the food, but until our land has recovered, I will not ask for payment."

During these dark days while Prince Olaf first secretly watched Agatha, another person assisted her most ably. That was Sylvia Hartly, the bazaar owner's wife. Even with provisions scarce and people starving, Sylvia and Elias managed to find some food. Many died. And yet Sylvia and Elias together saved the lives of thousands. To Agatha, every life was precious.

Even after all the years Agatha had spent with the common folk, Xana's population was far too large for her to know them all. Those unknown to her included even many who attended to the sufferers alongside her. Soon after Elias had joined her, there came a man Agatha did not know. Unlike most of the suffering people, he was clean, neat, and well-groomed, but he wore the clothes of a commoner. He said, "I am your prince, come to rescue all of Xana." What this man did not know was that Agatha had a rare gift of perception. Almost instantly, she saw the true character of everyone she met.

"You are not," Agatha snapped. In her anger, she demanded, "Confess, apologize, and promise you will never again try to deceive me. Then show me by your actions that you care more for our suffering people than for your selfish lechery." The man, pale with embarrassment, did all that Agatha required of him.

At night, Agatha returned to the luxury of the palace to sleep. On the very first night, Magi came to her, ravenous with lust. "My pretty one," he murmured to her, "come lie with me." He cast a spell meant to render a woman helpless, unable to fend off his advances. Lights flashed, but the spell failed. "Damn you," roared Magi. "Give me a fuck." He drew on all his malignant powers and cast one spell after another, each more powerful than the one before. None had its expected effect. Magi flew into a rage. He uttered a torrent of the vilest obscenities Agatha had ever heard. Abandoning his sorcery for the moment, he tried to use his manly strength to force himself upon her. He found his approach blocked by an unseen wall conjured by the fairy godmother's magic, even more powerful than his own. Yet on every night to come, he would try again to have his way with Agatha. And every night he would fail.

Each time he was thwarted, however, he took a terrible revenge. On that first night, roaring like a lion, he stomped out of Agatha's bedchamber and out the palace gate. Every night, he would use his spells to break open one commoner's home after another until he found a lovely young wife inside. His spells first stripped her naked, then rendered her unable to resist his assault. The husband, also helpless, was forced to watch. Magi roughly pawed her breasts and genitals. As he violated her and injected his seed, Magi reveled in her cries of anguish. In this manner, before the night was done, he ravaged more young women, all in full sight of their husbands or fathers, whom he had rendered unable to protect them. And he repeated this wicked sequence of assaults, night after night. As he ravaged his victims, Magi took care to inflict no lasting physical harm. He wanted to keep them beautiful for the next time he violated them. Yet, for all his magic, Magi's vile seed proved powerless. None of his rapes ever made a new life. None of his victims would give birth to the sorcerer's bastard offspring. But all these women suffered; all were bruised in spirit.

The most beautiful lady in all the land—Princess Agatha, whom Magi craved above all the rest—he could not touch.

The roiling anger born of this frustration perpetually tormented the sorcerer.

Agatha chose not to use the palace's huge main gate, but went in and out through a small side door. There, in the morning, she met Magi's first victim and her husband.

"It was horrible!" the young woman screamed, clutching at Agatha. "I couldn't stop him. I've always been faithful to my husband. Now he insists that I've been violated, and he can never love me again." In her anguish, she laid her head on Agatha's shoulder and bawled. Agatha wrapped both her arms around the wailing wife.

Agatha turned to the husband, a question in her eyes. He scowled and complained, "But she was violated. Soiled. I… I…" The husband's voice broke. He stood silent, trembling. Tears welled into his eyes, too.

"If you soil a dress," Agatha replied, "you do not throw the dress away. You cleanse the dress. Your love will cleanse your wife. Now, at the worst time of her life, she needs your love more than ever. Did she yield willingly? You know she did not. For you she is still pure."

"You think she is?" the husband asked. For the first time, a note of hope sounded in his voice.

"I am sure she is," Agatha insisted. "I can feel your love for your dear wife. Love can always prevail over evil. Show her how much you still love her."

"But…" He looked at his wife. "How can I ever lie with you again?"

"You not only can; you must," said Agatha. "Please, for all of us, do this. Cleanse your wife with your unconditional love. Don't just tell her; show her how much you still love her."

The husband stammered briefly, then, sobbing, threw his arms around his wife. "Elise, I love you."

Agatha joined their embrace, placing one arm around each. And in that embrace, she felt a change. "Your love is restored," she told them. "Please, forgive yourself for ever doubting her fidelity, and then, slowly, you will make the pain go away."

Every morning, Magi's victims from the night before flocked to the little side gate. And every morning Agatha gave them comfort. So soothing was her care and understanding that many went away with their hurt completely healed. To all she met, Agatha gave inspiration, sustaining them in these, their darkest days. Knowing well the palace's hidden chambers, she was able to find remnants of its once-vast wealth—scant treasure that Magi had overlooked. She gave these remnants to people who needed them most.

———

I have found only three direct references to Magi in the oral tradition. These include his appearance in the grand ballroom, his carnal lust for Agatha and other beautiful young women, and one other scene to be described later. I presume that he otherwise appeared before the people only rarely, and then to terrorize them with his vivid and destructive sorcery. Early on he probably infected people, animals, and crops with contagious disease and then let the disease run its course. After looting the homes of the aristocrats, he found few other items costly enough to interest him. I suspect he spent most of his time gloating over his stolen treasures as a pirate might spend his time admiring the stolen riches in his treasure chest.

———

Of the many acts of care and support Agatha gave to her people every day, only a few have survived the ravages of time. This account reveals much of her character. A young mother came to her, crying, "My milk has dried up. My baby is starving." Agatha looked at the little bundle nestled in the mother's arms, so weak as to barely whimper.

"Find a wet nurse," Agatha called out to the many people standing nearby. "All of you, go out and search. Somebody find a wet nurse."

"There is hardly a nursing woman left in our land," someone declared.

The farmer Elias was nearby and proposed another way. "Search the farms for a goat with a kid. This child can suckle the goat. My own farm is too far away, but I know many closer to here. I'll send couriers to all of them."

Four hours later a farmer arrived with a goat. Trailing it was a newborn kid. Agatha picked up the baby, but a glance told her it was too late. "The baby is dead," Agatha cried out.

"Please forgive me," the farmer pleaded. "I came as fast as I could."

"We must all forgive each other in these bad times," Agatha answered. Then she burst into tears. She knelt on the ground, lifted her arms in the air, and looked to the sky. "I promise," she yelled as loudly as she could, "this tragedy will never happen again."

But, soon after making her promise, uttered in raw anguish, Agatha recognized she could not fulfill it. Not directly.

But Elias had another thought. "Way outside the city at my farm, Magi's evil spells have little effect. I can feed and lodge at least ten nursing mothers."

The farmer with the goat and kid spoke up. "I can house two more. And I have farmer friends who can also help."

"What a wonderful idea," Agatha said. "But we must move the mothers stealthily so Magi will not notice. And let us also take pregnant women to the countryside." And so it was that this stratagem saved hundreds of precious babies.

The next morning, Agatha saw the bereaved mother sitting alone, weeping. She grasped the poor woman by the shoulders and lifted her to her feet. "Please," Agatha implored her, "you do yourself no good bemoaning your great loss. I, too, have suffered. Before my eyes, the sorcerer murdered my mother out of pure meanness."

Agatha paused for several seconds while the shock registered in the woman's eyes. Then she continued, "It hurts badly. My mother is as irreplaceable to me as your child is to you. But I must not allow myself to lapse into self-pity and inaction. All of Xana's people are hurting. I will feel far better, and my people will, too, by doing all I can to ease their suffering. Please, come with me. Share your loss with others and console them, that the healing will begin."

Under her fairy godmother's protection, Agatha herself never wanted for food. She never ate in the sight of her hungry people. She understood that to be able to serve them, she must stay strong. Each morning, in the privacy of her palace chamber, she broke her fast with a meal she cooked herself. Through every long day she went without food, but after sunset, again behind the palace walls, she cooked herself a nourishing supper. While the common people could not see her at these times, she could not hide herself from

Magi. Most nights he was nearby, leering and lusting after her. He uttered an incessant torrent of vile remarks about her breasts and her genitals and what he wanted to do with them. Such talk vexed Agatha, but she knew he could not act on his lechery. After a few days, she was able to ignore him completely.

Every day, from dawn to dusk, Princess Agatha was with her people. Immense was her pain as she saw more of them die each day. In her mind was the fairy godmother's prophecy, and the knowledge that she could not save any of them until she identified Prince Olaf and coupled with him. But she did not know that foreign prince, and did not know how she might come to know him. Many men offered themselves to her using many stratagems, but Agatha recognized their falsehoods. She delayed, even as her people suffered and died, knowing that if she mistook anyone else for the real Prince Olaf, the suffering and dying would never end.

Dressed as a poor peasant, Prince Olaf now spent his days near Agatha, but not so near as to be noticed. Having now resolved to behave like a true prince, he emulated her caring acts as best he could. He dared not look at her very often. Agatha's beauty, together with his love and fervent desire for her, would reduce him to complete helplessness. That was most so in the version of the legend that had Agatha naked, allowing Olaf to admire not only her face but also every inch of her ravishingly beautiful body. Unfulfilled love tortured him all day long, day after agonizing day. To his credit, he endured.

One day, Agatha was on a muddy street. Wooden shacks, their paint long since peeled away, crowded on both sides, all the more decrepit-looking by being within sight of the palace. Despondent commoners crowded the street, but Agatha was especially saddened when she saw a family that had been cruelly stricken. A poor peasant was crying profusely over a beautiful young blonde-haired woman. Agatha could see she was very sick and dying. Five starving children huddled nearby. The peasant had black curly hair, and must have been a strong, handsome man before Magi came. Now, his face wrinkled in agony, he looked years older than his likely true age. "Why," he asked, "is my beloved Betsy being taken from me? And my children have had no food for two days. I am just a poor crippled glassblower who never hurt anyone." He tried to stand up, but was badly bent over. He could barely walk, his limp was so pronounced.

"I know you are an honorable and honest man," Agatha said. "Who may you be?"

"Pedro Mendez."

Agatha lifted Betsy onto her lap and cradled her in her arms. The desperately ill young woman could barely speak. "My children and my husband need me," she said, whispering hoarsely. "I cannot afford to die and leave them all alone."

"No, I will not let you die," Agatha promised. "I will find a way."

Agatha had made this promise to many other people, and far too often had been unable to keep it. Agatha glanced up at the distant palace wall. Atop the battlements stood Magi, as if to proclaim to all the people below, "I rule this land, and I destroy it," casting his evil spells far and wide.

Agatha also noticed, not far away, a young man in shabby brown clothes and worn-out boots comforting a crying little boy and his mother. She had seen this man many times before, but never near enough for a good look at his face. Yet she perceived from his actions that he was an honorable man.

Agatha knew that her time was running out. She must make her desperate gamble, and make it soon. If she made the right guess now, she could save Pedro's family. If she guessed wrong, then Pedro's family, along with the rest of her people, were lost. Or, she reflected, she could wait, and though Pedro's family would surely all die, she might still save hundreds of thousands when she became more confident that she had correctly identified her prince. In her heart, though, she knew she must risk everything for Pedro's family. For if not for them, then for whom?

And so Agatha chose to trust her heart. Gently, she returned the dying Betsy to her husband's arms. Agatha stood, back straight, pulling herself up to her full, regal height. And turning to the shabbily dressed young man, she strode boldly toward him. Before he could back away to keep his accustomed distance from her, she looked into his eyes and spoke. "My sweet prince, come lie with me."

Agatha watched him carefully to gauge his reaction. If he showed surprise, then he had not expected the offer and was not the prince. Protected from all harm by her godmother's powers, she could safely renege on her invitation.

Instead, the man's face showed excitement such as Agatha had never before witnessed. In some versions of the legend, Agatha was already naked. As the story was told by others, she cast off her peasant dress and presented herself naked, an offering for all her prince's desires.

The crowd on the narrow street watched silently. Out of reverence for their beloved princess, they kept their distance. Nobody pushed in close from a lewd desire for a better view. In Xana's culture, everyone's first coupling was a defining moment in their lives. The people also knew full well that this defining moment in their princess's life might well be one for all of them.

Both Olaf and Agatha were virgins. Olaf knew nothing of lovemaking. Agatha, on the other hand, had been taught well by her mother. The young princess knew how to please a man. She could teach him to please her. Olaf, in his eager innocence, made the first move. He kissed Agatha on the mouth. A gentle touch to the lips was all the young prince imagined of kissing. When Agatha rolled her tongue inside his mouth, Olaf was electrified by the unexpected pleasure. As the virgin lovers proceeded to ever greater intimacy, things even more wonderful than either had ever imagined began to happen. Olaf kissed Agatha's breasts. Each nipple magically swelled and hardened, and she cooed musically. On sheer instinct, Olaf fell to his knees, pulled Agatha's belly toward his face, and tentatively kissed her genitals. Inspired by how she had responded to his first kiss, he resolved to explore with his own tongue. Soon he found her clitoris, an enchanting little button he had not even known women possessed. When he pressed his tongue to that precious spot, Agatha secreted a milky, sweet-tasting fluid. She quivered, and even the inexperienced Olaf sensed that his mouth's caresses were producing the most intensely pleasurable feelings in the princess. As both virgin lovers grew ever more fiercely aroused, neither noticed the dark cloud that was gathering over the palace.

Olaf, incapable of further restraint, struggled out of his rough trousers, freeing his insistent manhood. Gently but forcefully, he inserted it deep into Agatha. Lightning flashed continuously in the cloud, and thunder rumbled over the town. As Olaf's thrusts grew faster, so also grew the anger within the cloud. At the instant that Olaf planted his seed into his lady love, a terrible lightning bolt flashed from the cloud onto the palace wall. With a deafening roar, it struck Magi. A ball of fire enveloped the sorcerer, who screamed until every wicked inch of his body had burned into a blackened husk.

The Bad Times, as the people thereafter called them, which the sorcerer Magi had inflicted upon Xana's people, came to an end.

At that same instant a second lightning bolt passed between Olaf and Agatha, as intensely pleasurable to both as the first had been agonizing to Magi. Agatha felt a most delightful tingling between her legs. No, it was more than a tingling. Her orgasm was the most wonderful feeling she had ever known. The virgin lovers had each yearned for this moment, but neither had ever imagined how delightful lovemaking could be.

The cloud over the palace dissipated as suddenly as it had formed. On the rough, unpaved street, Olaf and Agatha lay exhausted in each other's arms, with Olaf's proud member still inserted into his beloved. They embraced tightly for several minutes, lost in ecstasy.

In the afterglow of their lovemaking, Agatha felt herself surrounded by an unnatural mist. Music filtered into her ears from afar, strange but melodious. Words came into her mind, she knew not from where. "You are now queen of Xana. As queen, no one can deny your dream of making the land of Xana happy and prosperous for all your people." Agatha thrilled to this realization. The next words that came to her, she realized, were her own. "The road will be long and arduous, but I will persevere until I complete the journey."

The people around her shouted, "The sorcerer is dead! The sorcerer is dead!" The crowd began to turn rowdy. With the fluids of their lovemaking still dripping down her thighs, Queen Agatha waved her arms over her head and managed to hush her subjects. "This is not the time to celebrate," she declared. "I know where Magi locked away the grain. We must break down the warehouse doors and deliver food to all our hungry people." Agatha led the way to the palace and showed her people the granaries. The starving masses quickly smashed them open. "Feed the people," Agatha commanded. "All the people."

Those who had gathered eagerly fed themselves first, but they obeyed. They spread food throughout the city and to the countryside. Agatha herself fed Pedro's children. With the sorcerer's death, Pedro's crippling injury instantly healed. He stood tall and straight again, the lines of agony vanished from his face. Once again the model of a strong, healthy young man, he begged a favor of his queen. "Please," he implored her, "I must nurse my wife back to health and strength, and leave distribution of food to others."

"I understand," Agatha said. "Your love will be her healing. Stay always by her side."

As Agatha was turning to leave, she heard one of the children ask, "Is Mommy going to die?"

"No," Betsy replied. "Mommy's not going to die."

As twilight settled over the town's streets, Prince Olaf accompanied the new queen to her modest door in the palace wall. As Agatha was opening it, she told him, "Good night, my sweet prince. Please meet me here in the morning." Before Olaf could decide how to answer, Agatha had passed through the door, closed it, and locked it from the inside.

Olaf was unhappy. His hopes for an encore of lovemaking had been dashed. Had Agatha rejected him?

She had not. But she herself was also preoccupied, in her own way, with what she had done. Agatha was in such euphoria that she could hardly have performed again that night. First was the lovemaking itself. Agatha had done this as a duty to her fairy godmother and to save her people. Yet, like her childhood duties in the palace, she had found making love to be pure pleasure. Her mother had told her that to couple with a man was "really nice." What an enormous understatement!

Agatha had found the feelings in her body to be the most wonderful she had ever known, far beyond anything she had ever imagined. These exquisite feelings were but a prelude to an even greater excitement—the recognition that not only was she queen of her people, but also that she could calm an unruly crowd, inspire them, and lead them in the urgent task of delivering food throughout the land. Most precious of all, she had saved the lives of Pedro's adorable children—two boys and three girls, from a boy of eleven years to a tiny girl of three—whom she had loved from the moment she saw them.

———

*D*isease does not spare the rich, but afflicts rich and poor alike. The common people, toughened by their hard lives, had suffered less than the aristocrats through the sickness, crippling, and hunger Magi had inflicted. Furmal Glender and Sebastian Malloy had both succumbed to malnutrition and disease. Sebastian's thuggish employees dispersed and would cause Xana's people no more trouble.

———

The next day, outside the palace gate, most of the few members of Queen Julia's inner circle still alive—haggard and emaciated—found the heiress. Hoping still to stave off her radical notions, the eldest pleaded, "You know the story of Cinderella. Now your prince has found you. Let him be king and rule with moderation, for he will treat you with all the kindness that befits his queen. We can advise him in the ways of the land of Xana."

Agatha burned with anger. Her whole body turned crimson. So immense was her rage that it is to her credit she did not explode. She took twenty slow, deep breaths before replying with resolve, "Cinderella and Snow White became pampered palace ornaments. Their lands were already prosperous and wisely governed. They also had wonderfully happy marriages and beautiful children." She assumed a dignified air of absolute authority. With all hesitation gone, Queen Agatha declared, "I have a destiny to fulfill. I must inspire my people to rebuild our ruined land into a prosperity such as the world has never seen. I must make sure that prosperity is shared with all my people. Not one shall be left out." Standing erect and regal, she pointed out into the town's streets. "Be off with you, naysayers, and never return to my palace. Among the humble and honest people I will find women and men with great talent to lead in this noble endeavor, people who never say, 'It can't be done,' but who will do it." Again, Agatha pointed away from the palace. "Go," she ordered.

An old woman who had been a senior member of Queen Julia's old council admonished the new queen. "Mark my words. Peasants can never govern a country. You may have some success for a while.

Though I may not live long enough to see it happen, I can promise that, in the end, you will fail. I will die in the serenity of knowing that the rule of Xana will be restored to its rightful ruling class."

"Your false words deceive me not at all," Queen Agatha said. "Rule by the common people, for the benefit of all, is a better way. And that way will endure."

Her mother's other advisers accepted their dismissal in silence. As they walked forlornly away into oblivion, Hector Ramirez stayed behind. He bowed deeply to Agatha. "As I served your mother without reservation, I offer equally to serve you in your vision of prosperity for all of your people," he declared.

"I thank you deeply," Agatha replied. "Your knowledge of our country's finances will have immense value. I ask you please to serve as my Master of the Treasury."

"I am honored to accept," Hector replied.

Agatha had already found most of the humble, honest, and highly talented people who would loyally serve her. Many she had known before the Bad Times; others had assisted her during the Bad Times. The most notable was Sylvia Hartly. With her husband's proud encouragement, she became not only one of Queen Agatha's first council of advisers, but also, on the strength of her skills, the chief administrator for the entire land of Xana. All the while, she continued to manage her charity. Sylvia is said to have once declared, "When Queen Agatha has a vision, I make it happen." Sylvia was not as arrogant as this statement may sound. Given her genius for organization, this is probably the best summary that could be given in a single phrase of the first twenty glorious years of Queen Agatha's reign. Many others capably served their young queen, but their names are lost with the passage of time.

———

L ater that day, the queen visited Pedro's family, entering their cramped house carrying a basket of food.

"Look!" one of the children said. "Agatha's come back with food." The children gathered excitedly around her, and Agatha filled their plates, first the five children's and then their parents'.

The oldest boy promptly invited Agatha to join them. "Please share this meal with us. We're so grateful."

"Thank you. You're generous. I'm delighted," replied Agatha, who sat down in the midst of the family and partook of the simple repast.

The oldest boy continued, "I'm Andre, and I'm eleven years old." He then extended his arm to each of his siblings in turn. "This is Susi, ten; Martin, eight; Charlotta, five…"

The smallest girl then interrupted. "I'm Anya, and I'm three," she announced cheerfully. Anya then climbed onto Agatha's lap. From a pocket in her dress, she pulled a very ragged doll, evidently her favorite toy, and handed it to Agatha. Immediately Anya held out her arms for the doll, and Agatha as quickly gave it back to her. Queen Agatha and humble Anya now handed the doll back and forth. Agatha gained the confidence not only of Anya but of all her brothers and sisters. By this simple game, she showed them she would never take from anyone what they considered precious. Under Queen Julia's reign, it had been common for aristocrats to seize from commoners any little baubles for which they had a fleeting delight.

Susi now offered Agatha a much larger doll. Anya placed her small doll close beside Susi's. "Mother and daughter?" inquired Agatha.

"No," Anya snapped, extending an arm toward Susi. "Big sister and little sister."

"Of course," Agatha replied, so cheerfully that harmony was immediately restored.

Agatha now learned that Pedro, humble and honest, was gifted with extraordinary insight into both people and events. He showed this talent to Agatha when he said, "You risked your country to save my dear wife and my precious children. I thank you eternally with all my heart. To show our appreciation, I promise that we will serve you all our lives in your quest to make our people prosperous and free."

"I am amazed and deeply moved," Agatha replied. "It is remarkable how well you have perceived my innermost thoughts and feelings. I thank you for your kind offer of service. I shall value your wisdom and sense of honor." Then she stunned the whole family with her invitation. "I wish for you to serve on my council of advisers. To be the opposite of my mother's council, it will be entirely composed of common, ordinary people like yourselves."

"I am humbled," Pedro stuttered in amazement. "As it is your wish, I will serve to the best of my ability."

Every day, Agatha visited Pedro and his family, and drew her own inspiration from seeing how quickly children and mother alike were recovering. The children loved Agatha almost as much as their own mother.

Queen Agatha cautioned herself that, no matter how precious they seemed, she must not favor the Mendez family exclusively. She had met many children in other humble families, and all of them loved her.

Queen Agatha, always leading in person, inspired as she had promised, and the people followed.

Prince Olaf joined her on these visits, and ever after he would be at her side. For Olaf, accustomed to princely pleasures, delivering wagons full of food to the poorest districts of the city and countryside must have seemed like the worst of drudgery. But pursuing the manly arts had given him strength and stamina, and one must not discount how his new connection with his beloved Agatha had inspired him. And so, just like all the queen's other people, he endured his new duties. The queen and her prince worked in the fields, joining in the planting beside the ordinary farmers. Soon the grain was ripening in the fields, and vegetables were growing in every household garden. Hunger and disease were quickly banished from Xana.

Agatha and Olaf also had to learn more about each other than just the magic of their bodies. As the first full day after their coupling ended, the queen and the prince talked outside the palace door for half an hour. They revealed to each other their stories of their lives. Then Agatha stepped through the door and locked her prince outside, just as she had the night before.

———

No record of their conversation exists. I presume that both talked about growing up in their respective palaces and learning to be courteous to the wealthy governing officials. It is likely that Agatha described learning the procedures of government from her service on the queen's council of advisers and in other palace duties. This included how she acquired an understanding of government financial management as a capable apprentice to Hector Ramirez; how she directed the entertainment for all palace functions; and, most important, how she connected with her common people. Olaf could describe much less preparation for ruling. What he told Agatha may have concerned his mastering the manly arts, tales from some of his many hunts, and probably his visit to the oracle. It is known that Agatha was distressed by his self-serving past, unsure whether to accept him as her true prince. But she had seen him behave honorably in Xana. She decided that she would test him somewhat longer to assure herself that he had matured. Thus it was that he accompanied and assisted her in her work among the people.

———

Though his toil was hard, Olaf found comfort in no longer needing to conceal himself from Agatha. Most of all, he was thrilled by always being near her, whom he loved so profoundly. Her initial misgivings about his lack of concern for his own country's people faded as she witnessed his willingness to work as hard as she did for her people. And, of course, she was delighted that he always treated her with great kindness. For his service to her people, even more than for the delights of their coupling, Agatha found herself falling more and more in love with him each day.

On their third day together, while hard at work delivering food, Agatha stole a kiss from Olaf. Throughout this day and the next, she stole more kisses, more and more often. With each kiss, she caressed him, thrusting her tongue deep inside his mouth. She wrapped her arms tightly around him, pressed her breasts onto his chest, and intertwined their legs. Olaf felt a heavenly bliss, and his mind filled with wonderful fantasies of coupling with his beloved Agatha again.

Hardly had this glorious dream squeezed out all other thoughts than Olaf would be jolted back to the hard world. Agatha would unclench, declaring, "We have much work to do." These brief romantic interludes were always witnessed by many of Agatha's humble and ordinary people. Nobody stopped and stared, teased, or jeered at them. Knowing how much Agatha had done for their happiness, they were all delighted that she had finally found her own.

The modern reader may feel that Agatha is tormenting Olaf, seeking to make him miserable by arousing him with deep kisses and much body contact, and then denying her most intimate favors. This interpretation is the complete opposite of both Agatha's character and Xana's social mores. She was teaching Olaf the arts of courtship, and Olaf himself was so much smitten by Agatha that he adored just being near her.

After five days, Queen Agatha invited her handsome prince to have dinner with her in the palace. Now, instead of cooking for herself, Agatha again enjoyed the services of the palace staff. As they dined, Agatha shared her ideas about how a monarchy should be governed. She was surprised by how little Olaf, having grown up as crown prince, knew about the mechanisms of governing. She mesmerized Olaf with her vision of wealth and power for the common, ordinary people. He declared, "Your vision is nobler than any I have read in any history book. People like Hector Ramirez, Pedro Mendez, and Sylvia Hartly can assist you far more than I can."

Agatha would invite all three, and others whose names are lost with the passage of time, to her first council. These advisers were to serve her ably for many years.

At that first dinner, Olaf continued, "I confess that, until I came to Xana, I had lived a hedonistic life. I am now ashamed of who I was. You have shown me that service to your people—*our* people, now—is far more rewarding. I hope you will still accept me if I stand back from government. I promise I will support you completely as my queen. I will be forever faithful to your vision. On occasions of ceremony, and when you meet your people on the streets, I wish to be at your side. I promise to greet them with the charm and dignity of a true prince."

Agatha considered this before answering. "You must still stand ready to do me, and our realm, one great service. I want you to promise me that when war comes to Xana—and war will come; the barbarians on our frontier have grown bold and make brutal attacks on the scattered settlements there—that you will stay here in the capital with me. I could not bear it if you should go off to battle and get yourself killed like my father."

"I promise I will be always at your side," Olaf readily agreed. "Hunting, archery, sword fighting, and jousting are the regal sports of princes and kings. Drawing the blood of people, and worse still, killing them, is not sport, and disturbs me greatly. The killing of game should be only for its meat. I will never willingly go to war."

Agatha, who perceived any person's true character beneath whatever facade he might have presented, recognized his sincerity. With this pledge, Agatha fell in love with Olaf as profoundly as he already loved her.

———

It has been suggested that in the eternal conflict between good and evil, personified by the fairy godmother and the sorcerer Magi, the fairy godmother perceived great good in the infant Agatha. She knew that she and Agatha together could prevail over Magi. But first Agatha had to prove her worthiness to rule. Protected from all harm, she could have spent her days reading in the vast palace library, abandoning her people to suffer outside without hope. Instead, she spent all day, every day, with her people, using all the resources she could muster to ease—in small ways—their suffering, and to inspire some measure of hope. But still, the young princess had to show both courage and wisdom. It has also been suggested that the fairy godmother detected great good in Pedro Mendez and his family, and placed Agatha close to them for her final and greatest test.

Chapter 3

The setting of all public events in Xana's capital city was the public square, nearly a quarter mile on each side. It was surrounded on all four sides by large buildings with elegant stone facades. One whole side was occupied by the royal palace. On the other three were public buildings and homes of aristocrats. Anyone inside this vast space would be awed by its grandeur and magnificence. Between the buildings, streets extended outward in many directions, like the spokes of a wheel.

Actually, the palace did not occupy one entire side, for the palace was in the shape of three sides of a rectangle. The open fourth side was adjacent to the public space but separated from it by a high wall. The palace thus had its own large private courtyard facing the town square. The palace itself and its wall had identical stone facades even more elegant than the other buildings around the square. To follow its corridors from one end to the other, around that vast circumference, was a walk of nearly a mile. The palace was thus large enough to house the government administration offices, spaces for royal entertainment, and the monarch's private quarters. A spacious balcony, about forty feet above the pavement, encompassing the entire width of the palace itself and the court-yard, overlooked the square. Centered on the balcony's railing was the royal symbol, a silver crown with five spikes, each topped by a little globe. It looked like the modern symbol for a chess queen. For generations, the monarchs of Xana had addressed their realm from behind that crown. Although many highly placed people often congregated along the balcony, the position behind the silver crown was reserved for the monarch alone. Directly below was the huge gate that led from the public square into the courtyard. Its rounded top was thirty feet high. The gate could be opened and closed only by several strong men using a pulley system. Most days it remained tightly closed. Except on ceremonial occasions, people entered and left the palace through small side doors.

In the land of Xana, it was the tradition—followed by Agatha's mother and all her ancestors—to be crowned inside the palace. Here only the aristocracy and visiting foreign dignitaries were admitted. Probably within a few days after Magi's death, Agatha had already decided to break with tradition and hold her coronation on the public square, where all her people could witness the ceremony.

It was four weeks after the sorcerer Magi died, and four weeks after Queen Agatha regained control of Xana and started her people on the road back to prosperity, that her grand coronation was held. A wooden platform was erected in the middle of the square.

A simple chair at its center served as a throne. To the chair, borrowed from a humble peasant, the symbol of the monarchy, the silver five-pointed crown, had been affixed. On both sides, shallow stands had been hurriedly built. With the coming of dawn, hours before the ceremony, the people of Xana began crowding into the vast public space. By mid-afternoon, they numbered in the tens of thousands—the largest gathering in the history of the land. Two lines of soldiers held back the people, clearing a line so the coronation party could walk unobstructed from the palace gate to the central platform. The weather was clear and warm with a slight breeze. It could not have been more favorable for an outdoor coronation.

The anxious, impatient crowd was electrified when Queen Agatha herself appeared on the palace balcony. The people cheered tumultuously. The deafening din went on and on. Agatha waved her arms over her head, and the people cheered all the louder. Finally she stepped back from the balcony and out of sight.

At that very instant the palace gates swung open. Prince Olaf carried the crown. He was followed by several of the queen's most trusted advisers and their sons, with Pedro, the humble glassblower, among them. They all walked solemnly from the palace gate toward the platform.

The crown was made of silver with two slender gold braids encircling the base. Ten triangular spikes extended upward and slightly outward around the periphery, each topped with a small globe. The actual crown thus enlarged into three dimensions the two-dimensional chess-queen symbol on the palace balcony. In private, of course, Queen Agatha had already placed the crown on her head and found that it fit securely, and that she could freely move around without its falling off.

Physically, Queen Agatha was petite but well proportioned, smaller than the average woman in Xana despite having eaten the best of food as she was growing up in the palace. Her smaller size was probably hereditary. In any conversation, her commanding personality compensated for her stature many times over. She dominated her much larger courtiers. Elias, for instance, was large in both height and girth, more than twice the queen in bulk, but he faded almost to invisibility when in the queen's company.

Elias had asked Queen Agatha for a central role in the ceremony. "I will be deeply honored to carry your crown to the coronation platform."

Agatha replied, "Prince Olaf is next in line to become king of Wan. It is proper for the crown of one monarch to be carried by another monarch."

"Please," Elias begged.

Agatha responded with the strength of will that characterized her entire reign. "I expect all the people of Xana to hear what I say. I remind you that I am monarch of Xana, not you. Now, you repeat to me what I just told you, or you're out of the procession entirely."

"You said that Prince Olaf should carry your crown," an embarrassed Elias replied meekly.

"And why?" Agatha insisted.

Elias hesitated, desperately trying to remember Agatha's words. "Because he will become the next king of Wan."

"Don't you ever forget," Agatha warned, "or ever again fail to understand all that I tell you."

"Yes, yes, your highness," Elias stammered, thoroughly mortified. But when the procession began, he maneuvered himself into second place behind Prince Olaf.

Prince Olaf himself wore a prince's tunic, but without decorations, epaulets, or other ornaments. Other men and boys in the party, of humble origin, wore peasant clothes. As soon as the entire party had emerged, the palace gates slammed shut. Prince Olaf ascended a short staircase to the central platform, leaving his retinue standing along the right side of the path. At that exact instant, the palace gates reopened, and the queen herself, followed by her ladies-in-waiting, stepped out to continue the procession. Attention was quickly diverted from the prince to the queen. With her handmaidens following her in a row, in simple peasant dress, Agatha walked at a stately pace. Her regal dignity held the people in awe. Among the handmaidens were Pedro's wife, Betsy, and daughters Susi, Charlotta, and Anya. Agatha did not hold her head high as if in haughty superiority to all those around her. Smiling slightly, she nodded alternately left and right. She connected with the people in her audience, looking directly into their eyes. She sensed their optimism, the promise that their lives would improve.

Someone in the audience remarked, softly, "Those little girls sure are cute. And well behaved, too."

Another replied, "The queen is so wonderful with children." In silence, the humble people of Xana watched her proceed to the platform. As her ladies-in-waiting lined up on the left side of the path, Agatha herself ascended the steps and sat on her throne.

The soldier at the head of the line now ascended the steps and gave a slow, deep bow to his queen. He was the commanding general of the army. He had displayed outstanding leadership by personal example, sharing with his men the discomfort of standing at attention all day to guard the path on which his queen would tread. "By right of primogeniture," the general announced, "I proclaim you,

Agatha, as queen of the land of Xana, to whom the army and all our people pledge our unreserved loyalty. To you, Queen Agatha, we look for leadership in securing the prosperity and happiness of our blessed land." The general again bowed deeply before his queen and returned to his post at the head of the line of soldiers.

Pedro's youngest daughter, Anya, who was only three years old, was next to ascend the stairs. Walking alone, she climbed slowly and gracefully. The crowd stood in hushed silence. This small child had an important role to play, but what was it? Would she make an embarrassing misstep? Anya first stood before her queen and made a deep curtsy. She grasped the crown from Prince Olaf. Would she drop it and spoil the ceremony's dignity? She climbed a set of small stairs, which hardly anyone had noticed previously, beside the throne. High enough now to reach, she very slowly lifted the crown onto Queen Agatha's head. Queen Agatha sat still, her hands on her lap, majestic in serenity. Would the crown fall to the floor? Would the queen have to grab it quickly as it toppled, marring the majesty of her demeanor? No. The crown stayed on Agatha's head. Little Anya stepped slowly down the stairs again and made another deep curtsy to her queen. Still alone and with the dignity of an adult, she descended from the stage and, from the ground below, curtsied to Queen Agatha for a third time. She turned toward the crowd on each side and curtsied twice more, first right and then left.

Then Anya ran to her mother. With Betsy grasping both Anya and Charlotta by their hands, and Susi holding Anya's other hand, together they walked back to the palace gate, so briskly that the two younger girls had to run. Protected from the crowd's excessive adulation by the line of soldiers, they were soon out of sight in the spacious palace courtyard. Anya's poise, remarkable for a child so young, quickly vanished in an emotional outpouring. Jumping up and down, she called out, "I crowned the queen! I crowned the queen!"

Her older sisters parroted her words. "You crowned the queen! You crowned the queen!"

Three-year-old Anya had played her role to perfection, and spontaneous cheering erupted from all the people of Xana. After several minutes, the cheering still would not stop. Queen Agatha raised her arms for silence. She rose from her throne, and as she waved both arms repeatedly over her head, the crowd gradually fell silent. While Queen Julia had addressed her people from the safety of the palace balcony, young Queen Agatha gave her coronation speech, entirely from memory, surrounded on all sides by tens of thousands of adoring subjects.

"The grain you have planted in your fields and the vegetables in your gardens will soon be ready for a bountiful harvest. You, the good people of the land of Xana, are, with your labor, ensuring that we will never go hungry again. There will be a surplus, which I will store in the royal granary, and if ever there be drought, you will all have food to eat.

"Now we will build schools. Each and every one of you will learn what only the aristocracy has learned before—to read and write. In the schools, we will do more than learn reading, writing, and arithmetic. We will learn the history, culture, and literature of the land of Xana as well as of the larger world outside. And we will study the wonders of nature to understand them and acquire a love for them.

"For centuries, my ancestors have been building the collection of the royal library to become as complete as any library in the world. Until now, only the aristocracy and a tiny community of scholars and teachers have been allowed to use it. I will open the library to everyone who can read, and to all school pupils. And I will build a grand National Library outside the palace and move all the books so they will be in easy reach of everyone. Most of the beautiful paintings and sculptures in the palace I will also move to the National Library. It will become an art museum as well, whose masterpieces you all can savor, even before you learn to read. The musical concerts that have been held each evening in the palace will henceforth be performed publicly, here in the city square. All of you, good citizens of Xana, will immerse yourselves in our cultural heritage. Here aspiring young people from the humblest of backgrounds will find mentors from among our land's finest artists and musicians, to build upon our heritage.

"But book learning is not enough. Each and every person will choose and then master a handicraft. With these skills, every one of you, good citizens of the land of Xana, will produce goods of great value. We will also teach cleanliness and ethics, for every citizen of the land of Xana will respect and honor every other citizen.

"With knowledge comes power. I have learned that in a faraway island kingdom, a parliament has been made to restrain the monarch. In that land, only the nobility may serve in parliament. But in the land of Xana, all people, upon completing ten years of education, will be eligible to vote and to serve in our parliament. Here the monarch will govern by consent, not by decree.

"And also from this distant land, I have learned of its Great Charter. Transformed in the land of Xana, this document will guarantee every citizen's right to have a free and dignified life, protected from oppression by all who would take from them what they do not deserve.

"Tomorrow I will marry Prince Olaf and unite the kingdom of Wan with the land of Xana. We will trade your crafts with the kingdom of Wan and throughout the world, and through trade, both our lands will prosper. Know ye all that by serving your queen in these great ventures, you will serve yourselves. Let us go forth together and make Xana a happy land."

Queen Agatha, with her royal crown on her head, then descended from the platform to meet her people. For hours, she talked with them, the simple and the humble, women and men in equal numbers. The first comment she heard was, "The little girl really made the show."

Agatha immediately replied, "You mean the dignified young lady." The correction spread quickly through the crowd. The queen was asked more questions about Anya: "How was she chosen? Did she receive a lot of coaching? Did she practice it over and over again?"

Agatha replied many times to the same questions. One of those conversations has survived the passage of time. She spoke with a very humble family she had once visited, and who had already witnessed Agatha's remarkable rapport with children. "I remarked to her good father that I wanted to be crowned not by the richest but by the humblest of our people. Anya was very eager. 'May I crown you?,' she asked.

"'Yes,' I replied, 'and I also ask you please to curtsy five times.'

"'Why?' she asked, as any child would.

"'Especially on the occasion of my coronation, it is very important for all our people to show respect to the monarch. Your curtsies will symbolize that respect,' I told her."

Someone interrupted, "Isn't that a very complicated concept for a child so young?"

"Perhaps it is," the queen replied. "But Anya is very perceptive. She may have understood more than we realize. Her parents certainly understood. And Anya knew that I wanted her to curtsy.

"She continued, asking 'If I drop the crown, will it break?'

"'Do not fear,' I replied. 'The crown is very strong. If you drop it as you practice with your mother, it will not break. But you must not drop it when you place it on my head.'

"That very day Anya started practicing. A few days later, I visited her family. The first thing she did when she saw me was to curtsy deeply, just like you saw today. She looked up at me, expecting my approval. I held out my arms to her, and she ran to me at top speed. I picked her up and said, 'Good job.' She wrapped her arms tightly around my neck. A minute later, I sat down and set her on my lap. Charlotta also climbed onto my lap, and my lap was full. Her older brothers and sister crowded around, and we had a lot of fun together."

Another person in the huge crowd, a craftsman who without any doubt had lost great sums to greedy moneylenders, approached the queen to ask redress. "I am just a potter," he said mournfully to the queen. "A good potter, I hope, but a very poor potter. The moneylenders take away all the profit I can make from selling my vases and figurines. Now that you are queen, can't you give back to me at least some of the money they took?"

"I am sorry," Queen Agatha replied, "that is a most improper thing for me to do."

Undeterred by the flash of anger Agatha perceived on the potter's face, she continued, "We should leave forever behind us the past and the ways of the past as we journey into the future of a new and better Xana. I have closed all the moneylenders' shops, permanently. I can promise that henceforth you and all the people of the land of Xana will keep the fruits of your labors. But as it is wrong for the rich to take from the poor, it is also wrong for the poor to take from the rich. Taking wealth from one person and giving it to another does not create wealth. It is your creations, the beautiful ceramics that you make, many of which we will sell at a good price to foreign traders, that create new wealth. I ask you, please, to join with me as together we bring prosperity to our land."

By now the potter's first flash of anger had subsided. He soon replied, "I am disappointed by your decision." After further hesitation, he stated, "Very well. I'll do it."

The next day, Agatha married Prince Olaf, again in the public square instead of the royal palace, and before a crowd as large as the one that had witnessed her coronation. Following their vows to each other, Prince Olaf delivered his first speech to the people of Xana. "My father, like Agatha's mother, is dead at the hand of the sorcerer Magi. I inherit the throne as king of Wan. Today Agatha becomes queen of Wan as well as queen of Xana." But Olaf was only the prince consort of Xana. Agatha was Xana's undisputed monarch.

Agatha then spoke. "According our marriage contract, we will spend six months each year in Xana and six months in Wan. From among you, the honest and humble people of our beautiful land, I am already finding capable councilors to lead you in carrying out my wishes during my months away from you. You will build schools, bring to Xana the finest teachers from all lands, harvest the grain and vegetables you have planted, nurture your animals, ensure that all our people have food in plenty, and start your education. And now—as in all lands and all times where bride and groom choose each other freely, like ourselves, instead of having the marriage arranged by others, we are eager for our nuptial bed to celebrate our love all night long by the joining of our bodies."

The gathered thousands cheered tumultuously as Agatha and her prince quickly descended the stairs and hurried inside a coach that had been brought close to the stage. The horses trotted off. As they approached the palace, the gates quickly opened, the carriage passed through, and, just as quickly, the palace gates closed behind them.

As soon as the carriage was safely inside the enclosed palace courtyard, Agatha and Olaf leaped out and ran together at top speed to the royal bedroom. Agatha may or may not have already been naked, but the stories leave no doubt that within a few seconds Olaf and Agatha were both totally naked, engaged in furious open-mouth kissing. Agatha guided Olaf's hand for him to fondle her intimately. Only five minutes after Agatha had publicly declared, "We are eager for our nuptial bed to celebrate our love all night long by the joining of our bodies," Olaf had already thrust his manhood deep inside her. Heaving and moaning, he required only one minute to erupt into a profound climax. The orgasmic delight spread over his entire body, and long afterward did he gasp in Agatha's tight embrace.

Their first round of lovemaking released only a small part of their arousal. Soon they were making love again, and Agatha discovered to her unexpected delight that she was multiply orgasmic. Over and over and over again, the royal couple exercised their passion for one another. Between couplings their bodies became each other's play toys, to be fondled all over and manipulated into every position they could imagine. But they did not continue all night long as the queen had promised. Eventually, utterly exhausted, they fell asleep in each other's arms.

———

There is considerable dispute among the different versions of her story as to whether this was their first intimate joining since Magi had been destroyed. According to some accounts, Agatha had kept her distance, so busy with the resurrection of her country that she took no time for her personal pleasures. Other accounts offer eloquent descriptions of their relations in the marital bed and in other convenient locations around the palace. One in particular offers beautiful detail of their coming together immediately after Prince Olaf finished his first palace dinner with Agatha. She had grasped his arm gently and invited him, "Please come with me to my bedroom and spend the night with me."

Prince Olaf had not expected Agatha to give so bold an invitation to fulfill his most cherished dream. He was so excited by the prospect of soon lying with Agatha that he could scarcely stand up. Agatha had to guide him by the arm as he stumbled toward the royal bedchamber. Agatha herself was either already naked or required one simple move to cast off her dress. Prince Olaf's hands were shaking so badly he could not undress himself, and Agatha had to do this for him. She dared not touch him intimately, for fear that he would explode almost instantaneously. After brief mouth to mouth kissing she guided his lips to kiss her in the most intimate manner possible and lubricate her for a smooth entry. As she expected, he erupted very quickly after entering. His entire body shook for several minutes afterward as they remained joined in tight embrace. Many times they coupled, always to the exhilaration of shared orgasms, before they fell into a restful sleep, secure in their love and in each other's arms.

The next morning, Agatha was back with her people. She was now Xana's true ruler. In the weeks that followed, her prince was always nearby to support her, yet always allowing Agatha to lead. Agatha and Olaf worked in the fields alongside the common farmers and helped with the bricklaying and carpentry to build the first schools. As queen, she had more official duties in the palace than when she had been only princess, but every day, she met and helped her people. In the land of Xana, Agatha was revered by the common people as no other ruler in the history of the world.

The day after Agatha and Olaf sailed away for their first six months in Wan, Elias visited several of her councilors, announcing, "There will be a meeting of the queen's council of advisers this afternoon." This body was charged with running the country in her absence. He then asked the councilors he had visited to notify all the others. When all had arrived in the council chamber, Elias arose, saying, "The meeting is called to order. Here are the items on the agenda." He had seized the initiative to assume the chair.

The meeting ended with most of the council's members assigned specific administrative tasks. Queen Agatha had asked Pedro Mendez and several of his fellow craftsmen to serve as councilors so they could provide wisdom from their understanding of the humble commoners' circumstances. They returned to their shops after each meeting. Pedro spent a few more minutes in a huddle with them. He observed, "Elias's craving to become the queen's favorite far exceeds his understanding or care for our humble and ordinary people."

After a brief hesitation, Alberto Sanichez replied, "With our queen away six months of every year, Elias can run the country half the time. He probably still has an ambition to take our beautiful young queen to bed."

"That's a delusion," Pedro responded. "She'll never let him. Fortunately he has no imagination. He's quite content to carry out our queen's agenda just as long as he is in charge of doing it."

John Siever then declared, "If he tries any actions harmful to our people, there are enough of us on the council to vote him down."

Pedro demonstrated his remarkable perception of Elias's nature as he continued. "True. Elias has no courage to withstand opposition. He retreats rather than standing to fight. We should not let a dispute among ourselves interfere with achieving our gracious queen's agenda. Allow Elias to chair the council. He knows that if he is to succeed as her favorite, when she returns she must find the schools functioning and the people healthy and well fed. Very simply, he must use his considerable administrative skill and ability to work hard to serve our queen."

His peers accepted the wisdom of what Pedro had said. And if Elias had been content merely to lead the country in the queen's absence, all might still have gone well.

But he saw the doors of the palace treasury standing open in front of him, and it was more than his weak character could bear. After all, he told himself, he was working harder on Xana's behalf than he had ever worked for himself. Didn't he deserve just a little something for all his toil and trouble? Elias figured that if he needed a bit of money now and then, certainly not much compared to what Agatha's many projects were costing, what was the harm? As long as he kept the social order functioning as Queen Agatha wished, at worst he could always pay back what he had taken. Surely the queen would not begrudge her chief councilor a small gift? At best, Elias became convinced, the queen would not even notice such a petty sum in all the realm's accounts. Others in the council, of course, soon noticed what Elias was doing. Many of them shared his justification for dipping into the treasury. Some, like the brick manufacturer Manuel Chan, soon followed Elias's example. Chan supplied all the bricks and capably oversaw the construction of Agatha's schools, a service that he believed entitled him to a proper reward. None of these councilors appreciated Pedro's acute perception of their character.

But Pedro was deeply troubled by this. After the council's second meeting, he came home and spoke very gravely to his wife. "Elias is stealing funds from the royal treasury, as are Manuel Chan, Horatio Lloyd, Aurelia Fernandez, and, I suspect, others."

"Please do not try to challenge them alone," Betsy pleaded. "Don't let them know you're watching them."

"I am not alone. I can trust John Siever, Alberto Sanichez, Sylvia Hartly, and Hernando Franklin. All will be able to keep quiet. They're absolutely loyal to our queen and her vision. And Hector Ramirez. He can find irregularities in the accounts. James Gomez, Helmut Giezech, and Nathan Wallace won't steal anything, but I can't trust them not to talk. About all the others, I am not sure."

After the next meeting, Sylvia motioned to Pedro. Unnoticed by others, she said in a low voice, "Elias is using his position as chairman of this council to take bribes. I can name others who are probably also involved."

"I can name all ten of them," replied Pedro.

Sylvia said, "If Hector will support us, he can search for evidence in the financial records."

Sylvia, Pedro, Alberto, and John went together to Hector's chambers.

"I am finding all of these drafts on the royal treasury," Hector assured them. "This was also a regular occurrence among Queen Julia's councilors."

"The aristocrats?" Pedro asked.

"Yes. Queen Julia was tolerant of such petty corruption so long as the amount stolen was not large and the culprit was also performing a useful service to the government. I reported these findings periodically to Queen Julia, who always thanked me for my service, ordered me to tell no one else, and usually took no further action. As with Queen Julia, I am carefully recording them and saying nothing. I will have all the accounts organized to present to Queen Agatha when she returns. I suspect our new young queen will be less lenient."

"Together," Sylvia suggested, "we must resolve, with utmost secrecy, to keep thorough records and collect eyewitness accounts. If we try to disrupt what these people are doing, we disrupt the whole country. We should keep the country running smoothly but also keep careful count of all of these unauthorized payments."

Pedro added, "Let us not again all be seen together, so as not to arouse their suspicions. When Queen Agatha returns, we will report everything to her. I am confident that she will do what is right."

Thus began a conspiracy within a conspiracy.

Chapter 4

The land of Xana is warm all year, which makes the assertion that Agatha was always naked believable. By contrast, the kingdom of Wan is cold in the winter, but Olaf and Agatha spent their time there in the warmest six months. During her first half-year term in Wan, Agatha entered the lives of the common people as she had in her own land. The people quickly came to revere her as much as did those in the land of Xana. Because the agriculture of Xana was vastly superior to what Agatha found in Wan, she introduced many improvements during her first seasons there. Also as in Xana, Agatha built schools for the common folk. Their six months in Wan passed quickly, and Agatha was happy they were sailing back to Xana.

A tumultuous cheering welcomed Agatha when she returned from her first term in Wan. Her ship, while still miles out at sea, had hoisted the royal flag bearing the silver crown on a background colored in the blue of sea and sky. As the ship approached the harbor, Queen Agatha stood on the deck, with Prince Olaf on one side and the ship's captain on the other. A huge crowd had gathered to see her arrive.

Agatha was first to descend the gangplank to the dock, meaning to greet as many of her subjects in person as she could. They looked well fed, clothed, and healthy, but Agatha detected a hint of unhappiness among them. A less sensitive monarch might have overlooked this completely. As she led the small royal party toward the city center, the crowds followed. There were far too many people for Queen Agatha to greet them all. Prince Olaf, at her side, delighted the people with his courteous and enthusiastic greetings. The queen and her prince together gave the people the attention they wanted. They felt valued and appreciated.

The first of the councilors to greet Queen Agatha was Elias. Although once he had desired to rape her, he had since given all appearances of being a hardworking, loyal, and competent administrator. "The harvest was good," he assured her. "The royal granaries are full. We have twenty schools already teaching our children, and twenty more are under construction. They are ready for your inspection."

"So you assure me I will be pleased by what I see?"

"Oh, yes, my good queen," Elias replied.

Similar reports came from others among her councilors.

From among the common people, however, came complaints. There were not enough teachers.

One case, especially poignant to Agatha, came from the mother of a five-year-old boy.

"My son, Michael Gant, is such a bright boy, so curious about the world," his mother cried. "He is full of distress that the schools have no room for him because there are not enough teachers."

"I am very sorry," Agatha replied. "We cannot build the land of Xana in a day or even in a decade. But I promise you that Michael will enter school next year."

The people also complained about Howell Granby, who had cajoled them to buy luxuries they neither needed nor could afford. He then lent them money for which he charged usurious interest.

———

For centuries, both the monarchs of Xana and their generals accorded high priority to feeding all the soldiers very well, even when many of the common people went hungry. This assured the army's loyalty to the crown and was the single most important factor in maintaining the country's long-term stability. Queen Agatha's first great achievement, completed in the first few months of her reign and aided by an abundant harvest, was to feed all her people as well as she fed her army. She earned her people's support and their subsequent understanding that she needed to keep the finances of her country strong. With full stomachs, the people were willing to be patient as the queen's other grand schemes proceeded more slowly than she would have liked.

———

At last, Queen Agatha and Prince Olaf reached the house of Pedro Mendez and his fine family. Pedro was the queen's most trusted and perceptive adviser. From him the queen would learn what had really happened in her land while she was away. As soon as she reached the doorstep, one of Pedro's five children called out excitedly, "Queen Agatha is here!"

All instantly rushed toward her, begging for her notice. Andre and Susi clutched her hands and led the queen to a plain, hard-backed chair. Charlotta and Anya leaped onto her lap, while Andre, Susi, and Martin crowded close.

Susi pulled out her large doll, which she handed to the queen. "Let's play school," she suggested. "Will you be our teacher?"

"I'd love to," the queen replied. "I can tell you like school."

Charlotta and Anya also pulled out their favorite dolls, which they clutched protectively.

Charlotta, speaking for her doll, said, "I learned how to spell your name: q-u-e-e-n-a-g-a-t-h-a."

"Correct," the queen replied.

Andre interrupted, "Shouldn't it be capital Q-u-e-e-n, capital A-g-a-t-h-a?"

Seeing how dejected that had made Charlotta, the queen asked, "Would you like to learn a queen's secret?"

All the children immediately said, "Yes," and good cheer was restored.

"In my first year of school," the queen continued, "I remember spelling Queen Julia without capitals. My very own mother. Would you like to learn another queen's secret?"

Of course the children all said, "Yes."

"I never let it worry me, and I never again left out the capitals."

Susi then spoke up, "My teacher says it's all right to make mistakes if we learn from them."

"And," the queen added, "we should also forgive ourselves completely."

Anya asked, "Was Queen Julia also a lot of fun for you to play with?"

"Not much," Queen Agatha replied. "She spent most of our time together teaching me how to be a good queen. Now, who would like to spell the name of your teacher? Show of hands."

All five children raised their hands.

"I know you all want to be first," the queen said. "But who will it be? I'm writing a number between one and twenty on this slip of paper." She folded the paper to keep it out of sight. "Whoever guesses closest is first."

"Fifteen," said Andre. "Fourteen," Susi said. "Seven," Martin offered. "Twelve," said Charlotta. "Six," said Anya.

"Here is the number," the queen declared, unfolding the paper so all could see.

"Eight," Martin cried out. "I came closest. My teacher's name is Daniel—d, I mean capital D-a-n-i-e-l."

"Wonderful," the queen encouraged him.

"I'm second closest," Anya chimed in. "My turn next."

These happy school games went on and on. Queen Agatha discovered what they had learned in school, confirmed that all had competent teachers whom they liked, and taught a few lessons of her own.

After half an hour, the children's exasperated mother, Betsy, called to them, saying, "Please let the queen have a rest. Your father has important business with her." As she led her children away, they all looked back at their queen until the door to the next room was closed behind them.

Pedro was very curious to learn what Agatha and Olaf had done in Wan. When Agatha entered his house to play with his children, Pedro invited Olaf into his glass shop next door. Olaf knew the art of storytelling, and charmed Pedro with his tales of Wan. Pedro in turn showed Olaf some of his glassblowing techniques, making a beautiful red goblet as a gift for the royal couple. The queen joined Olaf and Pedro in the glass shop.

"Betsy is with child," Pedro said proudly.

"And when is the blessed arrival?" Queen Agatha asked.

"In six months," Pedro continued. "The harvest was indeed good. The granaries are full, fruits and vegetables are abundant in the market, and the schools are filled with eager learners. However, we don't have enough teachers. Far too many children have been left out."

Queen Agatha and all of her councilors understood that Xana had far too few teachers to quickly achieve her goal of literacy for all. She had already sent agents to many foreign lands to hire more teachers.

"We should not get just any teachers," Queen Agatha reminded Pedro. "We need teachers both learned and compassionate with children. Years will be needed before we have enough of our own teachers. Good things cannot be quickly attained."

In a spirit of great humility, Pedro then said, "I thank you deeply for getting Anya enrolled in school."

———

Enrolling Anya had required the queen's personal intervention. Despite the shortage of teachers and therefore of classroom spaces for pupils, Pedro had no trouble getting all of his four older children accepted. But the school's headmaster had stated, "Anya is too young to go to school."

"Please," Anya begged. "I promise to study just as hard as Charlotta."

Her father then told the headmaster, "What would Queen Agatha say if you did not admit the young lady who placed the crown on her head?"

The headmaster stood his ground. "Queen Agatha herself set the minimum age of five for entering school. I am sorry, but I must obey my orders. I cannot admit Anya because she is only four. Next year."

Anya cried for hours. "I want to go to school. I want to go to school."

Her father Pedro was illiterate, but Sylvia Hartly wrote a letter on his behalf. "Pedro Mendez enrolled Andre, Susi, Martin, and Charlotta in school, but the headmaster denied admission to Anya because she is only four. The entire family, including the four older children, is terribly upset." The letter required two weeks to reach Agatha in Wan. When she read the letter, her face colored and she palpitated noticeably.

She had, however, learned to control her behavior when she learned of something she did not like. She took slow, deep breaths, and to those around her appeared to go into a trance, unresponsive to the outside world, while collecting her thoughts. Her husband, Prince Olaf, understood his beloved young wife. He could see that the letter had told of a problem at home. To understand what was troubling her, he gently took the letter from Agatha and read it. But he knew he could not offer advice about how she ruled her own land unless she specifically requested it. Only appearing to be in a trance, Agatha was actually devising corrective action. She wrote a letter on her royal stationery featuring the silver crown symbol at the top. "To the headmaster, as your queen I request you to admit Anya Mendez to school immediately. I promise that despite her young age she will perform as well as all of her siblings. She should attend class seated beside her sister Charlotta. To the captain of the queen's elite guard, send an observer to the school every day to ensure that Anya Mendez is attending class."

The letter took another two weeks to travel on the ship back to Xana. But Anya did not wait for its return to begin her education.

Every day when her older sisters Susi and Charlotta returned from school, they taught Anya all that they had learned. When Queen Agatha's letter arrived, Anya was already at the same level of achievement as her sisters.

The letter was delivered to Sylvia, who read it and then carried it to the Mendez family's home. Before Sylvia had time to gather the family, Anya started reading the letter herself. She slowly sounded out the syllables. "As... y-our... qu-een... I... re... qu-est... y-ou... to... ad... mit... Anya!" With a shriek, Anya dropped the letter and began jumping up and down. "I'm going to school! I'm going to school!"

Sylvia Hartly, accompanied by Pedro, Anya, Captain Miguelan of the queen's elite guard, and three other guardsmen, marched into the headmaster's office. Charlotta came with them. The captain handed the letter to the headmaster, saying, "Read aloud this letter from Queen Agatha."

The headmaster obeyed, and quickly turned pale. A few seconds later, he ordered an assistant, "Place another chair and desk in the classroom of Charlotta Mendez." To his credit, he continued, "I promise that Anya Mendez will attend class every day. You do not need to send an observer." Anya skipped, hand-in-hand with Charlotta, to her first day in school.

———

"And I think Anya is ahead of Charlotta," Queen Agatha told Pedro. "Anya is a precocious child. She should be encouraged in all she wants to do, as long as it is useful and honorable. Anya is destined for achievement far beyond anything we can now imagine.

"The school your children attend is superb," the queen added. "They have all learned more in six months than I did in my first six months of lessons."

———

For all ten years of their schooling, Pedro's five older children competed intensely to achieve the highest grades. Their father insisted, however, that they study together. Especially before examinations, they would ask each other questions they thought might be asked. Working together, they would try to find the best answers and make sure all five could answer them correctly. Pedro and Betsy both listened, and from their children's discussions acquired considerable knowledge of Xana's history and culture and even the outlines of its literature. Far into the future, when there were enough teachers, all the children of Xana would begin school at the age of five, as did Pedro's five younger children, who were yet to come into the world. Up to that point, children, and even adults, of all ages started school at the same time. Girls and boys attended the same class, but different ages had different classrooms and teachers.

———

When the discussion of his children's education concluded, Pedro's expression turned grave. "Your majesty, I am sorry to say we have discovered corruption at the highest levels. Your own administrators are involved—Elias and Manuel Chan." Pedro reeled off several other names. "They have stolen money allotted for the search for teachers and for building materials, taken bribes from builders and merchants, paid the carpenters and bricklayers only half of the amount you promised them, underpaid the farmers for their harvest, stolen grain, and overcharged the people for food. They have grown rich far beyond what they have rightfully earned. I felt I did not have the strength to stop them. My wife advised me to be patient, saying that you, my wise queen, would correct everything that has gone wrong."

Agatha flushed and rose in anger. "They have betrayed their queen. Indeed, they shall all return everything they have stolen and more. You and good Betsy were very wise not to interfere alone. I need you as my second set of ears."

Now, at his queen's side, Prince Olaf suggested, "Shall we have them publicly beheaded?"

"No," Agatha replied firmly. "I will bring them all before the people. They will publicly apologize and then give back to the people far more than the amount they stole."

"And what about Howell Granby?" Pedro continued. "He is the worst scoundrel of them all. He tormented me, saying, 'Surely you want this dress for your beautiful wife. Just sign these papers. She gets the dress now, and you can pay later. What more can you want than this beautiful dress for your wife?' There was something evil about his manner.

"I told him, 'I have the love of my wife and my children without the dress. I also have the respect and trust of Queen Agatha. These are surely more precious than all the costumes and jewelry in the world.' He cursed me, and he cursed you, too, my sweet queen. He said, 'Queen Agatha, Queen Agatha, everybody speaks so much of Queen Agatha. And where is she? Your so-called queen ran away to a distant land and deserted you. She is a disgusting pretender. Queen Agatha is not worth the breath you use to say her name.' And he cursed you with language so vile I cannot repeat it."

Queen Agatha replied, "All that he has done no one will ever repeat."

"My father taught me to never get into debt," Pedro said, "or else I will be poor the rest of my life. And now, my gracious queen, hundreds, perhaps thousands, are in Granby's servitude, drained of their funds and impoverished."

"I will have him seized, and he will return all that he has taken," Queen Agatha said.

So great was the greed of Howell Granby, so narrow was his vision, and so mistaken was he in his perception of Queen Agatha, that he lost much time that he could have used to escape. Too late, he came to understand that he could not continue his business now that the queen had returned. He spent more valuable time packing away as much ill-gotten money as he could. Already at the dock, loaded with luggage, he was bribing a foreign ship's captain to sail him away when the queen's soldiers found him.

A captain of the elite guard informed the queen. "We have captured Howell Granby and taken him to the palace dungeon. He insulted you repeatedly with the vilest comments I ever heard. My men wanted to break every bone in his body."

"Did you restrain them?" asked the queen.

"I told them that you forbid any form of corporal punishment."

"Then you maintained discipline?"

"Yes, my queen."

"I am pleased. You have all the money in these bags?"

"Yes, my gracious queen."

"And all the contracts, that we may know the names of every one of our good people to whom the money should be returned?

The amounts to be returned with interest? And his house, all the furnishings, his carriage?"

"Yes, dear queen."

Queen Agatha turned to Hector Ramirez. "It will be a big job for you and all your scribes, but I ask you please to examine and reconcile all the records so we may return to each of our citizens the full amount paid."

"We will start immediately, and strive to complete the accounting in three days."

After these revelations, Agatha consulted, in utmost secrecy, with Hector Ramirez. He had obtained a detailed, day-by-day accounting of all the illicit transactions by Elias, Manuel Chan, and other councilors. She also acquired a complete list of all the wealth they had obtained legally in the years before their conspiracy.

———

E lias and all the other embezzlers were blissfully unaware that they were being investigated. Queen Agatha also withheld Howell Granby's imprisonment from public knowledge. The queen invited Elias and often several other councilors, both honorable and corrupt, to meet her every morning at one of the small palace doors. From there the councilors walked all over the capital city to show off their accomplishments to their queen.

On the second morning after her return, a confident Elias asked the queen, "Will you call a meeting of your council of advisers?

"I wish to visit my people first, to inspect all that you have done," Queen Agatha replied.

"Haven't we told you everything we see?" asked Elias.

"You told all that you have seen. But do you see all there is? My mother rarely ventured outside the palace. She depended entirely upon her councilors to inform her of what was going on in our land. They didn't see, and my mother never knew, either our people's creative ability or their wretched poverty. I wish to see everything I can in our land with my own eyes."

Every day, Agatha visited farms, granaries, and schools, highly visible to the public, and usually accompanied by Elias and others who had embezzled royal funds. She connected with the crowds of people who gathered everywhere she went. At the schools, she talked with the children, and she was pleased by what they said. The pupils were eager to learn, the harvest had indeed been abundant, and the food had been safely stored.

But even at the first school she visited, Agatha saw several fully furnished classrooms, empty of people. At the second school, when she saw more unused classrooms, she queried Elias, "Why are these good classrooms vacant? I have met many parents who are unhappy because there is no room in school for their children."

"I am sorry, your majesty, we cannot find enough teachers."

Elias was unprepared for the vehemence of Queen Agatha's reply. "So you do not see all there is. You spent crown money constructing more schools than our available teachers can fill instead of finding more teachers? Don't you know that people are a more valuable investment than mere buildings?"

Elias, afraid of his queen's wrath, stepped back. "If you say so," he stammered.

"Pupils can learn from a caring and inspiring teacher, even without a classroom," the queen declared. "Pupils can learn nothing in the most luxurious of classrooms if they have no teacher to guide them. Your stewardship disappoints me."

"We'll expand the search for teachers right away," Elias hurried to answer.

"Indeed we will," the queen said.

At the farms and granaries, however, the queen found everything in order. She congratulated Elias on his competent management.

Every night, however, Queen Agatha draped herself in a cloak, slipped through one of the palace's back doors, and walked unnoticed to Sylvia's house. There she met with Hector Ramirez, Sylvia, Pedro Mendez, Alberto Sanichez, and several of the others who had been identified as completely trustworthy. Together, they assembled the documents and the testimony that would provide overwhelming evidence against all who had embezzled from Xana.

———

It was nearly a week after her return from Wan before Agatha called her first council meeting. The councilors had all assembled and seated themselves around the round table. Queen Agatha's chair was conspicuously unoccupied.

"Why is Queen Agatha late?" Elias voiced the thoughts of all who were present.

"Something is very wrong," said Manuel Chan, apparently the most timid and fearful of the embezzlers.

"Sylvia sure looks smug," somebody said. "Does she know something we don't?"

"And look at Pedro," said another. "Inscrutable as always. Sometimes I think he can see right through me and read my thoughts."

"I don't trust Pedro," added still another of the waiting councilors. "He's too honest. He can barely feed his family, but he won't take even one livre."

Then the door opened, but instead of the usual two army officers who would stand inconspicuously at the council chamber's corners, twenty soldiers marched into the room. They arranged themselves in two columns. Instead of the informality with which council meetings normally were held, the captain at the head of one column announced, "Her majesty, Queen Agatha. All rise and bow."

Between the two lines of soldiers marched Queen Agatha, carrying a stack of documents. These would prove to be very incriminating for many council members. As she proceeded to her chair, the soldiers formed a ring, surrounding the council table. Queen Agatha noted alarm on the faces of Elias the farmer, Manuel Chan, and others.

"We're in big trouble now," Chan whispered to Elias.

"Keep calm," Elias replied. "We'll get out of this."

Queen Agatha spoke angrily. "Elias, Manuel Chan, Aurelia Fernandez, Horatio Lloyd... " She continued, reciting the names, now lost, of others. "In these documents I have indisputable evidence that you have taken for yourselves royal funds intended for our people's welfare."

Queen Agatha's rage was terrifying to anyone against whom it was directed. The first councilor she interrogated was Elias the farmer.

"April 15, five thousand livres withdrawn for travel to the islands of the east; the purpose, to hire teachers; of this, four thousand five hundred paid to the ship's captain. Where is the missing five hundred livres?"

"I don't know," Elias replied. "There must be some mistake in the records."

"There is no mistake," Hector Ramirez said forcefully.

Queen Agatha continued, "And here is a four thousand livre withdrawal, in your name, Elias, to pay the bricklayers."

Pedro Mendez added, "The paymaster told me himself that only three thousand was delivered to him."

"The paymaster counted out the three thousand livres to me personally," Hector stated.

Queen Agatha read off page after incriminating page of treasury records. One after another, the contents of these papers negated Elias's denials. Queen Agatha's loyal advisers—Sylvia Hartly, Pedro Mendez, and others who had attended the secret night meetings—provided eyewitness testimony that supported what the documents showed.

After about fifteen minutes, Queen Agatha paused and looked directly at Elias. "I am tired of all your lies," she said. "With every accusation, I have presented documents and eyewitness testimony as evidence. You deny them all, yet you have presented not one bit of evidence in your defense. Remember that as your queen I can penalize you as harshly as I wish and as harshly as you deserve."

The queen could see that Elias was pale, sweating profusely, and trembling, his manner itself profound evidence of his guilt. Despite his physical bulk, Elias did not now look like a large man. Queen Agatha continued, "As you tell more lies, you earn for yourself an ever more unpleasant penalty."

Queen Agatha also perceived great unease in the mannerisms of everyone else she had named when the meeting began, against all of whom she had overwhelming evidence. The culprits were all behaving as if they felt guilt, shame, and remorse.

After another minute or two, Elias was unable to withstand the stress. "I confess. Every charge you make against me is true."

Manuel Chan, knowing he would be next, broke down completely. Before hearing the evidence against him, he sobbed, "I confess, I stole some money, too. Please have mercy on me and Elias. Remember, we built the schools and stored the grain, everything you wanted."

"I'll get to your case next. I have more thefts documented against Elias, and I expect him to confess to all of them."

Manuel Chan's face was soft and round, almost without wrinkles. His appearance was as meek as his manner. As the queen opened her case against him, he pleaded, "You do not have to recite every offense. I confess to all of them. Just add up the total amount, and I will pay it all back."

"You'll do more than pay it all back," the queen snapped. "I have the duty to present all my evidence, and you have the right to know that evidence and to challenge it if you can." The queen understood Manuel's shame, and that announcing his every misdeed to the country's leaders would deepen that shame.

After evidence of every one of Manuel's thefts had been presented, he stated solemnly, "I apologize for a great wrong. I promise never again to violate my gracious queen's trust. I also promise that henceforth I will persuade all others to be always honest and honorable."

"Aurelia Fernandez, the jewelry lady," Queen Agatha then inquired, "where did you get enough money to buy that elegant pearl necklace?"

Aurelia Fernandez was a beautiful woman with lovely brown eyes, full cheeks, brown hair full of ringlets, and a luscious figure.

She was a distinguished dressmaker who spent nearly all that she earned, plus as much money as she could borrow, beg, or cry for, to buy herself more jewelry. She went about the town bedecked with more rings, bracelets, and necklaces than anyone could reasonably count. She made elegant dresses for ladies of the aristocracy but also collected their used clothes and gave them to Sylvia Hartly to distribute to the poor. She had given her services without charge to Sylvia, making good clothes for the very poor and teaching them sewing skills. Agatha was uncomfortable with Aurelia's obsession with jewelry. But Agatha had also recognized that Aurelia was intelligent, worked hard, and certainly understood and sympathized with the needs of the poor.

In making the preparations for the queen's coronation, Sylvia had assisted most capably. In the version of the legend in which Queen Agatha wore clothes, Sylvia told the queen, "You have the dignity, bearing, self-confidence, and authority of a queen. But you also need to look like a queen. As queen, you are no longer one of us and should no longer dress as a commoner like us. It would never do at your coronation for me to be dressed more elegantly than you. You should wear a fine white dress of silk. You do not need any jewelry or fancy plaits—just a dress made of the finest of all fabrics. I suggest that Aurelia Fernandez can make you a gown regal enough for a queen."

Aurelia had sewed together a sleeveless, ankle-length dress of the finest silk, for which Queen Agatha paid her a good price. Some versions of the legend suggest that Queen Agatha wore such dresses in public for the rest of her life, and that no one in the land except the queen wore a dress of pure white silk.

Queen Agatha had to ask Aurelia a second time, "Where did you get the money to buy your necklace?"

After further hesitation, Aurelia replied, "I, I had to sew a lot of dresses."

"That's not all," Hector Ramirez interrupted her. "May 5, two thousand livres signed over to you, no account of your spending it as required."

"I can't be responsible for your losing the records," pleaded Aurelia.

"I do not lose records," Hector replied.

"Show us your records of how the two thousand livres were spent," Queen Agatha demanded.

"Ah, ah," Aurelia stammered.

Sylvia Hartly now interrupted. "May 8, the next council meeting after you acquired the two thousand livres, I saw you wearing the pearl necklace."

"And I also on that date," Pedro added.

"I, too, remember it well, all too well," said John Siever.

Sylvia continued, "Over the dinner table that night I remarked to Benjamin about the string of pearls Aurelia wore to the meeting. His face lit up as if he had received a profound revelation.

"'Pure white pearls?' he asked.

"'Yes,' I said.

"'Three days ago Aurelia came to the bazaar,' he told me, 'and gazed longingly at that string of pearls for half an hour. I knew how badly she wanted them, but I also knew that she could not afford them. Later that afternoon some man came in and bought them. Full price.'"

Queen Agatha scolded Aurelia. "Now I want your explanation of how you acquired the pearls."

Before Aurelia could dream up a reply, Pedro Mendez declared, "You were very foolish to display, if not stolen goods, certainly goods purchased with stolen money, so quickly after you obtained them."

John Siever continued, "Maybe you'll feel a little better if we tell you we'd have caught you even without that obscene exhibition."

"They're not obscene; they're beautiful," Aurelia whined.

"Obscene," John repeated.

"Stop!" Queen Agatha commanded with a voice of great authority. Instantly the room fell silent, and remained silent until the queen again chose to speak. "In my council everyone has the right to express an opinion. You have both expressed your opinions, and you should be respectful of each other's opinions even though you disagree. Our task here is to determine whether Aurelia Fernandez stole money that was meant for our schools. Your personal opinions about some ornaments are irrelevant to that task."

The queen's anger had not abated. "For the last time, Aurelia Fernandez, tell us what you did with the two thousand livres and how you acquired those expensive pearls."

"Ah, ah, ah," Aurelia sputtered.

Queen Agatha glared menacingly into Aurelia's eyes. "Are you ready to confess that you took two thousand livres of crown funds for your personal use?"

Aurelia then burst into tears. "I confess. I'll borrow money from friends right away and pay you back in full. But I will protect my friend who bought the pearls for me and will not tell you his name. I deserve the blame for persuading him to do a wrongful act."

"There is some honor in you after all," replied Queen Agatha. The queen continued, "Horatio Lloyd, May 26…"

Horatio Lloyd, a man with a cropped mustache and a sour face, rudely interrupted the queen. "Yes, I know, and there are two other cases. It's all Elias's fault. He set a bad example, and he deserves all the blame. If he hadn't started stealing, none of the rest of us would have."

"You are as much at fault as Elias," Queen Agatha scolded him. "You chose, most unwisely, to follow his example, and that places as much blame on you as on him. Many people here today had the good judgment not to follow his bad example. You, Horatio Lloyd, have been greedy and irresponsible—behavior as totally unacceptable as Elias's." Queen Agatha then presented each of her three cases against Horatio, none of which Horatio tried to deny.

After a long and bitter afternoon, Queen Agatha declared, "Elias, Manuel Chan, Aurelia Fernandez, Horatio Lloyd…" and all the others who had siphoned off royal money, "you are dismissed forever from my council of advisers, and you will appear before our people to atone for your high crimes. Captain Miguelan, have two soldiers accompany each of these criminals until sentences are passed and carried out."

After soldiers had escorted all of the embezzlers out of the council chamber, someone observed, "It seems very empty in here now."

"Not at all," the queen responded. "I see many capable and honest people whose advice I cherish. I thank you with all my heart for your support in these painful matters. Now we need a penalty sufficiently severe to deter others from trying to take for themselves the wealth that belongs to our people."

Pedro added, "As far back as even the oldest of my fellow artisans can remember, wealthy aristocrats have robbed and cheated us. Queen Julia sometimes pretended sympathy but never took any action to correct this. Our people expect you, are counting on you, to make all these thieves pay fully for their misdeeds."

Queen Agatha then spoke with a voice of great authority. "I suggest that we take from each of them everything they have, and invite our people to gather on the city square below the palace balcony to watch as the penalty is carried out. Does anyone disagree or feel this is too severe? I welcome all opinions."

James Gomez suggested, "This may be too harsh. I suggest they pay back twice as much as they stole, and let that be punishment enough."

Nathan Wallace disputed this. "Twice as much sounds like usury. We've closed down all the moneylenders. Let's not repeat their example. It would put us all in a bad light. We know how much each of them stole, and of course they should pay it all back. I understand you are more concerned with prevention than punishment. By removing them from this council, we have blocked their access to crown money. They will never be able to repeat their crimes."

Pedro Mendez disagreed. "My gracious queen, I understand that you intend to not only prevent the guilty parties from ever repeating their crimes, but also deter others who might otherwise attempt to do the same wrongs."

Queen Agatha complimented Pedro. "I never cease to be amazed by your deep understanding of my character and desires."

"You have earned my lifelong gratitude and my humble service." Pedro continued, "By taking all of these ten corrupt councilors' material possessions, we should convince others not to repeat their crimes. This should be our priority. These people still have all their talents. All of them can start over. They'll know they'll be watched, and are unlikely to steal again. As I said before, our people expect our queen to take strong action."

Alberto Sanichez supported Pedro's proposal. "Everybody I know will be delighted for you to take everything these thieves have."

"May I please have your vote on my request that the crown will assume ownership of all of the property of these ten criminals to use in educating our people?"

The vote in favor was unanimous except for two abstentions.

Sylvia Hartly said, "Please excuse me from your spectacle. Several of these people will come to me begging for charity. I will be ready to assign useful tasks to them."

After adjourning the meeting, Queen Agatha noticed that Hernando Franklin had remained in the room while the others were leaving. Before she could come to him, he came to her. "My gentle queen," he ventured, "an idea just occurred to me, too late to include in the discussion. If you disagree, don't hesitate to tell me."

"Hernando, please share your idea. I invited you to become a member of my council of advisers so I could hear your thoughts. I respect your understanding of, and sympathy for, the needs of our humble common people."

When she had heard him out, Queen Agatha complimented his suggestion. "That's a wonderful idea."

———

Hernando Franklin capably administered the direct commerce between the fishing people and the markets, completely eliminating the middlemen. Market owners or their agents would go to the docks, negotiate a price with the fishermen and women, and carry the fish to their market stalls in their own carts. His job completed by the time Agatha returned from her first visit to Wan,

Hernando soon afterward retired from her council of advisers and returned full time to the fishing he loved. However, it is suggested that Agatha and Olaf visited him several times every year at the dock, or in his home, where he served them a tasty fish dinner and charmed them with his tales of the sea.

James Gomez owned a small orchard. He treated the man and woman who worked for him like partners rather than just hired hands. After paying all his expenses, he divided his profits equally among the three of them, thus earning their lifetime loyalty.

Nathan Wallace was a commoner who had started his palace career as a sweeper. With hard work, courtesy, and diplomatic skill, he became a palace staff supervisor, respected both by his aristocratic superiors and by his commoner underlings. Agatha, while still a princess, had greatly valued his assistance in arranging palace entertainment. After advancing to the throne, she retained him in that position for many years.

The next morning, all over the city, couriers delivered the message, "Queen Agatha has caught several of her councilors stealing crown money intended for our schools. Please come to the city square in the afternoon to see for yourself how our young new queen deals with corruption and graft."

As Queen Agatha and Hernando Franklin had agreed, he waited until an hour after this message was delivered. Many people began gathering in the streets. To two different small groups of people he did not know, and who were talking about the invitation, he suggested, "Queen Agatha won't let them off lightly, as Queen Julia did." As Queen Agatha had foreseen, this rumor, like all rumors, spread quickly. The commoners were excited by the prospect that, for the first time in the memory of even the oldest among them, corrupt administrators would receive the punishment they deserved. They crowded into the city square in numbers as great as at Queen Agatha's coronation.

For centuries, Queen Agatha's ancestors had addressed the people from the palace balcony. Although Queen Agatha herself spent much of her time on the streets and in the common people's homes, she understood that the balcony was the best place to address the entire population. Tens of thousands could gather below to see and be seen by their queen.

The low wall that protected against falls onto the pavement far below rose four feet above the balcony's floor. The crowd cheered when at last Queen Agatha appeared directly behind the royal crest. In those versions of the legend in which Queen Agatha was naked, her breasts would have appeared just above that silver crown.

Elias was the first of the miscreants to be brought before the people. He was shaken to his very core by Queen Agatha's response to his crimes. He had expected a reprimand and perhaps a mild fine. Instead, she brought him before the huge crowd that filled the square. As he stood on the palace balcony, she publicly humiliated him. Queen Agatha proclaimed, "Your superb talent for organizing the harvest, distributing grain to our people, and storing the surplus has been of great value to our country. I am grieved that you have equally great talent for stealing royal funds. You stole fifty-one thousand livres, showing no concern to serve our people but only to enrich yourself. As atonement and compensation, you will apologize and give to the people everything you have."

Elias, a hardworking but morally weak man, had succumbed to temptation when faced with the money so readily available before him. He cried out to the people of Xana. "I have done wrong. I have taken that which I did not earn. I am sorry. I will return it all to you. I promise never again to violate my queen's trust."

"You will give everything you have to the people," Agatha announced. "You will give all your land, your property, your possessions, and even your clothes. You will keep only the clothes you are now wearing. Everything you have will be sold at auction. I shall use the money to find more teachers. They will teach arithmetic to all the people of Xana so they understand contracts and accounts. No one can shortchange them again as you have done."

"Everything but the clothes I am wearing?" Elias whimpered.

"Everything," Queen Agatha responded, as Elias was led away, weeping. "You leave in disgrace. May you one day regain your honor through service, humility, frugality, and generosity to your people." Agatha repeated, "*And generosity.*"

All the wealth he had accumulated in a lifetime disappeared in a flash.

Manuel Chan was waiting out of sight, the next embezzler to be brought before the crowd. When he heard Elias receive his punishment, he shuddered.

"Manuel Chan," Queen Agatha announced to the huge crowd below her. "You built the schools where our children are learning to read and write. And you betrayed the people of Xana. You took for yourself money earned by the people who worked for you. To repay our good people, my agents now take from you everything you have—your brick factory, your house, all your clothes except those you are now wearing."

The crowd below cheered its approval.

Manuel Chan gulped. But he had been forewarned when he heard Queen Agatha inflict the penalty on Elias, and was at least half prepared. He pleaded to the queen, "May I apologize to our people?"

"Of course," the queen replied sweetly. "Please do."

"I am sorry for having abused some of you. My brick factory was everything to me, and I have lost it. I become once more a simple bricklayer. I will use my skill to serve my queen, and all of you, to build more good schools. I have made the greatest mistake a man ever can, taking from others when I already had abundance. I implore of you, do not repeat my mistake. Serve our gracious queen in her glorious quest to make our land prosperous and free."

Aurelia Fernandez was next to be presented to the people.

"Aurelia Fernandez, no matter how much jewelry you wear, it is never enough. You have stolen money intended for our children's schools, so you could buy still more jewelry. The people of Xana need more teachers more than you need more jewelry."

Aurelia interrupted. "You know how many livres I have taken. I will borrow from friends and pay it all back. You have removed me from your council. Even if I wanted to steal more, I will never again have access to crown funds. I cannot repeat my crime. Just let me keep my precious jewelry and live in humility."

"You will pay me back," Queen Agatha snapped, "when I take all your jewelry and sell it at public auction."

Aurelia screamed, "No! Don't!"

Queen Agatha continued, "I will also confiscate your house, and my agents will search most diligently for any more jewelry you may have hidden away." To the palace officers standing on the balcony ready to serve their queen, Agatha said, "Remove all the jewelry."

"No! Stop!" Aurelia screamed again. She kicked and punched, struggling to the limit of her physical strength to protect her treasures. Three burly women were needed to hold her down while a fourth removed the jewelry item by item, placing it in a large basket. All the time Aurelia alternately screamed, "No!" then "Stop!" and then just screamed.

The crowd gathered in the public square started chanting, "Take it all! Take it all!"

Bereft of her jewelry and feeling as naked as the instant she was born, Aurelia had to be forcibly led away. Screaming, "Give me back my jewelry!" she was taken off the balcony, through the palace, to a small door close to the main palace gate, and pushed outside. The door was immediately afterward slammed shut and locked from the inside. Aurelia tried very hard to re-open the door and failed repeatedly. Then she started bawling her head off.

"Robber!" shouted someone nearby. "How does it feel to be robbed?"

"Look at the crybaby," said someone else. "Crybaby, crybaby," the crowd jeered.

Soldiers of the queen's elite guard protected Aurelia from any physical harm. But the taunts from the crowd of commoners inflicted excruciating emotional pain. They started chanting, "Lost it all. Ha ha ha! Lost it all. Ha ha ha!" The jeering stopped only when Aurelia had managed to push her way through the crowd and out of sight.

Crying profusely, Aurelia found her way to Sylvia's house. She screamed at Sylvia, "The queen took away all my jewelry. It was horrible. I didn't deserve anything this awful." Sylvia looked at her sympathetically, but said nothing. After a minute Aurelia continued,

"I have lost everything, and now I'm the poorest person in the land of Xana." She pleaded, "Please help me."

"You have not lost everything," Sylvia reminded her. "You still have your dressmaking skills. And the queen will let you keep your needles and threads." To one of her assistants, Sylvia then said, "Mattie, please fetch that pile of old clothes." Then to Aurelia, Sylvia continued, "Will you mend these clothes we are preparing to distribute to the desperately poor? You may keep for yourself any dress that you like."

"Yes, of course," Aurelia replied.

"And then will you help me prepare our dinner for the homeless, and yourself, to partake of?"

Aurelia was now only whimpering slightly. She answered, "Yes."

Back on the palace balcony, Horatio Lloyd was the next to be brought before Queen Agatha. Before the queen could even address him, Horatio shouted, "Your punishments have been much too severe. Perhaps not for Elias, who set a bad example, but certainly for the rest of us, who only followed his example."

"It was your choice," Queen Agatha admonished him, "whether or not to follow a bad example. And your display of bad judgment makes you just as guilty as Elias. I expect, and require, that all citizens of Xana will assume responsibility for their own acts. All the pupils in all our schools will learn from your example, which I shall include in their textbooks. Their lesson is that all must assume personal responsibility for their behavior. All will learn that the consequences of bad behavior will not be mild."

"I offer to pay it back, and I apologize," Horatio replied in a not very sincere tone. "And then I shall take my property before you take it away from me, and sail away from Xana forever."

"Even as I speak, my agents are taking everything you have except the clothes you are wearing," the queen declared. "If you are unhappy in the land of Xana, you are welcome to leave. You may pay for your passage on one of my ships by working as a deck hand."

Several people below started chanting, "Horatio, go away, go away, go away..." and more and more joined in until Queen Agatha waved her arms over her head. Slowly, the crowd fell silent.

One by one, the other schemers stood before their queen and the people, apologizing, some less sincerely than others, and all losing everything but the clothes they were wearing. As citizens of ancient empires had enjoyed the barbaric contests in their great arenas, so too did the citizens of Xana enjoy the humiliation of government officials found guilty of corruption.

———

Elias learned nothing from his penalty and changed his subsequent behavior not one bit. He simply cursed his bad luck in getting caught. Manuel Chan was truly repentant and thereafter probably lived honorably. Whether he ever got his brick factory back is not known, but possible. Aurelia Fernandez was otherwise an honorable person but had an addiction to jewelry. She used her female beauty and wiles to beg or borrow money from anyone she could charm. One can easily imagine one creditor after another whom she did not pay back. Queen Agatha would not have supported the creditor, perhaps saying, "I hope you learned your lesson and do not lend any more money to Aurelia." Horatio Lloyd was one of those people who blamed others for his own shortcomings and was forever evading his own obligations. Queen Agatha did not tolerate such behavior and demanded that all her people assume personal responsibility. Though nothing is known about how he served in Queen Agatha's council of advisers, he probably had administrative skill. If he did leave Xana, then Xana was better off without him.

———

The vilest villain of them all, Howell Granby, was the last to be brought before the people. When he appeared on the balcony, boos, hisses, and insults filled the air. Several days in the dungeon had soiled the elegant clothes, mussed the immaculately combed hair, and allowed stubble to grow on the handsome face by which the people remembered him. He now bore the evil countenance that matched his behavior.

Queen Agatha raised her arms above her head and waved them back and forth—her usual signal for silence.

"Howell Granby," the queen proclaimed, "you have lied, cheated, and committed the most dishonest acts in your business that I have ever heard of. You will return—"

And Howell Granby interrupted the queen. "I will not. You think you're a queen? You're not. You deserted your throne. You're a pretender, a traitor, a thief—probably a whore too. Well, I'm one honest businessman who will not be bullied by a stupid impostor like you; I will not be bullied to give away what I have lawfully earned, through honest signed contracts. And I demand compensation of one hundred thousand livres for the miserable nights I spent in your dungeon."

Shocked silence fell upon all who heard these words. Nobody ever insulted their beloved queen. Even the queen herself stood in stunned silence.

Within a few seconds, she spoke. In a rage no one before had witnessed, she responded, "I decree, even if no one has done so before, that any person who cannot read, write, and calculate numbers is not responsible for any written contract. Those contracts that you speak of are now null and void. Every one of them. My agents have confiscated everything given to you from these contracts, which we now return to their rightful owners."

Howell Granby then lost his temper completely. "You bitch! You common whore! How many tavern drunks did you lie with last night? May you burn in hell!" Howell Granby raised his fist and lunged toward Queen Agatha. He swung with all his strength, but stronger hands restrained him, and his swing missed Agatha's face by a foot.

Agatha flinched away from this first-ever attempt to do her harm.

All of the ten embezzlers understood that their deeds were wrong and, to a greater or lesser extent, were humbled by the penalties inflicted on them. Howell Granby remained arrogant and abusive. He believed that he was right, that he had the right to conduct his business in his abusive way, and that no one had the right to interfere. Queen Agatha could have shipped him away to a distant land, but she knew he would restart his wicked business anywhere in the world. He was, Agatha perceived, incorrigible.

Therefore, very calmly, she decreed, "Off with his head."

Howell Granby was quickly forced to lie face down on a nearby marble table. He raged on, saying, "You are an impostor, a robber, and a harlot!" He continued with language so vile and so depraved that no one in the land of Xana could ever repeat it.

The crowd below heard very little of what he said as they started chanting, "Off with his head! Off with his head!" Only the queen and those nearest to her heard Granby's ravings.

In a moment, Granby saw a large, strong man, whose face was covered with a black mask, approach with a large ax. At the sight, his tone instantly reversed. "No, I don't mean any of that. I'm sorry! I'll never insult you again. I'll give it all back. Please just let me leave on the next ship—" The crunch of the ax on the back of his neck ended his whimpering.

It has been suggested that the executioner looked hard at Agatha, hoping up to the last second that she would say, "Stop!" Agatha could not stand the sight of blood and had turned to look the other way. When the crowd below started chanting, "Off with his head!" Agatha knew she would look weak if she stayed the execution. She also knew she must be strong before her people. She had no reasonable alternative to proceeding with the execution.

Queen Agatha grimaced as she heard the ax fall. Seconds later, she raised her arms over her head. Obeying her signal, the crowd fell silent. "It is done," Queen Agatha said. "We will burn the remains and spread the ashes over the grain fields." A few seconds later, still with her back to the carnage, and in a voice too low for the crowd below to hear, she demanded, "Hurry up. Get the corpse out of here and clean up the mess!"

While some workers quickly moved the head and body out of sight, others scrubbed clean the bloody table. Queen Agatha addressed her loyal followers. "If there be any among you who had wished to enrich yourselves at the expense of your people, know that this will not happen." Queen Agatha did not say, "This will not be allowed," or "We will not let this happen." She stated the matter plainly and strongly. "This will not happen."

"In death, Howell Granby will serve the people of Xana as he never served them in life. When a man has no legal heirs, his estate goes to the crown. Therefore, I shall return to every one of you all that you paid Howell Granby, with interest. You may keep, as a gift, whatever he provided you in return. If he has wasted his ill-earned wealth so that what remains is not sufficient to fully repay you all, I will make up the rest from the royal treasury."

The people listening from the town square below cheered their approval, and a new chant arose: "Long live Queen Agatha! Long live Queen Agatha!"

Pedro Mendez stood in the square, among the crowd. A friend next to him remarked, "The more perceptive of the people understand our queen's message. We have to create our wealth through our own labor." Pedro nodded in agreement. "And taking even a little bit from someone else, or abusing them in any way, won't be allowed. And one more thing: she wants us to know that punishment will be swift, sure, and harsh." Pedro acknowledged this, too. "Nobody will get the chance to offend again," his friend concluded. "And when the consequences of those offenses are obvious, the queen won't haggle over questions of innocence versus guilt."

Pedro added, "Except for the headless Howell Granby, Queen Agatha always allows the opportunity for redemption."

"I don't understand," the friend said.

"Remember that she told each of the culprits, 'May you one day regain your honor with service to our people.'" Pedro was one of very few who fully understood his queen's message as soon as she delivered it.

—

A few days later, Queen Agatha's agents held the auction at which Aurelia Fernandez's jewelry was sold, one piece at a time, to the highest bidder. In the way of a beautiful woman whose sense of courtesy and tact allows her to get people to do almost anything she wants, Aurelia borrowed money from friends and attended the auction.

One of the first items offered was the pearl necklace. Tragically for Aurelia, Helmut Giezech kept bidding up its price. Helmut was a trader whose business had prospered once Queen Agatha freed him from the moneylenders' yoke. He paid his workers well and always treated them with dignity. He found that he made much larger profits for himself by treating his workers and his customers well than Queen Julia's aristocrats had ever made by cheating them.

"Five thousand six hundred livres," said Aurelia, in obvious duress.

"Five thousand seven hundred," Helmut responded.

"I don't have five thousand seven hundred livres," Aurelia cried out in desperation. "Put this offer on hold while I try to borrow more money; you can sell some of the other items in the meantime."

"Five thousand seven hundred, cash, ready for immediate purchase," Helmut replied, holding the money high enough that all could see it.

"Sold for five thousand seven hundred livres," the auctioneer announced. Aurelia screamed at the sight of Helmut taking the necklace in hand.

Aurelia shed copious tears, but she had the presence of mind to buy back several of her other favorite ornaments until her money was used up. Mercifully for Aurelia, Helmut did not bid on any of them.

After the auction, Aurelia came crying to Helmut. "Why are you so cruel? You know how much I want that necklace. Now you have taken it from me a second time."

"The necklace is useless to me personally, except as an item of trade," Helmut replied. "Your treasure is my trash. And I suppose some of my treasures are your trash. I make you two promises. I will keep the necklace safely until you pay me seven thousand livres up front. I also promise to give the additional one thousand three hundred livres to our glorious Queen Agatha's schools. I will not earn even one livre for myself."

Several weeks later, Aurelia returned to Helmut Giezech. She proclaimed, "I have borrowed and begged and cried for seven thousand livres. Here they are. Will you please give me back my pearls?"

Helmut counted out the money, slowly and carefully. Poor Aurelia watched in dreadful anxiety. "Yes," he finally replied, confident he had the full amount. Then he withdrew to another room, closing the door behind him. Aurelia had a sickening feeling that Helmut was taking all her money for nothing in return. But a minute later, he came back with the pearls in hand.

"Thank you," Aurelia managed to say weakly, grabbing the pearls out of his hand. She admired them for a minute, placed them around her neck, and ran out of the house.

The next day at the council meeting, Helmut declared with great fanfare, "At the jewelry auction I bought the notorious pearl necklace for five thousand seven hundred livres. Yesterday Aurelia bought it back from me for seven thousand livres. Here are the additional one thousand three hundred livres, which I am donating to support our gracious queen's schools." He walked around the table to hand the coins to Hector Ramirez. Hector immediately began riffling through the stack of ledgers and reports that he brought to every council meeting, preparing to make the appropriate entry in his accounts. Helmut then pulled another sack of coins out of his pocket and handed them to Hector. "And here are another one thousand three hundred livres of my own money, which I am donating for the education of the children of Xana."

After the meeting adjourned, Helmut himself wrote the public report of the proceedings, ensuring that all of Xana's people would know about his donation. In later years he amassed great wealth by shrewd trading, and frequently, with great fanfare, gave large sums to Sylvia Hartly and other charities.

Helmut Giezech, as a member of the queen's council of advisers, guided the growth of a market economy for Xana. The rigors of the market were tempered by strictly enforced laws to protect both customers and workers. Likewise, new laws required that both workplaces and neighborhoods be kept clean. Severe penalties were decreed for all violations; in consequence, there were very few violators. People who lost or could not find work with merchants or craftsmen were set to useful tasks by the queen's agents. Most toiled at cleaning the city or building roads or other structures. Some, with more ambition, were apprenticed to master craftsmen.

Over the years, Aurelia regained some respectability—as well as a huge collection of jewelry. If she owed money to buy ever more baubles, it was a private matter between herself and her lender. It is suggested in a very few sources that she became the queen's dressmaker, and that the queen paid her generously. But Aurelia was never again able to touch crown money.

During Agatha's second six-month absence from Xana, no one dared steal money she had intended for the common people's welfare.

———

In Wan, though not in Xana, Olaf was king. During Queen Agatha's second summer in her husband's realm, King Olaf had arranged a swordsmanship contest, and he himself entered. Contestants were not supposed to harm each other, but accidental injury, and even death, was a common consequence of the flailing blades. Agatha demanded that all contestants wear the armor of jousting and that a scrape of sword on armor over a vital spot would constitute victory. The contestants complained that covering their arms with armor would inhibit their agility with the blade. Agatha relented, but only on the condition that if an arm was cut, the injured contestant would be declared the winner.

Of the more than one hundred swordsmen, mostly noblemen and army officers, King Olaf and his younger brother, Ivan, were truly the best in the land. The royal brothers were always the winners. Finally Olaf and Ivan alone were left undefeated. For half an hour, their blades flashed against each other without any nicks on their armor. At that time, Agatha walked unprotected between them—in some versions totally naked—gently pushed them apart and insisted, "This match is a tie. Shake hands on it." Olaf and Ivan meekly obeyed.

Soon after the match, Prince Ivan poured a glass of wine for young Baron Tomas, his favorite childhood playmate. As he poured another for himself, he complained, "This one time I could have beaten my brother. But that Agatha bitch got bored and interfered. Of course I stepped back. You know as well as I that I would never slash a woman. But what made me agree to a tie? Why didn't I say, 'No, we'll finish this, one way or the other?' "

"It's almost as if Agatha has a charm about her," Tomas replied, "that she cannot be harmed or disobeyed."

"Ssh," Ivan admonished his friend. "I confess only to you that I believe the same thing. Just keep this between the two of us."

"You know I always support you," Tomas said. "You, Ivan, can be the great king Wan needs and deserves. These many years now, everybody has known what a weak king Olaf is, that the real power lies behind the throne, in those who support him."

"He has charisma," Ivan acknowledged. "He charms the barons. And as younger brother, I remain on the sidelines. But now Olaf bends to the will of his scheming foreign wife. She threatens the foundation of our realm! Her schools for the common people endanger our barons' very survival. For years, I have pondered how to unseat my brother and become king." Ivan fell silent for a moment. "Agatha may actually be my route to success."

"May I suggest, sir, that before you strike, you wait until Olaf and Agatha leave our country to return to Xana?"

"Oh, I agree with you. Before they depart, and in utmost secrecy, let me see how many of the barons I can persuade to join our cause."

Like Olaf, Ivan excelled at the manly arts of horsemanship, hunting, jousting, and swordsmanship. Unlike Olaf, he also engaged freely in the unseemly manly arts: gambling, drinking, and womanizing. He was adept with the dice and the cards, able to interpret his opponents' subtle signs, and he won consistently. Also unlike Olaf, he had studied, with great attention to detail, the art of ruling a country.

By the end of her second six-month stay in Wan, Agatha had converted her new land into a second Xana. The fields were lush with grain, vegetables and fruits grew in the gardens, and the children of peasants were learning to read and write. Queen Agatha was beloved by the people like no other ruler in Wan's history. Olaf might be king, but his queen was the country's real ruler.

However, many wealthy people in Wan besides Prince Ivan considered Agatha a usurper. In her absence, they usurped her and King Olaf.

Shortly after their return to Xana, Olaf and Queen Agatha were handed a letter from Wan, which read:

"My dear brother Olaf, I am now, by the grace of the barons whose names I have inscribed below, king of Wan. If you return, you will be placed in prison. Agatha, we will not let you again enter our kingdom. If you come, you will not be allowed to leave your ship, and you will be sent home at once to your own land. Your loving brother, Ivan."

Prince Olaf winced. "If I go back, Ivan will have me beheaded," he lamented.

Even before his brother sailed away, Ivan had convinced twenty of Wan's most powerful barons that their wealth and status were in grave danger. He was confident that those who assembled secretly before him would support him.

"Education for the peasants," he declared to them, "is the ruin of us all. How can we keep them in servitude if they are educated? Agatha is our deadly enemy. We must not let her be the ruler of our land.

"My brother is a weakling. Agatha surely is not, but we dare not let her come to any harm. Should anything bad happen to her, the peasants will revolt, and we will surely lose."

"What are we to do?" one of the barons demanded.

"Our only chance," Ivan said, "is to keep her away from Wan. If she returns, we will be powerless to stop her from reducing us all to common peasants."

"Powerless?" another baron cried. "Haven't we a force of thousands to defend against her?"

Ivan shook his head, a frown on his face. "Her army is superbly trained and equipped, well disciplined, and intensely loyal. Every one of her soldiers from the general on down would give his life for her. Every one of her soldiers is equal to five of ours. Strong and determined is our foe, Agatha, and she knows that we dare not hurt her. But she has one weakness. She is squeamish about bloodshed."

At this, the barons exchanged knowing glances. They had all endured the stifling armor she had required during the swordsmanship contests.

"She believes her army's mission is to defend her land, not to invade another. I wager my kingdom that she will stay away if we warn her not to come. Though we do her no harm, we can threaten her adored Olaf."

The ship that carried Agatha and Olaf back to Xana was scarcely out of sight before Ivan made his move. He declared himself king of Wan. Instantly, as the news spread, the capital seethed with unrest. Within the hour, a large delegation of the common people converged on the palace to demand the restoration of Agatha and Olaf.

"Olaf is our king and Agatha is our queen," demanded the commoner Uriah Niessa, as hundreds stood behind him. Only a thin line of soldiers held them back from Ivan.

"I am your king and Mariel is your queen," Ivan shouted.

Mariel had been married to Ivan only six months. She was the daughter of Wan's richest baron. As Agatha was to the deposed King Olaf, so Mariel was always beside Ivan at court. Beautiful, polite, and cultured, in her eighteen years she had already become skilled in the feminine art of pleasing a man in the marital bed. Even so, Ivan kept several mistresses on the side.

"If you wish Agatha to be your queen," Ivan continued, "then we shall send you all to the land of Xana. There you can serve your traitorous Queen Agatha."

Uriah tried to protest, but Ivan decreed, "Every one of you shall go to Xana and never return. This is my command."

"My mother! My children!" someone whimpered in the crowd behind Uriah. "I cannot leave them to perish in this cruel land."

"Never let it be said that Ivan is a cruel king. Captain of the guard! Send five soldiers to accompany each of these traitors. Let them gather their families and any possessions they may cherish, then place them all on ships to Xana. So I, king of Wan, have decreed. So have it done."

Some of the protesters tried to flee, but, unnoticed while Uriah and Ivan spoke, hundreds of the king's elite palace guard had appeared in the streets behind the crowd. Outside the palace walls, the commoners found themselves surrounded. Inside, some of the barons questioned their new king's leniency.

"Don't you understand? Are you fools?" Ivan demanded. "Of course not. These are the leaders of a revolution. The rest of the peasants will not dare revolt after we send this rabble away. Agatha considers them her people. Imprison them, and she may return to free them. Execute them, and she may come back for vengeance—and her vengeance would be terrible indeed. Send her people to her, unharmed, and we are better off to have them gone. Make it clear, however, before they board the ships: anyone who dares to return will be immediately beheaded."

Ivan called for ink and parchment and, in his own hand, wrote a letter to Queen Agatha. Knowing that she knew them all by name and face, he listed every person he was exiling to the land of Xana.

Days later, as the first of twenty ships sailed into her harbor, Agatha stood on the wharf, her prince beside her and one step behind. Soldiers held back the crowd of admirers who always flocked when she appeared. A mass of anxious faces clustered along the ship's rail. She held her arms high to greet them.

Uriah, his wife, and their four children were first to disembark. He and his sons bowed before their queen. His wife and daughters curtsied deeply. "My queen, must you desert us? Please come back. The people will join you, and we will depose the usurper Ivan and restore you as our true queen."

"That will cause much killing and bloodshed," Agatha replied solemnly, "for Ivan will die fighting like a common soldier before he surrenders his crown, stolen though it is. I will not take wealth from my people and waste it in war. Queen of Wan I am not to be." And with outstretched arms she proclaimed, "I welcome you all as full citizens of Xana and implore you to use your talents to serve your new country."

As one ship after another docked, Agatha sought to give comfort and welcome her new citizens, greeting each by name. To those who questioned her as Uriah had, she replied, "Bloodshed does not win a kingdom, but you have a new land to build." Agatha's words traveled fast among the disembarking exiles, and most already knew her message before they stood before their queen.

———

B ack in Wan, Ivan proved capable as a king. By deftly playing the barons' ambitions against each other, he assured his own supremacy. Without acknowledging her role, he quietly welcomed the improvements to agriculture that Agatha had introduced. He understood that keeping the common people well fed but unlettered made it easier to hold them in obedient servitude. He also knew that making a country rich required trade. Thus did Ivan send out ships to trade with the land of Xana and other realms throughout the world. And so the land grew rich, but nearly all the wealth accrued to himself and his barons. Wisely, both Agatha and Ivan, though for different reasons, kept the peace and elected not to interfere in the affairs of the other's land.

Chapter 5

The day after Queen Agatha returned from her second and final visit to Wan, she was in the city square, speaking with her people. A woman and her son came to her, in tears. Agatha recognized them as Michael Gant, who wanted so much to go to school, and his mother.

"Gracious queen, they would not let my son enroll in school again. You promised…"

"I remember my promise as well as you do," Queen Agatha replied. "Your grief is healed. Let us go together to the school, and I will have Michael enrolled."

"And you still remember my son's name!" his grateful mother replied, astonished.

Queen Agatha held Michael by the hand for the half-hour walk to the school. "What am I going to learn in school?" Michael asked.

"First you must learn to read and write. Then you can read any book in the entire land of Xana."

Michael's next question was profound for a six-year-old who had never been to school. "I heard someone talking about King

Lars and Queen Lara. I've been wondering about them. Who were they and what did they do?"

"King Lars and Queen Lara were my grandparents," Queen Agatha replied. "Yes, their names differed only in the final letter, a rare coincidence. Their subjects frequently commented on this. Side by side, they ruled the land of Xana wisely and kept our country tranquil. This was in spite of a huge gap between aristocrats' wealth and the common people's poverty. They were already more than fifty years old when their fondest wish was finally granted. Queen Lara delivered a healthy baby girl, and they had an heir to the throne. They named their daughter Julia, and coddled and pampered the girl with every imaginable luxury."

Michael interrupted. "If King Lars and Queen Lara were your grandparents, Julia must be your mother. She became Queen Julia!" The boy's pride at this deduction shone on his face.

"Yes, Julia was my mother. And even though they pampered her, King Lars and Queen Lara did teach their daughter to be courteous, and they found kind teachers to educate her well. They encouraged her to play with the daughters of the aristocrats. Young Princess Julia quickly became the leader of all the playmates' games." Little Michael gazed up, wide-eyed, as he took in what the queen was explaining to him. "When Julia was fifteen years old," she continued, "her mother died, and she stepped into her mother's place as co-ruler. When, three years later, King Lars was himself on his deathbed, Julia was at his side. King Lars's final words to Julia were, 'You have learned all that I taught you. I know you will be a wonderful monarch.'

"'You have been a good teacher,' replied his daughter, who continued, 'I promise to govern by the wisdom you have taught.'

"For ten years, the rich and handsome young men of the land sought her hand in marriage. But she rebuffed them all. Queen Julia simply had no interest in romance. But then Captain Marcel Gregorius, who had been protecting our frontier, was assigned to the grand palace as a member of the queen's elite guard. His duty was to guard Queen Julia's person, but he soon did more than this. The young captain became enamored of her and begged for her hand in marriage. Though the queen did not share his passion, she admired his handsome face and courteous manner and admired his bravery on the battlefield. His ardor in her bedchamber gave her great pleasure. Marcel's bid to marry the queen was encouraged by his father, the commanding general of Xana's army. General Herbertus Gregorius was excited by the prospect of a future grandson becoming Xana's king someday. And so an extravagant royal wedding was held in the palace."

Queen Agatha's tone then became very cross. In a disgusted voice she continued, "From what my mother told me of her wedding, the pure waste, even allowing for a dignified ceremony, could have supported a thousand families like yours."

Returning to the solemn tone of a teacher of history, Queen Agatha continued, "Four months after the wedding, a barbarian horde crossed Xana's borders, seeking pillage and destruction. 'I must defend my country,' young Prince Marcel said. 'I must go with our army to repel the enemy.'

"His father protested. 'As prince consort, you need not risk your life in battle again.'

"Prince Marcel declared, 'A glorious victory over a deadly foe will enhance my standing in court. All my life, like you, I have trained to defend the land of Xana. I have fought other battles and have never been hurt. I promise I will return to you with news of a great victory.'

"His wife, Queen Julia, pleaded, 'I shall fear for your safety.'

"Prince Marcel replied, 'I promise to return to you safe and sound. For as long as they remember our victory here, the barbarians won't dare to come back. We will have a long and happy life together.'

"Queen Julia hesitated, but finally gave in. 'If that is your wish, then go.' Prince Marcel kissed his queen passionately. The prince was full of confidence as he departed. But Queen Julia had tears in her eyes as she watched him leave the room.

"Instead of resting on his rank as prince, Marcel returned to his old company as its captain, and marched into battle at the head of his men.

"In the palace's grand ballroom, Queen Julia was holding court with Xana's aristocrats and some foreign ambassadors when a courier arrived with news of the battle. 'We have repulsed the enemy,' he announced. 'Our land is safe. The number of our dead is huge, but our enemy has lost many more.' The courier hesitated before completing his report, but found the courage to go on. 'I am grieved, Your Majesty, to say that Prince Marcel is among our dead.'

"In front of her large and noble audience, Queen Julia leaped to her feet. She put a handkerchief to her eyes and stood some time in silence. Finally she sobbed, 'My worst fears are realized. I can never be the same again.' Queen Julia was again silent for a while. She continued, 'Now I myself know how all of you who have lost loved ones feel. Somehow, we must carry on.' The queen again brought her handkerchief to her eyes. After a short time, she laid her hands on her belly and spoke once more, 'And yet, amid our grief, I also have good news. I am with child. Our child will be my husband's legacy, and our line will continue as monarchs of Xana.'

"General Herbertus was torn apart by conflicting emotions. His grief at the loss of his son was keen, and yet he was elated at the coming birth of the grandson he had yearned for, the future king of Xana. His excitement overcame his decorum, and in the midst of this somber assembly, he cried out, 'My grandson will be the next king of Xana.'

"A courtier seated near the queen asked, in a more seemly fashion, 'Did Prince Marcel know you were carrying his child?'

"'Yes,' the queen replied. Then, in her sorrow, she fell silent, but soon continued, 'He wanted so much to announce both our child and our victory while standing by my side. But now,' and her voice broke again, 'I must do so alone.'"

Little Michael's gaze widened even farther, and his mouth fell open. "That child must be you!" he cried.

"Yes," Queen Agatha replied.

The boy's brows knit as he thought of something else.

"Then you never knew your father?"

"No. He died before I was born. But throughout the land he is remembered as a hero. My mother never married again. She spent the rest of her life teaching me how to be a good queen."

"Did you know your grandfather, the general?"

"I saw him, they tell me. But I have no memory of him," the queen said. "They say he was at first unhappy that Queen Julia bore him a granddaughter instead of the grandson he had expected. But within days he changed his mind. The general understood what we should all know—that a girl baby is as precious as a boy baby. He delighted in playing with me when I was just a babe in arms. And so I delighted in him, they tell me. I reached for brightly colored ornaments that he held, or for decorations on his uniform. I am told that I recognized both him and my mother and smiled at their approach. But when I was just four months old, my grandfather died in his sleep. Nobody did him any evil; his death was natural."

"So you were too little to remember him."

"Yes."

"Do you remember your grandmother?"

"My grandmother, General Herbertus's wife, died giving birth to my father, Prince Marcel. He was her first and only child. My grandfather was grief-stricken. He threw himself into his duties with the army, trying to bury his immense sadness. As my father grew, the old general trained the boy to follow him as an officer. If my grandfather had had a loving wife to care for, he probably would never have become commanding general."

As she walked, little Michael's hand in hers, Queen Agatha also spoke to him about Xana's Great Charter, and other tales from their land's history. Before she had time to say all that Michael wanted to hear, they reached the school.

The headmaster, Lan Weili, had been hired at great expense from a faraway land for his skills at administration. His assistants were all lifelong citizens of Xana.

Queen Agatha, little Michael, and his mother strode right into the headmaster's office, interrupting a meeting. "I promised Michael Gant," Queen Agatha proclaimed, "that he could start school this year. He is now enrolled." This, as the assistants all understood, was their queen's style. She didn't say "This is what I will do," or "This is my wish." She stated her wishes as actions already achieved.

Lan Weili replied, with the authoritarian arrogance typical of his native land's culture, "He has applied late. The first-year class for six-year-olds is filled."

The queen's anger flared. "Do I have to enroll him on your roster myself? Since you cannot do your job, you may return home across the sea."

One of the assistants quickly interceded, saying, "I will enroll Michael. Please do not be so harsh to Lan Weili. He has never known adversity, but he is a brilliant scholar and leader for our teachers. I suffered with you through the Bad Times, and I know you always do the right thing for our people."

"And I promise you," Queen Agatha replied, "that Michael Gant will be your best pupil."

"That is up to Michael Gant," Lan Weili declared.

Agatha snapped back, "You question the honesty of your queen?"

Before more heated words could be exchanged, Michael said, "I promise I will be your best pupil."

Queen Agatha turned to leave, but Michael called out, "Queen Agatha!"

"Yes?" Agatha replied encouragingly. She turned back and, as she so often did with children, squatted so she could look directly into Michael's eyes.

"Dear queen, I never had so much fun in my life as when I talked with you. Will I ever talk to you again?"

"You will. I promise. Not tomorrow or even next year. There are many people in our country, and I have the duty to make all of them happy. But some year, we will talk again, and you can tell me all the wonderful things you have learned in school."

What Queen Agatha did not know was that in the nights to come, Michael would stay awake, memorizing every word that she had said.

———

This event is the second in the record in which Queen Agatha intervened to enroll a talented pupil in school. She probably did so on other occasions, but if so, the stories are lost with the passage of time. On the first occasion, when she enrolled Anya Mendez at age four, she may be faulted for breaking her own law that children should start school at age five. But the result was happy, as Queen Agatha, with her great insight into human character, had foreseen. With Michael Gant, the queen only bypassed bureaucratic obstructions to enroll a six-year-old in the class for six-year-olds.

———

In her fifth year of school, when she was only eight years old, Anya Mendez barged into her headmaster's office, telling him, "I'm going to the queen's council meeting today with my father. I am sorry to miss class, but I will learn so much about government just by being there."

The headmaster knew that several of Pedro Mendez's children attended his school, that they were all excellent pupils, and that Pedro was one of Xana's leading citizens. After some hesitation, he replied, "Well, so be it."

Anya ran home to tell her father, "I'm going to the queen's council with you today. The headmaster said it would be all right."

Pedro also hesitated, but soon acquiesced. "Come along. But be sure to behave yourself, and don't interrupt or talk out of turn. Two army officers are always in the room, and they'll remove you forcibly if you disturb the meeting."

"I promise I'll be on my best behavior," Anya replied. "Surely you know I would never do anything Queen Agatha didn't approve of."

"Of course," Pedro said. "I'm sorry I spoke harshly. I guess I got too anxious."

Thus came Anya uninvited with her father to the queen's council. Pedro explained, embarrassed, "Anya absolutely insisted on coming. I remember you saying, 'Anya should be encouraged in all she wants to do, as long as it is useful and honorable.'"

"My wise Pedro," Queen Agatha reassured him, "you always do the right thing." Turning to Anya, she cautioned the girl, "I know you are brimming over with good ideas, and the council will hear them and act on them. But I will call upon you last. Please listen patiently to all the other council members and absorb their wisdom. You should know how council is conducted before gushing forth." What Anya might have said is lost, but it is known that the queen's council attended primarily to improving education and how best to profit from foreign trade. Anya would certainly have contributed enthusiastically to these discussions.

The next day, Anya told an assembly of all the pupils and teachers in her school about the council meeting. Her friends were not envious of her special privilege, but proud that one of their classmates had actually served on Queen Agatha's council.

Several members of her elite guard always accompanied Queen Agatha on her daily forays outside the palace to connect with her people and to visit the schools. They not only guarded the queen, but also ran errands at her request. She would ask one to deliver a message or fetch a particular person. As she always addressed a soldier very graciously and by his own name, each considered it an honor to fulfill these extra services.

Queen Agatha did not visit little Michael Gant's school again until the year after Anya Mendez had become a member of her council. One of the soldiers opened the door to Michael's fifth-year class and announced, "Her majesty, Queen Agatha." As they had been instructed, all the pupils and their teacher stood up. The boys bowed and the girls curtsied as Queen Agatha entered. She pulled up a chair and sat down amidst them, her head level with theirs, and outstretched her arms, palms up. Instantly all in the room relaxed.

"What have you learned in class recently that you think is important?" the queen asked.

Several hands went up. She chose a boy on the far side of the room. "Memorizing facts is necessary," the lad answered, "but we also need to learn to reason and to think critically if we are to make the correct decisions for our lives."

"A pretty important fact we all need to memorize, don't you think?" a girl interrupted. "Queen Agatha, I suppose you have to think critically all the time to rule our country."

"I do," the queen responded. "Every day, new problems—or new facts, I should say—arise. I need all the ability I can muster to think critically if I am to find the best solutions. Sometimes I make mistakes. That is one reason I need to be with my people every day. Only by listening to all of you can I quickly learn if things are going wrong. The sooner I find out, the more easily I can correct a wrong."

She switched tracks. "Who is ready to answer a simple reasoning question?" After a few seconds she continued, "I see nearly every hand in the room is up. I hope you're as pleased as I am."

The children lowered their hands and listened expectantly. "Here's the question. Alphonse sometimes brings marvelous, elaborate toys and shows them off in class. You keep begging to go to his house to play with them, and finally he says, grudgingly, 'Come over today after school.' Very sternly, he adds, 'But you'd better not break any of my toys.' You've heard rumors that Alphonse gets very mean when he can't get his way. Soon afterward your old friend Georg says, 'Mama has invited you to dinner tonight. Why don't you come over early and we can play.' Georg is the sweetest, kindest person you have ever met. He doesn't have any fancy toys, but for him a simple block of wood becomes a carriage with horses in which you can journey to a faraway and enchanted land. Would you rather go to Alphonse's house or Georg's? Why did you make this choice? Who'd like to answer?"

Queen Agatha expected the pupils to hesitate, but after a moment a few of them raised their hands. Agatha was careful to choose from among this much smaller band of volunteers.

The boy she chose said, "This is my one and only chance to play with Alphonse's toys. But it sounds like he won't let me do more than look at them, and I've already seen them at school, and I won't ever be his friend. I think friendship is more important than fancy toys. And I like Georg's imagination. I'll go to Georg's house."

Solemnly, he added, "I think you must have to make harder choices than that."

"Good reasoning," the queen said, applauding as she spoke. "I certainly do have to make harder decisions. You have chosen a wise value, friendship over riches. So long as I always make my people's happiness and prosperity my priority, I can guide myself to a good answer."

Another boy spoke up. "I'm Jere, and I have a different answer. Seth is right: this is my only chance to play with those toys, and I have to be very careful not to break them. But this is my only chance; so I'll go to Alphonse's house. Georg seems like a nice boy, and he's a good friend, too. So I'll ask him if I can wait until dinner to come to his house. I'm sure we can play some other day."

The children looked at each other uncertainly. A boy asked, "Who got the right answer?"

Queen Agatha replied, "Seth and Jere both gave good answers. You both wisely weighed the evidence. Then you both listened to your hearts as you decided. This made the choice more comfortable for each of you. In everyday life, there are different ways to do things, all of which will work. Seth is a peaceful boy, faithful and trusted as a friend. Jere is more adventuresome. Different people can be comfortable dealing with the same situation in quite different ways."

The teacher broke in, "How did you learn these boys' personalities so quickly?"

"I listened to my heart," the queen replied. "I had already endorsed Seth's answer, and then Jere was bold and confident enough to suggest that a different response was correct for him."

Then Agatha asked a very difficult question, appropriate for the tenth year of school, but way beyond the fifth. It was not about obscure facts; rather, it involved thinking through how to deal with a specific situation. Agatha sensed unease in the teacher as well as the pupils. And she locked eyes with Michael Gant.

"An alchemist tells you he has invented a method to turn iron into gold. As proof, he shows you a tiny gold saucer. He asks for a loan of one hundred thousand livres to develop his process, and promises to return two hundred thousand to you in six months. He knows you have that hundred thousand livres to invest."

"What is his proof that he didn't make the saucer out of gold in the first place?" Michael asked. "Or that he didn't put a thin gold foil over the saucer?"

Queen Agatha responded as if she were the alchemist. "I can assure you I am telling you the complete truth. You can trust me."

"I don't trust him," Michael responded. "I never read about anybody doing this, and it just sounds too good to be true. So I tell him, 'If I bring you an iron nail, can I watch you turn it into gold?'"

"Oh, no," responded the queen-cum-alchemist. "It's a very secret process. I'll have to charge you four thousand livres. But if you bring me the nail, tomorrow I will show it to you turned to gold."

"And you keep the four thousand livres? If you can turn it into gold, you don't need any more money from me. And I'll give you the nail, free. No deal."

"Very well, no advance payment." Michael marveled at his queen's marvelous impersonation. "But I keep the nail."

The alchemist turned back into a queen as Agatha continued. "You bring him the nail, and the next day he shows you the nail now colored like gold."

"Does it have the same size, shape, and weight?" Michael asked. "Maybe he switched nails. Or just put a thin gold film on it."

"So far as you can tell, only the color has changed. But the alchemist says, 'See, I turned your nail into gold. One hundred thousand livres? Deal?'"

"I'll have to think about it," Michael insisted. "I want to read all the evidence I can find in the National Library."

"Right now, or I'll make the offer to someone else," the queen growled, still pretending to be the alchemist.

"Not now. I'll come back if I decide on it, and take my chances that no one else has taken your offer in the meantime." And then, speaking to the queen instead of the alchemist, Michael interjected, "He sounds like a swindler. I think he'd take all my money, and then board a ship to a distant land, and disappear. If I had one hundred thousand livres, I would find young craftsmen just finishing their apprenticeships; any of them ingenious enough to make better new products could use my money to make those things. That would bring real wealth to the land of Xana. And I would get back my money with a profit!"

One of Michael's classmates murmured, "He's such a brain."

Another asked, "Did he get it right?"

And another said, "As far as I can tell, he did."

Queen Agatha responded, "Michael gave a very good answer."

As she was leaving the room, she overheard one of the pupils say, "How'd she know his name?"

The reader will recognize that the queen was testing her young scholar for both his knowledge of facts and his reasoning ability. Why did she choose a question from the sciences?

While she was growing up, Agatha would have read writings from ancient societies about their science and philosophy and, from some of them, their democratic politics. The ancient authorities were mostly wrong about physics, but the archers of later kingdoms did not need to understand action and reaction and parabolic trajectories to know how to adjust their bows' elevations for varying target distances, or how much to lead a moving target. The ancient concept of an earth-centered solar system was also wrong, but the astronomers of ancient lands had prepared fairly good star charts and had found the motions of the moon and planets with moderate accuracy. As a seafaring nation, Xana would have had sailors who knew how to navigate by the sun and stars. Agatha, in her childhood, would have stood on the palace balcony at night. She would have watched how the moon and planets moved, seen how the moon's phases were related to the angle between moon and sun, and learned to identify some of the brighter constellations.

What we now call chemistry did not exist. Agatha would have read about alchemists' claims of turning base materials into gold. But she also used her critical intelligence to deduce that because this supposed conversion had never become widely used, the efforts had failed. Thus, she knew, the alchemists' claims of success were fraudulent. Young Michael's performance on her test was superb.

In the headmaster's office, Lan Weili said, "Queen Agatha, I owe you an apology. I made a mistake. I should not have questioned you. Michael Gant is more than the best pupil in the school. He is the most dedicated young scholar I have ever known, in my land or yours."

Queen Agatha replied, "I accept your apology graciously. Early in my reign, I made an even bigger mistake, and it cost many of my people their happiness. Several of the people I entrusted to run the country during my first sojourn into Wan robbed the people and the treasury in my absence. I perceived correctly that they were competent administrators. Looking back, I now see that I also perceived their dishonesty. The signs were all there. I became careless and ignored those signs. I'm more observant now. It won't happen again. My story, like Michael's, has a happy ending. I was able to return to my people all that my unworthy councilors had stolen, and added a generous rate of interest."

Even as the headmaster was singing his praises, Michael Gant himself was devastated that Queen Agatha had given him so little of her time. As class was dismissed, one of the soldiers, always nearby to protect and serve his queen, called out, "Michael Gant."

"Yes, sir."

"Queen Agatha says, 'I made you a promise.' Please come with me so our gracious queen may fulfill her promise." Michael's exhilaration could hardly be imagined.

The soldier escorted Michael to a classroom, now empty of pupils, where the queen was seated alone. Michael bowed before his queen as all school boys were taught. Then he sat down comfortably beside her. "You have learned so much," the queen said. "Please share with me what you know."

"I can do long multiplication and division in my head," he said

"You're ahead of me," Queen Agatha replied. "I need a pen and parchment."

"I've memorized the Great Charter, too." Michael fell silent a moment. "But my classmates all know I'm different. That somehow I'm above them. I feel like I have to answer some questions wrong, so they won't turn their backs on me completely. Of course, I made sure I answered your question as best I could."

The queen nodded sympathetically. Encouraged, Michael let his pent-up thoughts pour out.

"I get bored in class. I read as much as I can in the library, and I already know everything the teacher is going to say. So instead of listening so much to the lesson, I concentrate on how the teacher is giving the lessons, and how the pupils respond. I've figured out how different ways of teaching can work differently with different pupils. Some learn better from some kinds of teaching, and some learn better from other kinds. I guess what I mean is that what we really need is for each of us to have a teacher for ourselves. I know that can't happen. We don't have enough teachers. I've tried to help—to tutor some of my classmates, to help them learn the way they need to. But they don't like this very well. They think I'm being bossy, trying to act like a teacher. The headmaster doesn't give me any encouragement, either."

Michael looked at Agatha expectantly, as if seeking confirmation of whether he had gone too far. She smiled encouragingly and he went on.

"In class, they teach us your vision for the land of Xana to prosper and be happy. I have my own vision. May I tell you what it is?"

"Yes, of course," the queen said.

"My vision is to arrange for every pupil to have a personal tutor, to teach face to face. The higher-level pupils would tutor the lower-level ones, in every school, everywhere in our land.

"And I know how we can do this! In every school in Xana, you can have the headmaster find the best pupils in the upper classes. The headmasters can invite these pupils to be tutors for everyone in the lower classes who is struggling with their lessons. Give them a week or two to decide. Some of them may not be comfortable as tutors. And they should be allowed to say no. But I'm sure many of us will be eager to accept. My dear Queen Agatha, if you decree this, it will happen!"

She gazed joyfully into young Michael's eager face, but shook her head slowly.

"With matters of policy," the queen said, "I can't just wave my hand and have a thing happen. Yet with the wisdom of our council, I promise you that we'll find a way."

"I have learned that there is another pupil, Anya Mendez, on your council," Michael said. "She is a year younger than I am, yet I know she has told you some useful things—things that a pupil knows best."

"She certainly has," replied Agatha. "Anya has a brilliant future. And yours, Michael—yours holds just as much promise."

"My queen," Michael said, working up his courage. "I would like to serve on your council. Let me help you find a way to make this tutoring a part of every school in Xana."

What profound insight for a fifth-year pupil! Queen Agatha marveled. "How you have discerned my will," she said. "Even before you spoke, I was ready to invite you. I can just wave my hand," which she did symbolically, "and declare, 'You are now on my council.'"

Queen Agatha returned to the headmaster's study. The door had been locked, but she heard talking inside. The soldier at her side said loudly, "Open immediately to admit her majesty, Queen Agatha."

A sound of footsteps was heard, and the door swung open. Queen Agatha, with Michael at her side, strode briskly into the room. She issued a decree to the school's headmaster, Lan Weili, saying, "I have appointed Michael Gant to my council of advisers. When the queen's council is in session, Michael Gant is excused from class."

The queen turned away, expecting obedience. But as she passed through the door, she heard one of the assistants speak. Because she always wanted to know what her people were saying and thinking, she stopped to listen.

"This is a typical decree from Queen Agatha," the assistant said. "Once proclaimed, obedience is mandatory. She puts on such airs as the servant of her people; but Agatha is as authoritarian as any other monarch in the history of the world."

Lan Weili answered this, "I have learned much about the ways of Xana since Queen Agatha visited us four years ago. We should never dispute the queen. She must always be obeyed. Where Queen Agatha stands above other monarchs, past and present," he said, "is that her every act has the sole purpose of increasing the happiness and prosperity of the common people. Never once does she enrich herself personally."

———

A week later, an officer of the army, especially chosen for this particular duty because of his humor, courtesy, and ability to keep sensitive matters secret, escorted Michael to his first meeting of the queen's council.

"This is not the way to the palace gate," Michael said, confused.

The officer replied, "The queen will use one of the side entrances when she has an important meeting. This lets her go in and out without drawing attention."

"I feel sort of intimidated," Michael confessed, "all by myself, with the people who run the whole country."

"You know," the officer replied genially, "I've been one of the guards of the queen's council for nearly twenty years, for both Queen Julia and Queen Agatha. The councilors now are all very ordinary, humble people—friendly and approachable, just like the folks in your own neighborhood. Queen Julia's councilors were an arrogant, stuffy lot. When Agatha was only a teenage princess, a child hardly older than yourself, her mother put her on the council to learn government. Agatha didn't like the other councilors, and they didn't like her. They would argue violently, and Queen Julia had to ring a bell to shut them up. I remember what she said one time: 'Mind your manners, all of you, especially you, Agatha. This discussion is finished.'"

The officer then changed his tone. "Now that Queen Agatha runs the council, everybody is a lot friendlier."

"So you've known both Queen Agatha and Queen Julia, and all of their councilors?"

"Sure. My job is to be ready for any service, be impartial, and keep confidences. I knew them all."

"How does Queen Agatha compare with Queen Julia?"

"I think, if anything, Queen Agatha is even more autocratic. Whatever she says, the whole country has to follow. But Queen Agatha is much wiser than her mother. She has a sense of fairness and justice. She listens to all opinions, considers them carefully, and finds the best features in each. Then she makes her decision, and that's it."

"In school, they tell us she wishes for the monarch to rule with the consent of parliament. We won't have a parliament until the first pupils complete their ten years, and then we'll need to have enough voters and candidates; but what if parliament refuses one of the queen's decrees?"

"We won't find out until it happens. I'm guessing Queen Agatha's sense of fairness will prevail. You've probably never been in a confrontation with her. Everyone who has always backs down in the end. She gets her way with everyone, every time. In the end, everyone benefits."

Michael responded, "She sure got her way when she enrolled me in school. I'll never dispute her."

The officer asked him how that had happened. Michael repeated verbatim what had been said that day between the queen and the headmaster.

The officer affirmed, "And there you have Queen Agatha's sense of fairness and justice."

Michael turned to another matter. "And I understand that there is another child on the council, Anya Mendez. Can you please tell me about her?"

"Anya is a charmer," the officer said, "full of wit and vitality. She has so much tact, diplomacy, and poise. There is a story I'd like to tell about her. Everybody on the council knows it, because they saw it happen, but please don't repeat it in school or to your neighbors."

"I promise," replied Michael, by now feeling quite inferior to all the other council members and more than ready to be obedient.

"A few weeks ago, three of the council members were in the heat of an argument, shouting at each other. Anya jumped onto the center of the table and yelled, 'Shut up!' It became so silent, we could hear birds chirping outside. Anya promptly sat back down, crossed her arms on the table in front of her, and stuck her nose up in the air, as if to say, 'I sure showed you.'"

"What happened next?" asked Michael.

"Queen Agatha let them all sit in complete silence for a while. I think she wanted this to be a lesson to be remembered. Usually the queen responds by summarizing each person's arguments, but this time, she asked each of the members involved to explain their opponents' arguments. They couldn't do it. Queen Agatha was quite cross. I've forgotten what the argument was about—it was completely trivial—but I remember exactly what Queen Agatha said. 'You expect me to listen to everything you say. I expect you to listen just as carefully. You each state your position in a calm, low voice, and then repeat each other's position quietly and respectfully.'"

"Did the queen rebuke Anya?"

"No," replied the officer. "After the meeting, as the other councilors were leaving to carry out their duties, I saw Queen Agatha, Anya, and Anya's father chuckling together. I couldn't hear what they said. But I can guess. Our queen has a great deal of respect for people who do the right thing without being asked."

Despite the officer's jovial character, Michael's arms and legs were shaking as he opened the door to the council chamber and caught his first sight of the people who ran the country.

He was surprised. They didn't look like dignitaries. They wore plain commoners' clothes and stood about in little groups, talking to one another. Queen Agatha herself was with one of those groups. In the room's center was a large round table surrounded by chairs.

Michael could have stood silently at the doorway all day but didn't have time to be shy. He had just entered the room when Queen Agatha herself saw him and came to him. "Welcome to the council, Michael," she said.

Reassured, the boy ventured to speak.

"I see King Arthur's round table," he replied, showing his mastery of the world's history and lore. He quickly corrected himself, saying, "I mean, Queen Agatha's round table. Is this where all members sit as equals? But I thought you made the final decision."

Queen Agatha smiled. "Yes, but I govern with my council's consent. Often, though, in a matter of importance to a single person or family—as when I needed to get you enrolled in school—I act on my own, and act quickly. But when a policy concerns the entire land of Xana, I never make a decision against the advice of my council.

"All members of the council are equals in their right to speak freely, to be listened to by everyone, including myself, and to receive a courteous reply." She bent down so she could look Michael directly in the eye. "You understand that the council's decisions are made public, but our discussions are held in confidence. That is to ensure each member speaks freely and honestly. If a proposal made in good faith is found, after free discussion, to be unworkable, there should be no censure. That would inhibit free speech." Sensing Michael's anxiety, she spoke directly to what she knew was on his mind. "Oh, don't worry. Tutoring is such a good idea that we will find a way to make it happen. In every school in the land of Xana. I promise."

The queen went on to explain that the decisions of her queen's council of advisers were posted in the National Library and announced in every school.

"I read the decisions in the library," Michael replied. "Now I understand why we read only the final action, but nothing about the discussion. I noticed something else. On different days the handwriting is different. Different people must write it each day, but 'Agatha, queen of the land of Xana,' at the end is always in the same handwriting. I think it must be yours?" he said tentatively. "That you are endorsing whatever the council decided?"

"Very good reasoning," the queen responded.

Concluding this private conversation, Queen Agatha invited all the members to convene. "Please take your seats." She escorted Michael to his chair. "Let us all welcome Michael Gant to the council." Every council member clapped. "He has a proposal that I am sure you will find so valuable that its merit needs no discussion. We need only to find the means for its implementation."

All the dignitaries were now gazing at Michael, and this made him very nervous. He took comfort, though, feeling the queen's hands on his shoulders.

Queen Agatha continued, "Each of you, in turn, please introduce yourself to Michael."

Already, in the library, Michael had learned and memorized the councilors' names. Now he concentrated on connecting each name with a face. Going clockwise around the table, each member rose in turn and stated her or his name. When they had progressed a quarter of the way around, a distinguished middle-aged lady, who wore the most dignified clothing of anyone in the room, arose and said, "Sylvia Hartly."

"And she runs the whole country," Michael said to himself in utter amazement.

And about halfway around the table, a humble-looking man arose and, standing tall, said, "Pedro Mendez." A little girl seated next to him stood next, rising barely higher than when she was seated. "Anya Mendez," she announced, with poise and grace.

Thus did Michael meet Anya for the first time. He marveled even as she said her name, murmuring to himself, "She's so pretty."

Then it came his time to speak. Michael presented his vision for tutoring to the council exactly as he had presented it to Queen Agatha a few days earlier.

Anya endorsed the suggestion with bubbling enthusiasm. So much, indeed, that the queen could see how shy, studious Michael had been overwhelmed. Agatha realized her hope that something special would develop between the two children on her council would not happen. Michael and Anya talked well about policy, but although Anya became a friend to everyone she met, Michael's friendship with her would never become more than casual.

Anya endorsed Michael's idea by recounting her own family's experience. "We've already been tutoring Henri at home," she said, "and he's the best reader in the whole first-year class. And we're teaching Patrick to read even though he's only three. Some of my classmates are planning to be teachers ourselves after we finish our ten years. Tutoring now will be such wonderful training! After two or three years of this, our teacher shortage should be solved."

Another council member objected. "I am not in favor. While this idea has some merit, we should not tell the headmaster how to teach his pupils. Long ago, we accepted our gracious queen's wisdom that any person does a job best when he is free to perform it his own way."

"But," said another, "each school and its headmaster are required to include all the subjects that we believe to have value. Tutoring could be one of these subjects."

Michael Gant interrupted. "The headmaster of my school believes that teachers, and not pupils, know what should be taught. He will allow tutoring at our school only if this council requires it."

"I congratulate your quick thinking and boldness to speak up," Queen Agatha declared.

Another councilor asked, "Remember Headmaster Johann Johannssen? He demanded that pupils obey their teachers so rigidly that he would not allow any pupil's critical thinking to challenge a teacher's authority. We sent him home."

Queen Agatha added her observation. "I visited that school recently, and found the pupils had become strong critical thinkers, with their new headmaster's encouragement."

"We can go even further," another councilor added. "I suggest that, maybe in the ninth or tenth year of school, pupils who plan to become teachers can practice teaching entire classrooms in the lower years. Of course, this would be under the regular teacher's supervision."

"This sounds like a good idea," Anya replied. "I don't plan to become a teacher, but I'll certainly try your practice teaching."

"You might change your mind about not teaching."

"We will see."

Queen Agatha then spoke. "I agree pupils should wait until their ninth year before they teach a whole class. Even our most advanced class is only in the sixth year now. We can defer a full discussion of this proposal to a future meeting. But the sooner our pupils start tutoring one another, the better for everybody."

There were a few more comments, mostly agreement with points already made. Queen Agatha's second endorsement had concluded the discussion.

Sylvia then arose and spoke with her usual quiet dignity. "It will be easy for us to begin tutoring nationwide. I'll instruct my staff to write a letter to every headmaster in the land. This will describe our policy and instruct them to reply, in due course, with the name and year in school of each volunteer. Each school will still have complete freedom on how to carry out our policy."

By unanimous vote, the council then adopted Michael's proposal.

A fter the council meeting adjourned, Pedro immediately escorted his daughter back to school. Anya burst into her headmaster's study with her usual exuberance. "This is so exciting! The council has approved a new teaching program for every school in the country. Please call an assembly of the entire school tomorrow morning; I can explain it then."

Hesitating a moment, the headmaster replied, "I should know about this program before I call an assembly."

"I'm not supposed to talk about actions of the queen's council," Anya said, "before they're officially posted in the National Library this afternoon."

Standing in the doorway behind her, Pedro affirmed, "Yes, I can vouch that this program will be an important improvement to our children's education."

Reluctantly, the headmaster agreed. Anya nodded in satisfaction. By now, she knew that with her vigor and vitality, along with the value of her suggestions, she could always get her way with the headmaster.

That evening at the Mendez family home, the dinner-table discussion was especially lively. All five of Pedro's older children, now in the sixth year of school, wanted to become tutors. Henri, though only in the first year, wanted to join them. Even Patrick, only three years old, said, "When I go to school, I will be a tutor, too."

Pedro's oldest child, Andre, who was the children's natural leader, proposed a strategy all could accept. "Anya, as a member of the queen's council, should announce the tutoring program. Then let us all volunteer together. Each of us should say, 'I am the first person in this school to volunteer to become a tutor. I am not tied for first; I am the first.'"

"Not so fast," their father cautioned them. "You should invite your classmates to come to the assembly room platform and volunteer with you."

The next morning Anya, Charlotta, Martin, Susi, and Andre marched together to the assembly platform. Ordered by both height and age, standing side by side, they looked like stair steps. As planned, Anya explained the tutoring program. Then, on Andre's cue, the five Mendez siblings declared in unison, "We can be the first pupils in the entire land of Xana to volunteer to become tutors. If you are ready, come to the platform and volunteer with us."

The hall remained silent. Nobody moved.

Andre was unprepared for this lack of immediate response. Queen Agatha, however, would have expected the pupils to hesitate, to think critically and listen to their hearts before making such an important decision. Within a minute, two pupils stood and came to the platform. Others followed them in a modest trickle. By the time two weeks had passed, enough volunteers had come forward that every lower level student who needed a tutor had one.

Several weeks later, while Queen Agatha was visiting the Mendez home, Henri proudly told her, "I'm tutoring, too. In my class, I'm helping several children with their reading and their arithmetic."

This did not accord with Michael Gant's proposal, by which older students should tutor younger ones. But Queen Agatha replied, "That's wonderful!"

Henri went on, "My big brothers and sisters will have only five years to tutor before they finish school. I will tutor for ten years. And then I will become a teacher."

"Henri, you'll be a wonderful teacher," the queen said.

———

Michael was only in his second council meeting when a proposed trade mission to Karma was discussed. Even the council's experts on foreign trade seemed confused. Nobody understood which of Xana's products the people of Karma might desire. Michael suggested, "I can go to the National Library and read everything I can about Karma. Then we'll know what to do next."

"What a wonderful suggestion," Queen Agatha said. "We look forward to your report at our next meeting. But please don't wait until then. As soon as you have finished your reading, write what you have learned. Then immediately take that report to the trade office."

Michael's contributions to Queen Agatha's council of advisers were just beginning. He was learning from the inside how a country is governed. Much of the council's time was spent increasing the profits from foreign trade. As the delegation from each new country was received, Michael would go to the National Library, study that country's culture, and prepare his report. Decisions on trade greatly improved based upon that knowledge. Michael Gant conducted all his research while still a pupil, and so learned much about the world.

After completing his ten years of school, Michael would be assigned to Xana's trade delegations and visit faraway lands. His duty was not to negotiate, but rather to travel around each foreign country to learn its culture and mores. He could not imagine a better way both to serve his queen and satisfy his curiosity about the world. Even during his sea voyages, Michael was learning.

As each delegation departed, Queen Agatha would escort her envoys to the ship and introduced them to the captain. At the start of Michael's first voyage abroad, she said, "Captain Antony Barra, this young man is Michael Gant." The two shook hands. "I instruct you to keep Michael in your company while at sea and teach him the skills of sailing. You will find he learns fast. It may suit you, as it will certainly suit him, to assign him a cabin boy's duties. This will teach him humility. But only for an hour or two each day. For the rest of the day he should be on deck with you."

"I have a most able cabin boy in Willis Tomkins," Captain Barra replied. "Mr. Gant can assist him and learn his duties during those times when we have little to do on deck."

By the end of his voyages, Michael understood navigation and ship handling, though not the diplomacy a captain requires to maintain discipline and morale among the seamen. That, he humbly understood, would require many years' service at sea.

At the tender age of twenty, Michael Gant would found Xana's first university. Queen Agatha herself attended his class on the history and culture of foreign lands. It was her wish that her artisans' creations should be more desired abroad, thus bringing even more wealth to Xana's people. When he had achieved his twenty-third year, Michael acquired a fancy for one of his pupils. Although, by his own decree, relations between teacher and pupil were forbidden, he bided his time. Only after the course was finished and the grade assigned would he court her and, finally, make her his wife.

Chapter 6

Prince Olaf was never interested in running a country. Losing his own land to his brother's ambition came as a secret relief to him. He was quite happy to let Queen Agatha reign supreme in Xana. As prince, he acted as her gallant, able to satisfy Agatha's lusty and voracious appetites. Hardly any married couple—surely no queen and her prince—could have coupled more joyously and frequently than Agatha and Olaf.

But Olaf was more than Queen Agatha's gallant. He was always ready to be her companion and to comfort her, to relax her from the stresses of ruling. He did not participate in government, but when his queen visited schools, craftsmen, the homes of commoners, and especially military barracks, he often accompanied her. His charisma and enthusiasm made him an outstanding consort for the queen. Together they could greet many more enthusiastic citizens than could the queen alone. The queen and prince together knew how to dazzle delegations of dignitaries from abroad. Queen Agatha learned how to use Prince Olaf's charm to negotiate deals more favorable to Xana than foreign traders had intended.

Queen Agatha busied herself much of each day in affairs of government. These were Olaf's free times to engage in his own interests. Early in Queen Agatha's reign, he established a royal stable and invited his queen to visit. A stable boy led several horses in succession to his queen and the prince. "This horse is suited for the cavalry," Olaf described the first. Of the second he said, "This horse will be good for pulling a carriage." Of a third, "A wonderful horse for pleasure riding." And of a fourth, whose behavior was surly, he said, "This horse is best returned to pasture."

"How can you say all these things about horses you've never seen before?" Agatha asked.

"I know horses," he replied. Queen Agatha never could understand how he did it. But for his part, Prince Olaf never could understand how his queen could just as quickly sense the true character of any person.

The stable boy then led a pure white mare to the queen. "This mare is especially gentle and obedient. I invite you, if it please your majesty, to learn to ride her."

Queen Agatha hesitated, thinking about the many times she had walked through the city like any commoner. "I don't need the luxury of riding when my people all have to walk." But suddenly a new thought struck her and her mood perked up. "On a horse I can travel all over our country in just a few hours," she exclaimed.

"And you can ride when you visit the barracks and review your soldiers," Prince Olaf added. "As you know, all of your soldiers can fight equally as cavalry or dismounted as infantry."

Queen Agatha embraced the white mare's head, and the horse sensed her kindness.

With a gentle hand on her back, Olaf directed Agatha to the mare's left side. "Place your left foot in the stirrup," the prince instructed her. Seeing Agatha hesitate, he continued, "The horse always expects to be mounted from the left side." Agatha complied. "Now lift your body up and onto the saddle."

In the saddle for the first time in her life, Queen Agatha said, "This is fun. How do I make the horse go?"

"Kick her gently on the sides."

"But won't that hurt?" asked the queen.

"Not at all. The horse expects it. A gentle touch is all you need."

Responding to the pressure of Agatha's heels, the horse started a slow walk. "How do I make her stop?"

"Pull back on the reins," Olaf answered. "Pull the reins left to make the horse turn left, and right to make her turn right." Agatha experimented with this and grinned broadly as she discovered how readily the horse followed her lead.

Agatha reined her horse in behind Olaf's as he rode into the courtyard. They took a leisurely half hour's ride together, and Agatha quickly gained confidence in guiding her horse.

After Queen Agatha became proficient at riding, she chose to go mounted whenever she visited her army. At the camps and forts, she reviewed her soldiers while mounted regally on her white mare, with the commander on her left and her prince on her right, both mounted. When all the soldiers were assembled in formation, the commander ordered, "All bow to her majesty, Queen Agatha." Then they raised their swords at 45 degrees above the horizontal and called out in unison, "Hail to her majesty, Queen Agatha." Their next action was to recite from memory the Xana Soldiers' Pledge: "I pledge to obey my queen and the orders of my superior officers. I will protect the people of Xana ahead of saving my own life. I will support my comrades in battle, no matter how great the danger." Every soldier, up to and including the commanding general, repeated this pledge at least once a year. Whenever she was present as the pledge was recited, Queen Agatha would dismount and show her own humility by doing a slow, deep, and graceful curtsy to her assembled soldiers. With the formalities concluded, Queen Agatha walked through the ranks, talking with individual soldiers about their private concerns, whatever those might be. The soldiers loved her for her personal attention. After each visit, they were better motivated than ever to obey the Soldiers' Pledge.

At the start of her reign, Queen Agatha journeyed to Xana's far corners as her ancestors had done, in the royal carriage. But now, only a few weeks after she first climbed into the saddle, she was making her forays on horseback, galloping beside her prince, arriving in just two or three hours at distant destinations that required the whole day's ride by carriage. In later years, as the land of Xana grew ever richer and more people could afford horses, Agatha rode more often in their midst. Through Olaf, the royal stable provided horses to the people, charging only the sum needed to maintain the mounts.

As for Olaf's other interests, Agatha prohibited jousting. Such tournaments killed or injured good people to no gain. Olaf, dressed in an officer's uniform, frequently visited military bases to teach his skills in sword fighting, archery, and horsemanship to soldiers. Agatha, however, never touched a sword or any other weapon. Olaf hunted without her. While Agatha had no qualms about eating venison Olaf had killed, she could not kill any living creature.

Agatha and Olaf rode across the country mainly to visit the schools. She tried to visit every school at least once every three or four years, making all her visits unannounced. This imposed a wholesome discipline on all headmasters, teachers, and pupils. Agatha expected the classrooms to be immaculately clean and neat, and so they had to be kept every hour of every day. Pupils were expected to know their lessons, and every day, most of them complied.

———

On one of these school visits occurred an event that is worth recounting because it reveals so much of Queen Agatha's character.

"Now be sure to make the room tidy," a teacher named Jane directed her pupils. "We never know when Queen Agatha will visit our class, and she wants to see everything in place."

Alan Turot was the smallest boy in the class, but he was also one of the most eager. He straightened his desk to be in line with those next to him, and he put his slate and chalk and all other possessions in their proper places.

"Come on, Tommy, do your part," Jane pleaded.

"Aw," griped Tommy, who was the biggest and heaviest boy in the class. He put up one or two items, but someone else had to move them to their right places. One of Tommy's classmates also had to move his desk into line.

The class returned to its history lesson about when their kind Queen Agatha had been crowned. The children heard how the queen had delivered her speech about building schools for all of Xana's children and bringing prosperity to even the humblest of her people. In doing this, the teacher explained, the queen had been immensely successful.

Just as Jane was telling the children how the people came to revere their compassionate monarch above all others in their land's long history, the classroom door opened. A man stood there, in a splendid officer's uniform. Jane recognized, although her pupils did not, that this was no ordinary soldier, but Prince Olaf, the husband of Queen Agatha.

This officer, the prince, announced, "Her Majesty, Queen Agatha."

As they had been taught, the pupils and their teacher rose to face the door. Even Tommy, grumbling, stood up. Then gracious Queen Agatha entered. Again, as they had been taught, all the boys, even Tommy, bowed deeply, and all the girls curtsied. Queen Agatha held out her arms. Immediately the children rushed to her, sensing that their queen radiated their happiness back to them. Queen Agatha loved all children.

"How do you like your teacher?" she asked.

"She makes learning fun," a boy replied.

"And what is one of the fun things you learned?"

A girl waved her hand vigorously, eager to answer the question.

"That a three-year-old gir—uh, dignified lady—put the crown on your head."

A boy next to her added, "I did my arithmetic, and she's eleven years old now. Do you still keep track of her?"

"All the time," Queen Agatha replied.

"And I believe she's at the top of her class, too."

"She is. You're very perceptive," the queen said. "How did you know?"

"The textbook says crowning you was something she very much wanted to do, and she did it all perfectly. She even did all five curtsies she had to do, and knew when to do them, and where!" The boy was breathless with excitement at the chance to show off his knowledge. "So if she could do all that when she was three, she must be doing a lot more now."

"Excellent reasoning," Queen Agatha replied. Then a girl named Veronika started waving her hand. Everybody in the class admired Veronika. She was forthright and bold and didn't let anybody get in her way. "What do you like about school?" Queen Agatha asked.

"I love school and learning," Veronika replied with a smile. But it quickly turned to a frown. "But I don't like Tommy. He is a bully." The girl's statement distressed Queen Agatha.

The queen asked the teacher and several other children about the supposed bully among them. They were afraid to answer. But from their silence, wise Queen Agatha perceived the truth.

"Which one of you is Tommy?" the queen asked.

No one replied. Agatha stood and surveyed all the pupils. On the face of the biggest and most ill-groomed boy in the class, she saw a sullen look. Alan and several other children, sensing the queen was on their side, then nodded toward Tommy.

Queen Agatha approached the boy and addressed him sternly. "Henceforth, you will behave yourself. What does Article 7 of the Great Charter say?"

"Uh, uh," he stammered.

"You'd best learn and never forget." Queen Agatha then approached Iva, a very pretty girl but the shyest in the class. "Would you like to teach him?"

Iva palpitated, and after a short silence, managed to reply, "Ye-yes, my queen."

Queen Agatha laid a comforting arm on her shoulder. "Please don't be shy," she said. "We both know you know the answer."

Thus calmed, Iva replied proudly, "'Treat every citizen of the land of Xana with the same courtesy and kindness as you treat your queen.'"

Queen Agatha turned her attention back to Tommy. "Have you bullied your classmates?" she asked him directly. She looked at Jane, the teacher, who now dared to nod slightly.

"I don't do no bullying," Tommy muttered, looking at the floor.

"Double negative," Queen Agatha snapped. "You don't do your lessons, either. Confess, apologize, and promise you will never bully anyone again. That is not all! Promise also that you will come to the aid of anyone you see being bullied. Look at me." The boy lifted his eyes, now moist with tears. "Lie to your queen, and you will spend the rest of your life wishing you hadn't."

The learning was instant. Queen Agatha was kind and compassionate, but, if angered, became as strong as an ox.

After several seconds of shocked silence, Tommy sputtered, "All right, all right. I've been a bully. I'm sorry."

"Your promise," Queen Agatha demanded crossly.

"I won't be a bully anymore."

"And…" Queen Agatha insisted.

Silence.

"And… what else do you promise? Who knows the answer?"

Nearly every hand in the class shot up. The queen selected little Alan Turot and squatted next to him so she was at his level. "We both know, don't we?" she said. Alan beamed with pride at sharing a secret with Queen Agatha. This one instant—an unlikely event, for Agatha could have selected any one of many other pupils— changed Alan's life, completely and forever.

Alan said proudly, "I promise that I will never bully anyone—I'm not very big—but I promise I'll do what I can to protect anyone I see being bullied."

Queen Agatha smiled at Alan and patted him on the back. As she turned to leave, Alan called out, "My queen, I know now what I want to do when I grow up. I want to be a soldier. I want to be strong and protect my land and my people."

Queen Agatha turned and patted Alan on the back once again. "You'll be a wonderful soldier."

An hour later, school was dismissed for the day. Pupils and teachers alike were congregating in the large courtyard between the school building and the road. Alan saw that Tommy had already broken his promise to Queen Agatha and was tormenting little Raul Benshev, a boy half Tommy's size.

"Leave him alone," Alan demanded.

"Get lost, runt," Tommy said.

Angered, Alan hit Tommy on the chin as hard as he could. Unfortunately, given his small size, that wasn't very hard.

Tommy turned on Alan, and Raul, unhurt, ran away. "Take this," said Tommy, and his first blow knocked Alan down. "And this," Tommy said as he hit Alan again. "And this, runt." Alan, already lying on the ground, received blow after cruel blow from Tommy. And it hurt badly.

Then Alan heard a distant shout. "Seize that bully!" It was Queen Agatha. Tommy had heard her, too. He ran away as fast as he could. Agatha hurried to Alan and lifted him to his feet. Wiping dirt from his eyes, he recognized his queen. "I am sorry, my queen," Alan cried. "He was just too big and strong."

Queen Agatha took Alan into her arms. "I forgive you," she assured him. "Please tell me what happened."

"Tommy was being mean to little Raul Benshev. I told him to stop. When he wouldn't, I hit him. Tommy turned on me, and Raul ran away. Raul was scared, but he didn't get hurt. I just wasn't strong enough. I…"

Queen Agatha interrupted. "You are very brave, and your heart is kind and pure. You have already protected one of your classmates. You will grow strong. You know what a wonderful soldier you will become."

Prince Olaf and two of the queen's elite guards were bigger and in far better condition than Tommy and could run much faster. They quickly caught up with him and grasped his arms. Prince Olaf was much too polite and diplomatic to make such a statement, but one of the soldiers at his side stated bluntly, "The queen doesn't like what she saw you doing. You won't like how she'll punish you." They brought the boy, tightly secured, to confront his queen. She still had her protective arms around Alan.

"I didn't do nothing," Tommy protested. "He started it."

"Double negative again," Queen Agatha scolded him. But this was no matter of mere grammar. Her eyes narrowed, the queen's fury descended. "You tell nothing but lies. Whatever you say, I know the truth, because it is the opposite. You have proved yourself unworthy to be in school. You shall go now to a farm. There you shall cooperate with everybody. Never again shall you ever abuse anyone. You shall work hard from sunrise until sunset. For this, you shall receive nothing but food and water. You can sleep in a hayloft, and you shall work every day—no days of rest—until the meanness is worked out of you."

"I promise I won't bully anymore," Tommy whined as he was led away.

"At last you tell the truth," Queen Agatha replied, "because everyone else on the farm is twice as big as you are."

All the school's people, young and old, had gathered. Agatha listened carefully as they reacted to what she had done.

An older child said, "I'm stunned. What a severe sentence! How can our loving, compassionate Queen Agatha be so harsh?"

"I don't feel sorry for Tommy," another said. "He deserved it."

"I'm glad we're rid of him," said yet another.

Then an older person, a young adult, spoke with firm authority. In the early years of Queen Agatha's reign many children started their first year of schooling well beyond age five, and were fully grown up while still in school. This young man seemed to be a leader among the pupils. "Our queen has taught us a great lesson today. We all want to make sure it doesn't happen to any of us. There must be no more bullying at our school."

All the pupils thereafter treated each other with the courtesy and kindness they expected from their queen, and that she expected from them.

———

Inspired as never before in his life, and determined to become a soldier, Alan did not go home that day. Instead, he went straight to the barracks of the queen's elite guard. Seeing his cuts and bruises, the sentry at the gate remarked, "Kid, you sure got the worst of that one. What happened?"

"I got beat up, and Queen Agatha rescued me."

"Queen Agatha herself?" He spoke in a tone of marvel. The soldiers had a special reverence for their queen. "Tell me what happened. Everything."

After Alan had finished, the sentry replied, "That's an amazing story. Kid, I think you're telling the truth, because it sounds just like what Queen Agatha would do. You're a good kid. Come in and meet my buddies."

Inside the barracks, Alan repeated his story to the fascinated soldiers. He finished by saying, "I'm here because I want to be strong like a soldier."

A grizzled old sergeant approached him. "Kid, whatever else you do, be sure to finish your schooling. If I had the education you're getting, I'd be a general right now. I'm not permitted to teach you how to use weapons. Queen Agatha says only soldiers can use them. But I can show you how to make yourself strong." He demonstrated push-ups, sit-ups, deep knee bends, and chin-ups. "Do each of these twice a day. Finish as many as you can without wearing yourself out. Each time, try to do one more than you did the time before. You won't be able to every time you try, but as the days go by, you'll do better. And run around the block at home as many times as you can. Like everything else you do, try to go around once more than you did the time before, if you can."

Alan devoted himself to his lessons more assertively than ever. Over the months, the number of times he could do each exercise steadily rose. On days off from school, he often visited the barracks and would run with the soldiers. On his first day, he ran until he dropped. The sergeant stopped and returned to Alan to find his face pale. "Don't overdo it," he cautioned. "When you get tired, stop. You'll need years of training to run as far and fast as we do."

Alan was one of several boys of different ages who enviously watched the soldiers practice with swords, lances, and the bow and arrow. They were prohibited from using lethal weapons until they finished their schooling and actually enlisted in the army. But these schoolboys often exercised and even practiced martial arts with the soldiers. Queen Agatha approved this quasi-military training and discipline as a means to improve the boys' physical and moral strength.

Queen Agatha required every pupil in Xana's schools to choose and master a manual trade. This was an essential part of every child's education. The products of their craftsmanship brought prosperity to Xana. Alan chose metalworking because he believed this skill would enable him to make the best weapons. He had watched real soldiers working to hone their swords, sharpen arrowheads, and make strong bowstrings. In school he had taken up wrestling, and after a time he became the school's champion. Through it all, he remained courteous, helpful, and, when needed, protective of his classmates.

When he completed his ten years of schooling, Alan enlisted in the real army. His years of ever more strenuous exercise made him the strongest in his recruit company. He still ran strong after all the others had stopped.

———

After completing his military training with distinction, Alan Turot's first assignment was to the frontier. For generations, bandits had been marauding Xana's frontier communities—stealing and pillaging, and capturing citizens to make them slaves. Alan's frontier post was a simple stone structure with low stone walls, defensible against a small band of raiders but certainly not against a massive assault. The forest had been cleared on all sides of the post, so no one could arrive undetected. The commanding officer addressed Alan's small troop. "I hope you enlisted to fight. Because here you're going to fight. The barbarian raiders are becoming bolder and more brutal, killing and kidnapping from isolated farms. I don't have enough men to protect them all."

"I enlisted to protect my people," Alan declared.

Ignoring Alan's words, the commander went on. "Two days in the fortress to get acquainted, then four days on patrol. Two days of rest, then four on assignment. That's the routine here. Expect a lot of hardship."

Excited voices and the sound of horses interrupted the commander's oft-repeated speech. A woman holding a small child was sharing a horse with a soldier. She moaned, "They took away my husband and our three workers. I managed to hide in the cellar with Ramon, and they didn't find us."

The commander's wife placed the woman and her son under her tender care.

Alan spoke up. "If they took them alive and didn't kill them right away, we can rescue them."

"No chance," said one of the returning soldiers.

"Why not?"

"Can't do it." The reply came with no explanation.

"I learned in school," Alan declared, "that Queen Julia's councilors would say, 'Can't do it,' to whatever Princess Agatha proposed. And yet she found people who did those things anyway. I will be one of those people."

To this assertion came no reply.

By the start of his second day in the little fortress, Alan had memorized the maps of the country that surrounded him. He had questioned veteran soldiers about the lay of the land. He was granted permission to explore the countryside on horseback but cautioned that if detected he must disappear into the forest and return to the post.

The countryside of Xana was mostly rolling land, hilly but rather dull scenery, with no high mountains or waterfalls. Much was in subtropical forest, but not dense jungle, so that both foot soldiers and mounted cavalry could pass through readily, and with enough brush to provide cover. The forests were interspersed with grasslands and some farms. The rivers were shallow enough that men and horses could cross. Those rivers were wide enough that invaders would be slowed down and exposed to arrows as they waded across. The rivers would be natural lines of defense.

On his solitary patrol, Alan was nearing the top of a hill when he heard voices of both anger and pain. Creeping to the edge of the forest, he saw ten slaves tilling a field under overseers' whips. He identified them as citizens of Xana by their now tattered clothing. For several hours, watching from cover, he familiarized himself with the armed guards' locations and movements. Finally, as the sun reached the horizon, he watched as the slaves were herded into a low building. There, he presumed, they were locked up for the night.

Back at the outpost, Alan was pleased that five of the comrades he had trained with were eager to join him in a rescue mission. Together they sought out the commander.

"I don't know," the commander replied. "I don't have enough men here, and I can't afford to lose you." But after some hesitation, he agreed. "Give it a try. It might work if you can get in and get out unseen. If you encounter any significant resistance, leave as fast as you can." He barked, "That's an order. Understood clearly?"

"Yes, sir," Alan replied.

The patrol took ten extra horses for the ten slaves. They timed their movements to arrive at the bandit settlement after dark. The first quarter moon gave enough light to guide them but, they hoped, not enough to make their approach visible. Leaving one man and all the horses hidden under trees, Alan and four companions advanced across an open field. A bandit sentry appeared, only to fall noiselessly to the ground when Alan shot an arrow through his heart. A second sentry appeared at closer quarters. One of Alan's companions likewise killed him with an arrow before he could sound the alarm. The five brand-new soldiers reached the prison building without other encounters. The door was locked with a massive padlock. With one swing of his sword, Alan broke it open, unfortunately making a loud noise. Posting his four companions to stand guard outside, Alan entered. A single torch burned inside, but it gave Alan all the light he needed.

One of the ten emaciated men inside cried out, "A Xana soldier."

"Ssh," Alan admonished him. "Quiet. We're getting you out."

It took Alan about two minutes to roust the weary men out of their uncushioned beds. During this interval, two other sentries came in sight of the open door. Alan's companions quickly knifed them to death, but one gave a shout before expiring.

The five soldiers and ten rescued men hurried across the field toward where the horses were sheltered. More shouts came from the bandit post. Arrows swished through the air, but the bandits could not see their targets, and their arrows fell harmlessly into the plowed soil. The soldiers of Xana turned around just long enough to loose their own barrage of arrows and see four more bandits fall, presumably dead. Soon they reached the waiting horses, mounted, and galloped away through the brush. A minute later, one of Alan's men said, "They're not giving chase."

"We're going home," a jubilant Alan announced.

The raid had received only grudging approval from the commander. But after its success, Alan, often single-handedly, began to make daring inspections of other bandit settlements. He led his companions on dangerous raids to rescue more of Xana's abducted citizens. His self-confidence and seeming lack of fear inspired his comrades. Stories of his exploits began to spread to other frontier posts. Other eager young soldiers began to emulate him and conduct similar raids, often with great success.

Then, one night, Alan learned the truth of warfare. Not only did his raid fail to free a single slave, but he was seriously wounded. Three arrows penetrated his armor, one on the left forearm and two close together on his left side below his heart. Two of his faithful companions were killed, both by arrows in the chest. Despite this raid's catastrophic failure, Alan's comrades testified to how bravely he had fought. His leadership, they reported, was all that enabled any of them to survive. It took him a while to recover, but his officers prescribed counseling from older soldiers who had seen the true horrors of war. He was given rest and then promoted to a position from which he could plan larger raids. But Alan did not stay behind fortress walls hunched over his maps. He still led his soldiers in combat with skill, courage, and understanding that earned the highest respect from all who fought with him. Chastened by bitter experience, he determined to drive the bandits forever away from Xana's frontiers. Senior officers who commanded other frontier outposts began to take notice. One of them dispatched a courier to the capital city to present a detailed report to Queen Agatha.

———

*A*t this juncture in Alan's life, it is appropriate to learn how, upon being crowned queen of Xana, Agatha needed only two years to completely reform the army. What had been a group of undisciplined drunkards became an efficient and deadly fighting machine. Through the whole process, she consulted continually with a selection of soldiers from the full range of ranks, from the commanding general down to new recruits, succeeding in reaching a near consensus among them. Her first act was to prohibit all hazing and corporal punishment. Offenders were immediately discharged from the army and sent to farms for hard labor to correct their moral improprieties. Very soon, these offenses ceased altogether. Officers' orders were required to be reasonable and intended to accomplish useful goals. In return, obedience remained mandatory. Discipline, though mild, was strictly enforced. Next, instead of endless parades, she prescribed a regimen of physical exercise and daily practice with horses and weapons, and hand-to-hand combat. Drunkenness is endemic in all armies, but Queen Agatha greatly reduced its incidence in hers by bringing the soldiers' families to their fortresses or encampments. This practice allowed soldiers, when not on sentry duty or military operations, to spend their nights with their wives and sweethearts. In the barracks themselves, soldiers were expected to hone their weapons instead of shining their boots or engaging in drinking bouts. The camp followers—prostitutes—who had served lonely soldiers were taken to the cities to be housed and given honorable work.

When he arrived at the palace, the courier searched for and finally found Queen Agatha meeting with the staff of her Foreign Trade Office.

"Excuse me, your majesty," he interrupted. "I have a report straight from Captain Severen about some important developments on the frontier."

The queen grabbed the report from his hand and unfolded it. When she had finished reading it, she demanded, "Why wasn't I informed of this sooner?"

"No excuse, your majesty."

"It's not your fault," the queen said. "Thank you for delivering this important message. Please send my personal congratulations to every participating soldier."

"Glad to, your majesty."

Queen Agatha patted him on the back, and he hurried on his second mission of the day for his queen—and second long horseback ride.

Then Queen Agatha went into one of her trance-like modes, becoming almost motionless except for deep, slow breathing.

"What is the queen thinking?" one of the trade office officials whispered.

"Probably something most profound," suggested another.

Suddenly the queen burst forth, "We can stop the barbarians without a costly pitched battle."

Queen Agatha handed Captain Severen's message to another member of her elite guard. "Please take this to General Miguelan. Tell him and his staff to meet me in the war room within the hour."

With the senior army officers assembled, Queen Agatha added her unique insight into the military history of Xana that they all knew. "Our great battles of thirty-five years ago, in which my father was killed, and those of seventy-eight and one hundred twelve years ago, in which we lost most of our army but managed to repel the barbarians, occurred only after a charismatic leader united the many barbarian tribes. The tribes are still divided. Let us take the offensive now, attack and neutralize them one at a time before they unite against us. We will be spared the great losses of those battles, the many grieving families of our dead. I entrust all the tactical and logistic details to you."

"Very wise, my gracious queen," General Miguelan replied. "Our cities are still safe enough that we can send two thirds of each city's garrison to the frontier. In my years of service there, I have noticed the bandits never go out at night. At all our frontier posts, then, we will train all our men to move and to fight at night. To one bandit settlement at a time, we will send a large detachment under cover of darkness and overwhelm them."

"A sneak attack can be very effective," a staff captain commented.

"I'm sure it can," the queen said approvingly.

General Miguelan continued, "We'll keep them confused by sending out small scouting parties in many directions. They won't know where we'll strike."

Queen Agatha then ordered, "Send me a message after every raid, whether successful or not."

Thus were fought the Border Wars, as they would become known. Hundreds of slaves were freed, and, within five years, banditry had almost disappeared from the lands on Xana's borders.

General Miguelan was a career soldier whom the reader will remember from fifteen years earlier. When Queen Agatha returned from her first trip to Wan, he was a captain in an army unit temporarily stationed at the palace as part of the queen's elite guard. Later that unit was rotated back to the frontier, where he served with distinction. Impressed by his capable leadership, Queen Agatha had promoted him to general.

The story of Tommy the bully has a sequel. It has survived the passage of centuries, perhaps because it shows Queen Agatha's concern not only for people of humble and ordinary backgrounds who—like Michael Gant, Pedro Mendez, and Alan Turot—she identified as future leaders, but also for the common people of her land whose lives remained humble. After he had apprehended Tommy, Prince Olaf addressed the two soldiers in the queen's elite guard who had helped him. "I, of course, must return to the palace with my queen. I instruct you to take Tommy to say goodbye to his parents, feed him a good dinner at the barracks, and then carry him to the farm."

Now thoroughly humbled, Tommy plodded home with a soldier on each side. When his mother opened the door, one of the soldiers asked, "Is this boy your son?"

"Yes," she sputtered, "Yes. Tommy, what trouble did you get into this time?"

The phrasing of her question indicated that other people had complained about Tommy's behavior.

The soldier explained, "He was hitting a boy half his size, and I mean really beating him hard, and Queen Agatha saw it all."

"In front of Queen Agatha?" his mother gasped. "How could you?"

"I'm sorry, Mother. I didn't see her."

"The queen was furious," the soldier continued. "I can tell you just what she said. 'You shall go now to a farm. There you shall cooperate with everybody. Never again shall you ever abuse anyone. You shall work hard from sunrise until sunset. For this, you shall receive nothing but food and water. You can sleep in a hayloft, and you shall work every day—no days of rest—until the meanness is worked out of you.'"

Tommy and his mother cried on each other's shoulders. His mother managed to plead, "Can't you give Tommy one more chance? He's scared enough, now; he'll obey; he'll be a good boy."

"No," the second soldier said. "Queen's orders. We take him to the farm."

The other soldier explained more politely, "Queen Agatha visited his classroom today. She gave him another chance after he promised he wouldn't bully any more. And not an hour later, he'd already broken his promise. He wasn't just bullying, he was beating a little boy. Brutally. Queen Agatha certainly will not allow any chance whatsoever of behavior this bad happening again."

Both Tommy and his mother cried harder than ever. After a few minutes, the soldiers took Tommy away. The next morning, a courier came to Agatha, reporting that a mother couldn't stop crying because soldiers had taken her son. Agatha hurried to the woman's tiny house to comfort her.

"I am profoundly saddened by all that has happened," the queen said. "I know how much you love your son."

"My husband starved to death during the Bad Times. He gave his food to Tommy so our boy might live, but Tommy grew wild. I couldn't control him. Now I have lost my boy, too." The poor mother cried again.

"You have not lost your son," Queen Agatha assured her. "I sense that he is a good boy, but he has gone astray and must be corrected. No one can ever repeat what he has done anywhere in our beautiful land of Xana. The coming months will be difficult and painful for you both. Please do not lose hope. This, too, shall pass. I can promise you that one day, you will be proud of the man he has become."

———

The two soldiers of the queen's elite guard took Tommy to the barracks and offered him an excellent meal. Tommy, feeling bad, ate very little. Then they hoisted him onto a horse, lashed his legs to the stirrups and his waist to the saddle, and tied his hands behind his back. They saddled and bridled their own horses, and rode into the dusk.

In deepening twilight, they saw a pride of lions lounging under trees ahead of them. "Those lions will have you for breakfast tomorrow morning," one soldier taunted Tommy.

In a friendlier voice, the other advised, "Better not try to run away from the farm."

It was darker still when they saw a bear in a tree. "Give you two-to-one odds," one soldier said with an unpleasant laugh, "the bear eats him up before the lions find him."

"I'm betting he's sensible enough not to leave the farm," replied the other.

The lions and bear were probably both staged, but Tommy was appropriately terrified. As they rode on through the night, unfamiliar sounds from unseen animals kept poor Tommy in perpetual panic. Finally they reached the farm, where one of the soldiers knocked on the house's heavy door. The owner appeared, holding a lantern. "Queen Agatha requests that you strengthen this boy physically and morally," the soldier told him.

"He comes at a good time," came the reply. "I can use another hand at harvest."

The farmer led Tommy to the hayloft. After crying for more than an hour, the boy finally lapsed into a fitful sleep.

The food Tommy shared with his fellow farm workers was fine, far better than his poor mother could provide at home. At his first breakfast, he found the others to be friendly. As they ate, they explained how to harvest the grain. But as the rising sun's rays spread over the ripe wheat, the workers took up scythes and sickles and headed into the fields. After an hour, Tommy complained, "I'm tired," and sat down in the freshly cut stubble.

One of the workers grabbed his shoulders, yanked him to his feet, and yelled, "Get back to work." Five minutes later, Tommy again sat down to rest, only to be forced back to work. Agatha's prohibition of corporal punishment extended to people exiled to farms for correction. But the boy's misery was as great as if he had been beaten. He labored on, ever more slowly. Exhaustion overcame him despite incessant cries of "Hurry up!"

A worker suggested, "If he can't harvest the grain, let him clean the hog house." The combination of filth and stench made it a ghastly place to work. Nevertheless, being able to work at his own slow pace without constant demands to speed up, Tommy managed to finish before dinner. The foreman gave him his first compliment since he had arrived. "Good job, Tommy." Day after agonizing day passed. Even as he managed to work better, Tommy's life became ever more miserable as he yearned for home and painfully missed his mother.

As Queen Agatha had anticipated, Tommy toughened quickly. Within six months, he was working as hard as the others, who fully accepted him as another member of the farm crew. Queen Agatha's kind promise did indeed sustain Tommy's mother until her son had adapted to farm life. Tommy never completed his education, but remained a farmer all his life. He never married. To his credit, when he had a farm of his own, he built a house there for his widowed mother. There he took good care of her so she lived to a happy old age. She became friends with the neighboring farm wives and enjoyed lively times in her new home.

———

Sob sisters in our time may complain, "Tommy lost his father. He has had a hard life. Queen Agatha should have given him one more chance." I reply that many children lost one or both parents in the Bad Times. With the whole country nurtured by Queen Agatha, they showed marvelous resilience. Queen Agatha knew that if she gave Tommy one more chance, he would think he could keep on bullying forever. This the queen would not tolerate, and she stopped him. She told his mother, "I sense that he is a good boy, but he has gone astray and needs to be corrected." Her judgment of Tommy's character was once again correct. Hard work and discipline on the farm straightened him out, and for the rest of his life he lived honorably.

Chapter 7

One day the army sent its master of spies to the queen. "King Ibris of Mardon is amassing a large army to invade Xana," he reported. "He means to rape, pillage, and steal the vast wealth we have acquired."

"King Ibris, the robber king," Agatha replied. "He searches for small, weak countries, lands his army, steals their wealth and violates their women. He doesn't stay, but quickly takes home all the booty and many of the women. Though he keeps the costliest treasures for himself, he gives each of his soldiers a share of the loot."

"No one in Xana deals with Mardon," the officer said. "Few have even traveled there. I am amazed at your knowledge of that kingdom."

"Thank you for your kind compliment," Queen Agatha replied sweetly. "Please continue your report."

"King Ibris is raising an army of several thousand, both volunteers and conscripts, promising each of them vast treasure. But their training is short. Man for man, our soldiers are far better than theirs, but they have much greater numbers."

"We have the longbow," Agatha replied. "Along with the Great Charter and the idea of a parliament, I learned of this from a far-away island realm. As you know, I commissioned a trader to bring an example of the longbow all the way to Xana. My artisans copied it, and now we make our own, even stronger than the one we first obtained."

Knowing that the officer was expert at keeping secrets, she spoke freely. "Everyone in Xana knows I practice complete openness about all affairs of government—all those, that is, that directly affect all our people. This openness makes it easier for me to withhold certain facts that I wish not to become public knowledge. These primarily concern our army and some delicate matters of trade negotiations. As you know, few people outside our army even know we possess the longbow."

With steel tips fashioned by Queen Agatha's artisans, arrows fired by the longbow could penetrate all but the strongest armor from a great distance. The steel arrowheads were time-consuming and expensive to make. The enormous amount of practice soldiers required to become proficient with the longbow was done with blunt-tipped arrows.

———

Queen Agatha's army had the longbow but not gunpowder, which also would spread from the lands of its origin into distant places such as Xana. This enables us to approximately determine the years of her reign. We know the longbow was used with deadly success several times in a century-long war between rival kingdoms that began almost seven hundred years ago. Although gunpowder was used much earlier in one vast Eastern empire, it did not appear elsewhere until some five hundred fifty years before our time. Thus Queen Agatha must have reigned sometime around six hundred years ago.

———

With all its members sworn to secrecy, Queen Agatha called a joint session of parliament, her own council of advisers, and leaders of her army and navy. She decreed, simply, "Meet them at sea so the battle may be fought without harm to our people." Since no one could reasonably disagree, there was no further discussion.

In the war preparations room, Queen Agatha, the grand admiral of the navy, Gerd Alveria, and several other senior navy and army officers gathered around a large nautical map.

"I entrust completely to you," Queen Agatha declared, "preparation of the battle plan."

"We all know," Admiral Alveria said, "that you will pay very close attention and remember everything we say."

A naval officer drew a path on the map. "This is their only reasonable invasion route. We have twenty ships that can intercept them here." He drew a semicircle on the path. "Because we cannot learn their invasion route precisely, we will spread our ships five miles apart to cover a full hundred miles. The first ship to see the enemy fleet can relay its location to the next. Your majesty, we have perfected the system of flags you instructed us to devise early in your reign. These allow our captains to send complex messages from ship to ship, even miles apart. This will allow our fleet to assemble quickly to meet the enemy."

Another officer added, "King Ibris always times his invasions about one day before the full moon. Our spies tell us he seems to be deathly afraid of the dark. That makes him want to complete his looting and kidnapping when moonlight shines all night long. We have about two weeks to prepare."

Then Queen Agatha made her only comment. "We need a second line of defense at the shore, should some of the enemy ships get through. All our people along the coast should be moved inland, along with as many costly items as we can carry. Let King Ibris fight us in a city that is not only deserted, but is devoid of the treasure and women he came to take."

The army commanding general replied immediately, "Not in the city. We will attack them in the confusion of their landing on shore. We must not wait for them to form up a phalanx, for then the battle will be much more costly for us. Of course, move away all the people—both for their safety, and to ensure they don't interfere with our troops."

When the battle plan and provision for contingencies had been made, the officers began planning the logistics. Queen Agatha dismissed herself, saying, "I can see we have sufficient supplies for this mission. I entrust the details of loading the ships to your expertise."

Secrecy about vital matters cannot be long maintained by many people. Very soon, rumors of the coming invasion began to circulate. Queen Agatha wrote out the speech she herself would deliver from the palace balcony. She gave sealed copies to many couriers and sent them all over the land telling the local leaders to assemble their people, read the message, and then post it in a public place.

Though no rain fell, a low gray overcast sky accentuated the anxious citizens' gloom. Those in the capital who arrived early in the public square could see many people, including high-ranking army and navy officers, coming and going on the palace's wide balcony. As the crowd gathered, the spot behind the imperial crest, the silver crown, remained empty. At last Queen Agatha ascended from the courtyard behind the wall to appear at her place of honor. She waved her arms high above her head, and the hum of thousands of voices in the square below fell silent.

Queen Agatha addressed her anxious people, in numbers even greater than at her coronation. "The rumors that an invasion of our country is being planned are true, but, please, fear not. Even as I speak to you, King Ibris of Mardon is assembling an army to sail to Xana. He comes not in conquest, but to pillage, plunder, violate our women, and return to his home country, carrying our wealth with him. This enemy's preparations will not be complete for several days, and his fleet will need several more days to sail from Mardon to Xana. We have plenty of time to stop them. I promise you, no invasion will happen. We will not see a repeat of the Bad Times. Ibris and his army will never land on our shores. Instead, we will take the battle to him. We will inflict so many casualties on his army that he will never dare to return. Our soldiers and sailors are strong and brave, and our cause is pure." Her voice rising shrilly, the queen continued. "We will prevail. Have faith."

Queen Agatha concluded by recounting some of the preparations. "From the Border Wars we have developed the strategy of having the commanding officer at the scene of battle write a report. This report will be sent by a homing pigeon that will swiftly return the news to the palace. By act of parliament, I, your queen, shall be the first to open the message. I will then pass the news to parliament and all our people as quickly as possible."

By this time, Alan commanded a company of fifty men. His company was chosen to be among the land's thousand finest soldiers who would sail on Xana's twenty fighting ships. They would meet an enemy armada rumored to be much larger.

At the harbor, seated on her white horse with Prince Olaf on one side and the grand admiral of the navy on the other, Queen Agatha addressed the assembled troops.

"Today we call upon you to face the mightiest foe ever to threaten the land of Xana. All that we have acquired—our freedom, our prosperity, and our sense of fairness and justice—now depends upon your strength and courage. They have the numbers, but we have decency, honor, and courage. We will prevail." And after several seconds, as loudly as she could shout, she cried, "Show no mercy!"

The soldiers, in unison, shouted, "Long live Queen Agatha!" The fleet admiral joined the soldiers as they raced to board the ships. Observers from the foreign embassies who came to watch were astounded at the enthusiasm of soldiers facing odds heavily against them.

One of the ambassadors remarked, "I see worry on Queen Agatha's face. She delivered her speech with her usual bravado, in complete confidence that her people would carry out her wishes. Though no one but she will ever know for sure, I am guessing she is gravely distressed. No doubt she is wondering how many of these strong young men she is sending to their deaths."

To her prince and husband, Queen Agatha spoke grimly. "I have sent our grand admiral to command our fleet and possibly die in battle. Here at home, our duty will be the most difficult since the Bad Times. I must keep our people calm and their spirits high. I need all your love and support to sustain me, and our country."

"I give you my all," Prince Olaf replied. The royal couple watched the ships set sail. As the fleet receded toward the horizon, they silently rode their horses back to the palace.

How much anxiety Queen Agatha herself might have felt, she confessed to no one. She knew she must show complete confidence in her forces' victory, thereby inspiring the people's confidence. Over the next four days, Queen Agatha was able to do this by repeatedly reassuring them.

On the fourth day, Queen Agatha was visiting a humble blacksmith's shop. "How beautifully sharp and smooth you have made the blade," the queen declared as she watched him apply a fine polish. "You are a master of your trade."

"My dear queen, I owe everything to you," the blacksmith replied. "The free manual craft program in your schools is the only way I could ever have learned the art of smithing."

A clatter of hooves resounded outside the shop. A soldier on a brown horse was leading the queen's white horse. "The homing pigeon has arrived," announced the soldier, who turned out to be her husband.

"My sweet Olaf," Queen Agatha said, "bringing me news that the battle has been fought."

"Have we won?" the blacksmith asked.

"Have faith," Queen Agatha said. "Our soldiers are strong and brave."

Queen Agatha mounted her horse and galloped away at her husband's side.

Several people besides the blacksmith had been close enough to hear that the battle had been fought, but whether it had been won or lost they did not know. This tantalizing fragment of news spread very quickly. "Have we won?" citizens asked each other over and over again, and each offered an opinion.

"Queen Agatha will soon know," one said. "She promised to tell everybody."

"What if we lost? Does Queen Agatha have a second line of defense?"

"Surely she does," said another. "During the last several days, we've seen a good plenty of fully armed and armored soldiers on the streets. Surely they're ready to fight."

Innumerable times, Queen Agatha had repeated, "Have faith. We will prevail." But in the absence of news, the confidence these words had inspired in the people over the previous four days was quickly replaced by anxiety and fear.

———

A few days before he planned to set sail, King Ibris was holding court in his royal chamber. An orderly announced, "The ambassador from Wan requests an audience."

"Tell the ambassador he is welcome," the king replied.

The ambassador entered King Ibris's chamber and bowed deeply.

King Ibris addressed the ambassador. "Send my compliments to King Ivan. He is the wisest king Wan has had for many generations."

"I will deliver your message personally," the ambassador replied. "King Ivan requests that I deliver his message to you. It is this: call off your invasion of Xana. He warns you that Queen Agatha's soldiers are superbly trained, equipped, and disciplined, and are intensely loyal. Every one of them, from the general down, would give his life for her. With all respect, your majesty, my king says one of her soldiers is worth five of ours, or yours."

"With all due respect to King Ivan," King Ibris replied, "I believe he has greatly overstated Xana's capability. All my agents in Xana tell me that the Xanans are a peaceful people—industrious, yes, but not fighters. Lust for treasure and women drives men, and Xana has both in abundance. My soldiers will quickly overwhelm any feeble resistance the Xanans may offer. Call off my most profitable venture ever? Certainly not."

"Heed you not King Ivan's wise warning?" the ambassador chided him. "Beware, your majesty. Disaster awaits you." The ambassador turned and strode rapidly out of the chamber.

———

O n the morning of the fourth day after the fleet had departed, the watch officer on the Xana flagship greeted Admiral Alveria. "You are on deck very early, sir."

"If our estimate of their date of departure is correct, we should meet the enemy fleet today."

Soon afterward, the lookout reported, "A great mass of white sails is on the horizon straight ahead."

"It might be a patch of early morning fog," the watch officer suggested, "soon to disappear in the sunlight."

"Signal the fleet," the admiral ordered. "Order them to converge upon this point but keep their distance until all have assembled."

"So accurately have you predicted the invasion path," an officer commented to Admiral Alveria, "that our flagship, at the center of the squadron, has made the first contact with the enemy. The skies are fair, the wind behind us," he said. "Nature itself favors our cause."

Many miles to the east, aboard King Ibris's royal flagship, the lookout called, "Ship to fore."

"Whose?" the ship's captain asked.

"Sorry, sir, it is too far away for me to see the markings."

An hour later he called again, "It is a ship of Xana, sir."

"Then they know we're here," the captain replied. "Inform King Ibris."

King Ibris was in his luxurious cabin playing cards with his staff when the messenger made his report. The king chided the messenger, "Tell the captain not to interrupt my game with trifles."

Soon after the messenger returned to deck, the lookout shouted, "Ship to port." And a minute later, "Ship to starboard."

Little more time had passed before the ship's captain sent an urgent message to King Ibris. "More and more ships of Xana keep coming, twelve already in sight. I advise you to come on deck at once."

King Ibris laid his cards face down on the table. Without looking at the hands his courtiers held, he declared, "I win," and scooped all the coins from the table into his pocket.

As King Ibris stood on the deck, a grim scowl on his face, twenty ships of Xana had formed an arc around his tightly packed fleet.

"They may be only shadowing us," the captain said. "I have been considering what their movements may mean. Their ships are smaller, faster, and more nimble than ours. In any close ship-to-ship encounters, theirs will have the advantage."

"Keep our fleet together," King Ibris ordered. "Don't let them isolate and destroy one ship at a time. Let us prepare to attack at the first opportunity."

"Should I fetch your armor?" an orderly asked.

"Yes!" King Ibris replied with a flourish. His expression brightened. "What vast treasure in Xana will soon be mine!"

King Ibris, now resplendent in strong armor, stood by the helm of his royal flagship, watching the ships of Xana advance within a quarter mile. His captain advised him, "They really intend to fight us here and now."

"Then let us crush them here and now," King Ibris replied. He shouted so loudly that not only the soldiers on his own ship but those on other ships nearby could hear. "Their women are said to be very beautiful and to give wondrous pleasure in bed. Promise each man that he may pleasure himself with as many as he can handle. Each man may take one home as a lifelong slave and concubine. But I alone claim the right to ravage Queen Agatha. A reward of one hundred thousand acres of royal land to the soldier who brings me Queen Agatha unharmed." He shouted even louder, "Death by slow torture to any man who harms her body." After a few seconds, he concluded, "Promise each man as much of Xana's wealth as he can carry."

Hardly had King Ibris finished declaring his promise when Xana's soldiers loosed from their longbows the deadliest barrage ever seen in that corner of the world. King Ibris and his men were completely unprepared for this novel weapon. The Xanans were safely out of range of the king's ordnance.

Within seconds after he had promised each soldier as much of Xana's wealth as he could carry, King Ibris became one of the first to die. An arrow passed through his helmet's eye slit and penetrated the far side of his skull. Two arrows from the second volley struck the flagship's captain, one piercing his lung and one lodged in his groin. With that injury he could not even stand, much less walk, fight, or command. He could only lie in excruciating agony, watching Xana's archers slaughter his sailors and soldiers. Within minutes, hundreds had died. Hardly anyone above deck on the enemy's ships remained alive.

Shouting "Long live Queen Agatha," Xana's soldiers crowded the rails as the helmsmen directed their ships, aided by a favorable wind, toward the enemy fleet. The most skillful archers remained watchful to shoot any enemies who might venture within their sight.

As his ship came alongside King Ibris' flagship, Alan Turot, sword in hand, was the first to board. Four enemy soldiers who had hidden below the rail quickly surrounded him. But instead of overwhelming and killing him, the enemies were quickly dispatched by the swords of Alan's men. Similar scenes occurred on all of the enemy ships. The swords of the boarding parties took a fearsome toll on the shocked and demoralized enemy soldiers. The archers took deadly aim at any enemies who emerged from below decks or remained in the rigging. The next few minutes featured a slaughter by Xana's soldiers such as had never been recorded in the land's history. Survivors began surrendering, begging for quarter.

But the butchery had not ended. Xana's archers showed no mercy. The captives were lined up before execution squads, who killed the entire line in an instant with their arrows. Within an hour, an attacking force of more than five thousand had been annihilated to the last man. Thirty enemy ships had been captured, undamaged, to be added to Xana's navy.

For many of the surrendering enemy soldiers, their last moments of life were an interrogation, often rough. The wounded captain of King Ibris's royal flagship was taken to Admiral Alveria himself. He told his captor of King Ibris's arrogant final hours and ignominious death. Then he declared, "I am prepared to die. I have failed my king and my country. I implore you, allow my soldiers and sailors to return home. Like yours, they are only obeying orders. Disarm them and allow them one ship! Many in my country advised against this invasion. They urged our king to support our people's works to build our wealth, just as you have done in your country, instead of stealing it. Our failure will strengthen the hand of those who advised against this."

"Then you admit obeying a wrongful order, your act of cowardice," Admiral Alveria answered. "You deserve to die like a coward."

"I am not a coward. I am loyal to my king." Defiant, knowing he faced death, he challenged his captor. "And I suppose you disobey when your Queen Agatha gives a wrongful order?"

"Queen Agatha does not give wrongful orders," replied Admiral Alveria, who drew his sword to slay the enemy captain.

Nearly insensible as his life's blood ran out, the enemy captain croaked his final defiance. "I die as a hero and a martyr for my country!"

The execution of all prisoners may seem excessively harsh, particularly as Queen Agatha sought prevention above punishment. Admiral Alveria was surely one of the many military officers present on the balcony when Queen Agatha announced the imminent invasion. In that speech, she stated her determination to inflict so many casualties that the invaders would dare not return. When the troops assembled before boarding their ships, Queen Agatha's order was unambiguous: "Show no mercy." But the queen herself could not stand the sight of blood. She would have been useless had she been present at the battle.

Her duty was at home to maintain civilians' morale. It was Admiral Alveria's judgment alone how to interpret her order. He genuinely believed that Queen Agatha never issued wrongful orders. Whether Queen Agatha later regretted her words, or chided her admiral upon his return, is not known.

None of the people I talked to mentioned the following circumstance, but I find it noteworthy. Except for soldiers lost in battle, all the people who died directly or indirectly as a consequence of Queen Agatha's actions or orders were not citizens of Xana. These included the sorcerer Magi, Howell Granby, King Ibris, and his army. Of these only the execution of Howell Granby (who apparently arrived in Xana on a foreign ship at nearly the time Queen Agatha departed for Wan) was done by a specific order of the queen. Among her own people, Queen Agatha had abolished the death penalty.

After the slaughter at sea, the victorious Admiral Alveria penned his note to Queen Agatha. He attached it to a homing pigeon and released it to fly ashore.

On the voyage home, Xana's soldiers recovered as many of the costly steel-tipped arrows as they could. Before the enemy soldiers could be buried at sea, the arrows had to be removed from their corpses—a grisly task for the Xanans. Each blade had to be promptly scrubbed clean with oil to prevent rust. Admiral Alveria joined in this work, earning the lower ranks' respect by his example.

Two days later, an enemy soldier was found hiding in a ship's hold. Meekly, he tried to surrender, but instead he was stabbed through the heart.

It seems, however, that another enemy, a sailor who knew his ship, had hidden even more carefully. For four days, he went without food or water. When he sensed that the ship had been tied up at a dock, he waited until dark of night. He then stripped off his uniform, dived naked into the sea, and swam ashore. Finding some discarded clothes, he blended in with the populace.

This sailor had no quarrel with the people of Xana. He had never wanted to go to war anyway. Maintaining a low profile, he earned his room and board doing odd jobs. Even on his first day in Xana, he was impressed by how much happier and more prosperous the people were than those in his homeland. The entire city, he noticed, was kept beautifully clean. Queen Agatha, about whom nearly every conversation seemed to center, must be a far more capable ruler than King Ibris, he thought.

But he longed to return home to his beloved parents, who by now he presumed must believe him dead, along with the rest of the invaders. In a few months, the stranded sailor earned enough money to buy passage home. He returned to find his parents alive but more impoverished than ever, and his land now wrecked by civil war. Each of King Ibris's sons was vying for the throne.

It also seems that one of King Ibris's ships escaped. In the confusion of battle, its departure either went unnoticed, or was not reported to Admiral Alveria. Although stationed at the rear of the squadron, more than half the ship's complement, including both its ship's captain and the commander of its detachment of troops, were dead or dying from the barrage of arrows. But it was not boarded.

The army contingent's deputy commander said to the first mate, "They fight like devils. Their arrows of death go right through armor as if it were bare skin. We have been routed. It will be only a short time before we are all killed."

"Let us sail for home straightaway," the mate replied, "and at least save those of our men still alive."

It was from this ship's reduced company that King Ibris's subjects first learned of their king's death and the destruction of their invading force. The surviving deputy commander and first mate both told the tale of how the battle had been lost. Immediately thereafter, both were beheaded for desertion. The rest of the crew were spared, on the grounds that they had merely obeyed orders.

———

The homing pigeon's message from Admiral Alveria, still tightly rolled and tied, had been carried to the parliament chamber. Members were arriving, chattering nervously with each other, as the queen entered. "Her Majesty, Queen Agatha," Prince Olaf announced. All rose to bow.

If Queen Agatha feared what the message might contain, she dared not show it. As she walked toward the speaker's table where the message had been placed, she looked from one side of the silent chamber to the other and sensed her people's anxiety. Without hesitation, she picked up the note, quickly untied the string and unrolled the scrap of parchment.

Queen Agatha read the message aloud so that the assembled parliamentarians would learn the outcome of the battle as quickly as she. "Victory is ours!" she proclaimed. The members and visitors in the gallery all cheered. The queen raised her arms high and waved them back and forth, and her people fell silent. "This message comes from Gerd Alveria, commanding our forces." She read, "'The invaders have been annihilated to the last man. Twenty-five of ours are dead.'" Those watching from the chamber's front rows noticed her face turn red. Witnesses believed she felt both sadness for those lost and relief that the number had not been far greater, as most of Xana's people had feared. "'Forty-three have been badly wounded. We have taken thirty ships as prizes of war.'"

Before the ships had set sail, Queen Agatha had given Admiral Alveria another order. A sealed message was delivered to each ship's captain, to be opened only after the ships were at sea and secrecy was assured. Using the ship-to-ship signaling system, the names of soldiers and sailors killed and severely wounded would be sent to the flagship to be included by Admiral Alveria in his report of the battle's outcome.

"And now for the sorrow," Queen Agatha continued. She read the names of the twenty-five fallen and again her face flushed repeatedly. She continued, saying, "We will send couriers to their families, to assure them we all share their grief and honor their sons' supreme sacrifice. And now for the hope." She read the names of all the severely wounded. "We will send couriers to the families of the wounded; may the love of their mothers, wives, and sweethearts restore them to health and strength."

The parliament adjourned so the members could celebrate. As Queen Agatha and Prince Olaf were leaving the room, a courier met them to say, "A huge crowd is gathering in the square. They're frightened. They call out, 'Queen Agatha!' They want you to tell them news of the battle."

Agatha and Olaf slipped out of the parliament's rear entrance, hurried through back streets, and sequestered themselves inside the palace. Hardly anyone noticed their passage. *We should build a tunnel between parliament and the palace,* Agatha thought. Breathless from running, the royal couple sat on the first chairs they encountered inside the palace. The relief and exhilaration of victory had stirred their passions. They embraced and kissed, mouths lustfully open to each other. But after a few moments of this, Agatha drew back. She declared, "This is no time to sit and indulge ourselves. We must bring the good news to all our people!" A new thought crossed her mind. Agatha tied up Admiral Alveria's message, as if she had not yet opened it, as she hurried across the palace courtyard. Ascending to the balcony, she strode, message in hand, to the railing. She motioned to Olaf to stay behind, out of view. From the square below, the unceasing chant rang out: "Queen Agatha! Queen Agatha!"

The queen appeared alone. As the people caught sight of her, a hush quickly fell over the crowd. Agatha sensed her people's fear and anxiety. She also sensed how utterly they relied upon her leadership and strength in this time of crisis.

The suspense been long been building. Queen Agatha sought to relieve it as quickly as possible. She briefly held the sealed message aloft. Her people were unaware she had already read it. "The message from our commanding admiral," she announced, and quickly untied the string. By the time she left the parliament, she had memorized the message.

Looking directly into her people's faces, Queen Agatha announced, "Victory is ours. The invaders have been annihilated to the last man."

At the words "Victory is ours," a tumultuous cheering erupted. Hardly anyone heard the rest of the queen's words. Agatha waved her hands high over her head. This time, overwhelmed with joy, the people did not heed her usual call for silence. The queen never had the opportunity to read the rest of General Alveria's message above the public square. Unnoticed by the celebrants below, Queen Agatha beckoned a servant and directed him, "Place General Alveria's message in the foyer of the National Library. In the days and decades ahead, all our people can read of our great Victory at Sea." Thus the destruction of Mardon's army was thereafter described in public pronouncements and history books.

As the crowd celebrated, Queen Agatha noticed from high above, some turned rowdy. By this time, the queen's servants had now gathered behind her, ready for instructions.

Her first order was urgent. "Summon units from the elite guard into the square. Charge them with preventing destruction of property, both public and private." She added, "I must arrange an orderly celebration. Send couriers to assemble the palace musicians. Have them bring their instruments to the square as quickly as possible." Then she herself hurried from the balcony to the stage that faced the square.

Queen Agatha had directed the schools to teach the arts, including music and literature. All pupils were required to memorize several of Xana's most beloved patriotic songs and folk ballads. It is suggested that Queen Agatha herself had a fairly good singing voice. This generous education in music for everyone proved its value on this victory day. The queen directed the first musicians to arrive to play the nation's victory anthem. She herself led the singing. Other musicians joined the performance one by one as they arrived. At first, only the people who happened to be near the stage heard the queen begin to sing. But facing her people, she waved her arms vigorously in time with the music. More and more people noticed this and accepted her prompt to sing with her. The singing spread like a wave through the assembled multitudes. The victory anthem ended with a thunderous cheer. The queen then instructed the musicians to play several well-known tunes in succession. By now the celebration had become an orderly songfest. Those in the crowd who had been intoxicated with victory, and possibly other things, calmed down and joined in the music. After several songs, at first solemn and then more and more lively, the queen called for dance music. She and Prince Olaf had been trained since childhood in the art of the dance. They had honed their skills at the palace entertainments for visiting foreign dignitaries. Until now, Olaf had remained inconspicuous at one side of the stage, his usual practice when he was with his queen as she spoke to a large gathering. Agatha extended her arm, and he joined her. Together, they led the first dance, visible to all from the stage. At the queen's instructions, the musicians continued the dance music throughout the day and into evening twilight. And even before the darkness of night had fallen, the people celebrating had begun to feel the same passion that the queen and prince had felt earlier. Many of them began to do more than just dance.

After beginning the dancing, Queen Agatha and Prince Olaf quietly departed. It was now her duty to console the families of those who had died or suffered wounds.

The families of the dead had been escorted through the main gate into the palace courtyard, where Queen Agatha greeted them. "In this time of great pain, please do not despair. As you loved your departed, so have they loved you and our country. They willingly made their supreme sacrifice so you could preserve your life, dignity, and prosperity." Agatha could not hold back her own tears. The assembled mourners could feel how greatly she valued the lives of every one of her people. They knew her grief was as great as their own. "Their lives were not taken in vain," the queen said. "We will honor and remember their lives and their sacrifices forever. We open our hearts to comfort you."

Agatha had enlisted the land's most compassionate people. To them, she entrusted the bereaved families for consolation. With sympathetic ears to listen, the mourners could vent their anger and sorrow. This, the queen knew, would let their grief heal more quickly.

Queen Agatha now greeted the families of the wounded, who had gathered at the steps of parliament. "Be of hope and good cheer," she said to all. Face to face with each family, she said, "With your love, may they all recover. Be always by their side."

As darkness was falling, an anxious courier found Queen Agatha and reported, "Men and women are coupling on the public streets, some even in the city square, hundreds of them, maybe thousands!"

"Let them," replied the queen, who well remembered her first carnal congress with her prince. "What a wonderful way to celebrate. It's been a hard, exhausting day. Prince Olaf and I will do this, too, to calm ourselves."

"But surely you shall do this in the royal bedroom."

"Of course."

"Everything we've been taught says we are supposed to couple very privately."

"The loving couples," asserted the queen, "are too much wrapped up in each other to cause trouble to anyone else. When they're done, they'll be all worn out and will go straight home and to bed. Tomorrow, life returns to normal," and she raised her voice for her final words, "in our glorious land of Xana."

———

E arly in the morning twilight, four days later, the harbor watch spotted Queen Agatha's returning fleet while still miles out at sea. The huge size of the fleet amazed the sentinel. After sunrise on this bright, clear day, the fleet had come close enough for the watch to count fifty ships. Admiral Alveria's homing pigeon message about capturing thirty enemy ships had proved true. The queen and prince had plenty of time to reach the wharves and greet the returning soldiers and sailors, especially the wounded.

Queen Agatha had built many new wharves and piers to accommodate the huge increase in shipping that had followed her trade initiatives. A full mile of seashore was now built up, with enough docks for every ship in her expanded navy to tie up rather than cast anchor in the harbor. The crowds who gathered whenever their queen appeared in public spread out along this mile. Most of the soldiers assigned to defend the harbor were required to herd them back from the wharves. The queen and prince, together with the families of the wounded, were the only people admitted to the waterfront. From where they were held back, the onlookers could clearly see their queen consoling the families.

From her experience with the Border Wars, Queen Agatha had learned the importance of proper care for wounded soldiers. Though the medical arts in her time were simple, the queen had learned how to vastly improve the recovery prospects of the wounded.

Under former monarchs, severely wounded soldiers in Xana, as in most other lands, had usually been left to die in horrible agony. Queen Agatha's soldiers took the first opportunity to remove their wounded from the battlefield—or, at sea, to take them below deck. The first duty was to stop the bleeding as quickly as possible. The army and navy had established hospitals to care for the wounded and the sick. Queen Agatha had decreed three simple rules by which most would survive their wounds. The first was cleanliness, as she had also prescribed for the schools, city streets, and all her people's personal grooming. Her artisans had devised furnaces in which everything used to treat the wounded was heated above water's boiling point. Second, moderate exercise, such as could comfortably be performed given the extent of each man's wounds, was encouraged. The third, and most important, of the queen's tenets was that wives, sweethearts, and mothers stayed at their soldiers' sides to work the healing powers of love. The knowledge that, if wounded, they would get such excellent care greatly improved the morale of all fighting men as well as their courage and effectiveness in battle. Most of those who did suffer wounds would recover to serve their people again.

Queen Agatha enlisted the aid of the most sensitive people in her country to nurture soldiers who were permanently disabled. With their assistance these soldiers found handicrafts they both enjoyed and were able to perform despite their disabilities. Queen Agatha's government then provided the soldiers with free training, and they served their people with their new skills. This had also been the queen's humanitarian policy with disabled civilians. Before Agatha became queen most handicapped persons had been neglected and isolated. Providing the disabled with useful employment restored their sense of self-worth and integrated them back into society.

———

Before the fleet sailed, Queen Agatha had ordered Admiral Alveria to bring the wounded ashore immediately upon docking, ahead of all others, that they might sooner meet their families and be taken to a hospital for care. On each ship, a large placard was to be displayed, bearing the names of the badly wounded on board, so their families could find and greet them promptly.

The first ship to reach shore carried a placard bearing the name Manfred Niemann. As Queen Agatha approached the wharf, a beautiful blond-haired woman, slender and considerably taller than the queen, came to her side. "I'm Cara," she announced. "Manfred is my husband. I fear he may have lost an arm or a leg, or be crippled."

"I am sorry, I cannot promise that he has not," the queen replied. "I can promise that your love will heal him as fully as it is possible for him to heal. Can you give him your unconditional love, no matter how badly he is wounded?"

"Yes, yes, yes," Cara was quick to respond.

Manfred Niemann was carried off a ship on a litter and was greeted by both Queen Agatha and Cara as he came ashore. "Are you…" Cara started to ask, her voice trembling.

"I'm badly slashed up," Manfred said, as Cara gripped his hand. "But I'm still all in one piece, and I can move my arms and legs," as he promptly demonstrated. "David Sandry gave his life for me," he continued. "David had no wife and wanted me to return to my Cara. He held off three enemy soldiers long enough that others could reach me before he was killed."

To Cara, as to every wife or mother, Queen Agatha said, "Stay ever at his side. Your love will be his healing and will make him strong once again. We will give you food and a bed in the hospital, next to Manfred's. You will never have to leave him until you leave together when he is fully healed."

Manfred whispered to his wife, "Sweet Cara, as I lay on the ship, I had nothing to do but think about you and your sweet body. That often left me aroused." With a wink, he added, "That part of me still works fine."

Cara answered, "I'm so glad you are safe. Now that you are home with me, I will make your most cherished dream come true. Over and over and over again." Manfred's comrades lifted his litter and marched toward the hospital. Still gripping his hand tightly, Cara walked beside her husband. Queen Agatha smiled.

With the other soldiers' loved ones beside her, Agatha greeted every one of the severely wounded.

As the days passed, she made sure to visit each of them in the hospital every day until, one by one, each was discharged.

It is said that all of the forty-three wounded soldiers who had wives or sweethearts coupled with them in their beds, right in the hospital, within an hour of their arrival. It is also said, perhaps because of that physical loving, that every wounded soldier recovered.

Admiral Alveria had to sit impatiently for three hours before Queen Agatha was ready to receive his official report of the battle.

Eager as she was to confer with her general, her first sympathy was always with the humble people. Queen Agatha, who revered all life, shuddered at reports of bloodshed, even the enemy's.

After giving his report, Admiral Alveria identified Alan Turot as one of five junior officers to be commended for exceptional valor and leadership in the heat of combat. Queen Agatha herself decorated all of them. As she pinned the medal on Alan, she winked at him, and he winked back. Both shared the fond memory of the day she had inspired him to become a soldier.

The Victory at Sea was the last battle Alan Turot was to fight. And it was the last major battle Xana would fight in Queen Agatha's lifetime. She had established Xana's invincibility. After the horrifying end of King Ibris' attempted invasion, outsiders accepted the need to leave Agatha's beautiful land undisturbed.

As a member of the army's general staff, Alan Turot continued with emergency planning and army drills. Forty years, almost to the day, after Queen Agatha had promised him what a wonderful soldier he would become, she appointed him commanding general of Xana's army.

Chapter 8

Even at the age of four, Anya Mendez was already fulfilling wise Queen Agatha's pronouncement that she would have "achievement far beyond anything we can now imagine." In her first year of school, Charlotta took her younger sister into her care. In her second year, Charlotta was transferred to a different class, and Anya was on her own. Although she was always the youngest and smallest in her class, she also had the highest grades and was immensely popular. She made friends with everybody she met and joined in every event she could find. People often called her "whirlwind" because she was such a flurry of activity. Because all school children were required to learn a useful manual craft, Anya chose weaving and embroidery making. For all of her long life, she worked on her embroideries almost every minute that her hands were not otherwise engaged.

Always regarded in childhood as a very pretty girl with impeccable manners and immaculate clothing and grooming, Anya grew up to become a ravishingly beautiful and mature young woman. No matter with what clothing she covered her large, beautiful breasts, their shape was never concealed, to be admired—or ogled—by all. Hordes of men, enchanted by her enthusiasm and vigor as well as her beauty, sought romantic interludes with her. They held fantasies that she was as enthusiastic in her carnal activities as she was in every other aspect of her life. All the evidence suggests that Anya dressed as modestly as she did handsomely. She had just too many things to do to take time out for romance. She was a friend to all, but a lover to none.

———

Anya Mendez and her four older siblings were among the first two thousand of Xana's citizens to complete their ten years of school. Queen Agatha arranged a huge celebration for this auspicious event. The platform on which she had been crowned was assembled again in front of the palace's main gate. Enough of the stands from her coronation were set up to seat several thousand pupils, families, and friends, arranged in a horseshoe around the platform. As at her coronation, the weather was clear and warm. Soldiers of the queen's elite guard stood around the platform. The queen and Prince Olaf surprised everyone by emerging together from a modest side door. Hardly anyone noticed them until they were almost ready to ascend to the platform. The usual tremendous cheering arose, and Queen Agatha had to wave her arms over her head many times before the crowd gradually quieted down. Prince Olaf sat in a chair beside his queen.

She stood to address her large and attentive audience. "I congratulate all of you who have finished ten years of school with such great success. You now have both the privilege and the duty to participate in the affairs of Xana, to know the needs of all our people and work to satisfy their needs. You have learned so much about our culture and history. You have learned a useful trade that you will practice, and you will use it to increase both your personal wealth and the wealth of our country. You have learned how to conduct your business affairs honorably, never cheating another citizen and knowing how to prevent others from cheating you. Most important, you have mastered the fine art of critical thinking: how to examine evidence and pursue the truth by following wherever the evidence leads. You know there are dangers in wishful thinking, and that the struggle to see the world as it really is, rather than how you wish it to be, will be your lifelong personal challenge. Graduating from school is not the end of your education, only a certification that you have obtained the skills to keep learning throughout your lives. There is so much that you still do not know, ready and waiting for you to discover.

"Today is the beginning of a new age in which you, the educated citizens of our land, will govern Xana alongside your queen. I call for elections, thirty days from now, to our long-awaited parliament. You will select from among your own peers fifty educated people who understand your needs and will act upon them. I pledge complete openness of the crown's public affairs. I will seek the parliament's approval of all measures to tax and to spend money; on all matters of education; and on all trade agreements before they take effect. If, in your judgment, any of these measures are not proper, those you elect will have the power and the duty to recommend suitable amendments to the crown.

"We now put into action articles 12 through 18 of our Great Charter, which deal directly with parliament. I remind you first of all of Article 12. 'All people who have completed their educations have the privilege to seek election as members of parliament, and both the privilege and duty to vote for those candidates they believe can most effectively represent the well-being of the citizens of Xana.'"

One of the graduating pupils grumbled, "We all had to memorize Article 12 in school. What's so important that the queen is repeating it now?"

One of his classmates immediately rebuffed him. "This is so important—I'm glad we're being reminded."

Queen Agatha continued, "People who were educated in the reign of Queen Julia are included, as are members of the old aristocracy. Though they no longer have the right to acquire wealth by cheating their fellow citizens, they still deserve to have their legitimate interests represented."

Queen Agatha, followed by Prince Olaf, now descended from the platform to greet and congratulate individually the assembled graduates, families, and friends. So large was the audience that the queen and her prince needed several hours to speak with nearly all who attended. By all accounts, they did so with charm and enthusiasm.

Following the graduation ceremony, Anya's many friends and classmates persuaded her to stand for a seat in the first parliament. She won the election overwhelmingly and, at age fourteen, became the youngest person to serve in Xana's first parliament. Nobody younger would ever be elected in Xana's long history. Two of Pedro's other children, Andre and Charlotta, were also elected to that first parliament. Altogether, over many years, eight of Pedro's children were chosen by their peers to serve one or more terms, and all ten were loyal advisers to the queen. Each year, as more pupils completed their ten years of school, so increased the number of people eligible to vote and to serve in parliament.

Anya served off and on as a member of parliament for nearly eighty years. She became known there as "Embroidery Anya," because all through parliament meetings, and even on the many occasions in her later years when she served as the speaker, she worked on her embroideries. Traders from foreign lands desired them for their beauty and paid the high prices that she asked, and more wealth flowed into Xana.

———

Queen Agatha addressed the parliament's opening session. "We now put into operation Article 13 of our Great Charter. 'It shall be the duty of members of parliament to consider actions of the monarch, approve those that they believe will advance the welfare of all the citizens of Xana, or, alternatively, to amend or reject those they believe are not conducive to the citizens' best interests. In these discussions, members of parliament will engage in courteous and reasoned discourse with the monarch. If at any time members of parliament quarrel with each other and neglect the welfare of the citizens, the monarch may dissolve parliament and call for new elections. If the monarch, at his or her discretion, believes that the quarreling has become irreconcilable, he or she may also prohibit the entire membership of the dissolved parliament from ever again serving as its members.'

"In the next days, I will present several proposals for your reasoned consideration. They will deal specifically with hiring teachers and building schools; providing for the army and the navy; grants to craftsmen; building roads and public structures; agriculture; grants for artistic creation in literature, music, and art; appropriation of funds; and miscellaneous endeavors. The ministers in charge of the relevant offices will present them to you."

The first few ministers presented brief summaries. All invited questions, as their queen had requested, but members of parliament asked very few. On the day Hector Ramirez, as the chief financial officer of the realm, presented the budget, his presentation was minutely detailed, very different from all the others.

When Ramirez ascended to the speaker's platform, he began with a summary of the principal items, which included a surplus. The members listened eagerly, then soon realized they were being subjected to a line-by-line itemization. Ramirez' speech was tedious in the extreme, a recitation of page after page of obscure numbers, delivered in the dullest possible monotone.

Members of parliament had more and more difficulty paying attention. One man seated next to Anya Mendez expressed everyone's opinion when he complained, "He's a financial genius and a horrible speaker. Anya, you're on the queen's council. Perhaps you could tell me what he's saying."

Anya replied with her usual cheerful voice. "We all know how Queen Agatha travels all over the country listening to people explain their unmet needs. But she also learns about wasteful spending and duplication. She huddles many hours with Hector Ramirez and his staff to prepare a budget. As much as possible, we increase spending on these unmet needs. But it's even more important to balance the budget. Increased revenues from foreign trade have enabled us to increase spending every year. Any spending increases beyond this must be compensated by reductions elsewhere. We talk about all of this in council. I pay close attention to all the expressed unmet needs. We often debate their relative merits, and may make a few budget adjustments. I don't pay any attention to the numbers, however. I trust the competence of our Master of the Treasury, and endorse the budget that we approved in council."

"Maybe there's too much openness," the man suggested.

Another member of parliament interrupted to ask about where the navy would obtain the timber, iron, ropes, and sails for a new warship that was being recommended.

"My staff in the treasury office is prepared to answer your question," Ramirez said. "Please visit them. I am sure Queen Agatha will not object, if you wish, that you in parliament defer a vote on the budget until the answers can be presented." Though dull in his speech, Hector Ramirez was courteous and helpful.

The questioner didn't bother to investigate the matter further. The parliament approved the budget the same day with no more questions.

At the next meeting of the queen's council, it is said, fourteen-year-old Anya Mendez herself reported, "Everybody in parliament admires Hector's ability at managing the treasury. But he's a terrible speaker. Nobody can understand what he's saying."

Anya's oldest brother, Andre, joined the queen's council in the same month he was elected to parliament. Asked why he had not joined with Anya years earlier, he had remarked, "My little sister's so eager about everything. Before I took on this awesome responsibility, I wanted to prepare myself by finishing my education first."

Andre continued, "I suggest that instead of the queen's ministers giving speeches to parliament, they should write reports and recommendations for us to read at our leisure."

The patriarch of the illustrious Mendez family, Pedro, still illiterate but wise to the ways of his country, suggested, "The members of parliament may be overwhelmed by all the reports that will come to them. I will suggest that each member should select one branch of the government's work, something the member finds interesting or important. It might be the schools, support for artisans, agriculture, the army, public works, and so forth. Each member should carefully study the reports of this one branch, discuss it with others who have the same interest, and make recommendations when the parliament meets next."

Queen Agatha responded, "As always, Pedro, your wisdom guides our country. Parliament in Xana represents all the people, not just the aristocracy as in some lands. We will modify our procedures in accord with our own experience."

———

The government of Xana had independently, centuries ahead of its adoption elsewhere, invented the system of legislative committees.

———

When Anya was twenty years old, a new member—also twenty years old, handsome, and elected from the hinterlands—attended his first day in parliament. Throughout the meeting both Anya and the young man kept exchanging glances across the crowded chamber. Anya felt a sort of glow—something she had never felt before—inside her.

Anya and the young man both gave attention to each other instead of the deliberations. One member after another added money to projects in their own neighborhoods, which added up to exceed the expected revenue. Anya also did not notice her brother Andre arise and rebuke parliament, "And where do we get the funding for these excesses?" When the final vote came, Anya voted in ignorance for the extravagant final proposal. She also failed to notice that her siblings Andre and Charlotta had both voted "No."

When parliament adjourned for the day, Anya and the stranger immediately sought each other out.

"Hello," he said, somewhat cautiously. "I'm Leon Levinsky, elected from the town of Joslin. That's on the frontier."

"I'm Anya Mendez. Welcome to parliament."

Leon wasted no time in describing his background. "My family has always been very poor. We worked hard but remained as poor as ever. Then a school was built in Joslin, and I had the great good fortune of being selected to attend; so many others were not. School opened a whole new world for me. It gave me the chance to escape from poverty. We can build more schools, but we just can't get enough teachers. I was elected on my promise to bring more teachers to Joslin."

Anya was about to tell Leon that he could become a teacher in Joslin, but then she had a selfish thought. She wanted him to stay in the capital. "You could become a teacher yourself, right here," she said. "Take the place of one of our local teachers, and still serve in parliament."

"What a wonderful idea!" Leon replied. "I'll do it."

Anya continued, "I know quite a few young women and men, many of them my own classmates, who are looking for a change of setting. I'll introduce you to some of them tomorrow. I'm sure we could find somebody who would go to Joslin to teach."

"We need not just one teacher in Joslin," Leon insisted, "but several more."

"Let's go out together and find them," Anya suggested with her usual enthusiasm. "Also, you should talk to the pupils in some tenth-year classes. Tell them what a nice place Joslin would be to start their teaching careers. You have the vitality."

"Is there something I could do in parliament, to get more money for schools in the frontier towns?"

"There's never as much money for teachers as Queen Agatha would like. She and our Master of the Treasury, Hector Ramirez, agree that we must balance our budget. Borrowing now means the people must carry an added burden in the future. There's endless bickering among members of parliament for how to spend the limited money at our disposal. Your best way to bring new teachers to Joslin is to talk to teachers here about all the excitement of going far away into the countryside. Queen Agatha says every teacher has the right to move to a new position, if there is a vacancy, before the start of the school year."

Shortly afterward, he continued, saying, "Anya, I feel something very wonderful about you. I feel as if we're both headed in the same direction…"

"To serve our gracious Queen Agatha," Anya finished the thought, "and to make her dream of education for every child come true."

"And we'll work together in parliament for our glorious queen."

211

And then they put aside talk of schools and parliament and the queen. They looked into each other's eyes.

Anya and Leon kissed. Anya had never before kissed a man; for her, this was entirely new. Leon, for his part, possessed some experience in pleasing a woman, having had a few brief affairs before leaving his distant home.

In the foyer of parliament, anyone could have watched the risqué show these two members put on. But in the spirit of the Great Charter's Article 7, they mostly looked away. Upon seeing the intensity of their kissing, one of the bystanders commented, "It looks like Embroidery Anya just met her fate."

It was already late afternoon, and Leon invited Anya to dine with him in a tavern whose cook was highly renowned. They talked for hours. Leon, like everyone else who had attended school in Xana, had been taught that a dignified three-year-old lady named Anya Mendez had crowned their blessed Queen Agatha. He remembered the "dignified three-year-old lady" phrase but, like most other people in the hinterlands, years earlier had forgotten her name. Only in the capital city did most people know that the famed three-year-old was Anya Mendez, now grown up to be stitcher of beautiful embroideries, a member of parliament, and one of Queen Agatha's closest advisers. Leon was amazed when he realized who he was with. "You are the person who crowned our queen?"

"Oh, yes. I've known Queen Agatha as far back as I can remember. She probably comes to our house more often than I go to the palace."

Leon was even more astounded. "I never knew you were royalty."

"I'm not royalty. My family was once as poor as yours. Thanks to our gracious Queen Agatha's trade missions, we now can sell abroad much of the glassware my father and brothers make, and many of my embroideries. We have become prosperous. We are blessed that our queen values our advice and counsel! We are doubly blessed that we can do so much to help her make our land happy and prosperous."

Leon and Anya found they had so much to share. Both wanted a large family with many children, like the one in which Anya had grown up. Leon was delighted to learn of the queen's vision firsthand, from one of her inner circle. Anya's exuberance made her queen's vision Leon's vision as well.

Early the next morning, Anya met Leon at his lodgings. Together they visited several schools. Leon was as enthusiastic as Anya as they spoke with teachers who had become bored with life in the city. They also talked to tenth-year pupils about the excitement of teaching in Joslin. Nearly forty people wanted to know more. Although many later declined the invitation, Leon did obtain several new teachers for Joslin, more than he could have done from his seat in the parliament hall.

Going from one school to the next, Anya and Leon showed growing affection for each other, walking hand in hand. When away from too many curious eyes, they would stop to kiss passionately, and to caress one another's bodies.

Anya and Leon attended the parliament's afternoon session, this time seated side by side. As the speaker called the house into session, Queen Agatha ascended to the platform. When she spoke, everybody listened. In a low voice, Anya confided to Leon, "Queen Agatha. Something special is about to happen. She doesn't come to parliament very often."

"I am greatly saddened," the queen said, "by the spending measure you approved yesterday. While all of the additions to spending are useful, our country would become indebted if we retained them all. Our future living circumstances will decline as our revenues must pay off the debt instead of improving the schools and the new building you have so eagerly endorsed. Many of you remember how you or your parents remained impoverished having to repay the moneylenders. Surely you are wise enough not to let this happen again, and this time to the whole country. I ask you please to reconsider the motion you passed yesterday."

Anya immediately arose and said, "I move we reconsider the spending bill passed yesterday."

Leon was still not sure of what he was voting on, but was hopelessly besotted with Anya and wished to support her. He was one of several members to second the motion. The queen listened to the discussion but did not need to speak again. Perhaps because all members knew the queen would remember who voted "No," parliament unanimously approved the queen's original spending proposal.

Dining together after adjournment, Leon asked Anya, "What, really, does parliament do? Do its members initiate any big or meaningful measures?"

Anya replied, "Parliament has the duty to approve, amend, or reject all the initiatives that Queen Agatha sends for our approval. But the queen makes her requests to parliament only after listening to each argument on her council. She takes care to heed the needs and wishes of every element in our society. In her wisdom, she finds middle ground that may at least partly satisfy diverse interests. Too often, the members try to get more for their own neighborhood, as we did yesterday." Anya blushed to say this, abashed at how careless she had been in her vote. "This often requires taking money from someone else. These quarrels get nowhere. In the end we usually approve the queen's original proposal with little dissent."

"So the real decisions are made by the queen's council before they ever reach parliament," Leon surmised. "Could you tell me about your debates in council?" Anya spent most of their dinner together telling Leon how Xana's real government, the queen and her councilors, worked.

After dinner, Leon took Anya to the little room he had rented upon arriving in the capital. They had been there for only a few minutes when Leon turned away to gaze briefly over the housetops from his tiny window. He turned back to see Anya, for the first time, naked in front of a man. With her legs spread wide and arms resting over her head, she invited him. "My sweet prince, come lie with me."

"I am not a prince," Leon stammered, even as his body responded to the sight. "I am a humble commoner who loves you very much."

"You are my handsome prince, just as Olaf is Queen Agatha's handsome prince. Come to me."

"Please let me explain," Anya had offered after their first coupling and shared orgasms. "'My sweet prince, come lie with me,' were Queen Agatha's first words to Prince Olaf. Though many people watched them couple and thus end the Bad Times, my father was one of the very few close enough to hear her invitation. I was there, too, but I was too young and too weak from starvation to remember. As each of us children grew mature enough to understand the act of love, and responsible enough not to tell anyone else, as my father demanded, he told us the whole story."

As the next day's dawn came through the window, Anya and Leon found themselves still naked together and instantly resumed their coupling. They spent their next four hours in each other's arms, their bodies mingled and their passion unabating.

Late in the morning, hunger rather than loss of passion finally drove them to the tavern. They visited more schools and attended another session of parliament. Throughout the session Anya and Leon held both of each other's hands, but on this day Anya paid close attention to the proceedings and made some comments in support of Queen Agatha's ideals. They gulped down their dinners so they could leap naked together into bed for another night of flaming passion.

At the end of this second night together, Leon begged, "Please marry me, Princess Anya."

"Yes!" Anya replied with a happy shout. "And we'll have Queen Agatha herself marry us."

"Our queen?" asked Leon, surprised.

"Surely. She presided when Andre, Susi, Martin, and Charlotta married."

Leon repeated their names. "Who are they?"

"My older brothers and sisters, in order of their ages."

After their first nights and days of passion, Anya took Leon to her home to meet her large family. Her father, Pedro, and older brothers, Andre and Martin, were all at the glass shop, but her mother, Betsy, gave Leon a warm welcome. Now nearly fifty years old, Betsy was still beautiful—tall and slim, her golden hair fashioned in lovely waves. She was the picture of stately elegance. Charlotta had her mother's golden tresses, but Anya had inherited jet-black hair from her now-graying father. It was so dark it had a blue sheen, enhanced by the blue of her eyes. Anya, always aware of the harmony of colors, often dressed in blue. Her younger siblings, Henri, Patrick, Lillian, Flora, and Jerome, all liked Leon from the instant they set eyes on him. After half an hour, Pedro came home from work while Andre and Martin went to their respective homes.

"Darling, I'm home," Pedro announced, and promptly disappeared.

"He went as fast as he came," sputtered an astonished Leon. "What happened?"

"Father always wants to clean up after working all day in the dirty glass shop," replied Anya. "Soon you'll be seeing him at his best."

Ten minutes later, he returned, clean, fresh, and neat. Pedro rushed to kiss his wife. Leon was amazed to see how intensely they kissed. Politely, he looked away. Soon Betsy started giggling merrily. Leon couldn't resist a quick glance, and he saw Pedro's hand stroking below her belly, while his other squeezed her bum! Betsy was obviously enjoying this love play immensely. Leon was shocked by such a display of intimacy in front of the whole family.

Anya noticed his expression, and nothing about her was the least bit timid. She whispered to Leon, "My parents have been kissing and caressing each other all over, in front of us children, as far back as I can remember. We grew up believing this is the normal thing for parents to do. When they retired to the privacy of their bedchamber to couple, they would explain, 'We are making you a new brother or sister.' From all the giggling and laughing, from both Mother and Father, that filtered into the hallway, we knew that making new babies was great sport. And we all learned, very young, the details of how they did it. We are blessed to have such loving parents. They taught us how to behave—to be kind and courteous, helpful to each other, and ready to work hard for anything worthwhile. What wonderful models they were for all of us children. Just as much as my parents love one another, I will be your loving wife."

At last, Anya was able to introduce Leon to her father.

A father's approval of the man who wishes to marry his daughter is a theme which seems to transcend all cultures. When Leon came before Pedro, he quickly sensed that this illiterate glassblower had a mind that could perceive one's true character as keenly as Queen Agatha did. Pedro asked the most penetrating questions Leon had ever heard.

"My daughter is not the first woman you ever possessed," he declared.

"How do you know?" Leon asked.

"I know," Pedro replied. "Since you've already done it, just be honest with me. What makes Anya very special?"

"Anya is smart, she's creative, uh, uh, and she does what she really likes, uh, and is good at, uh, uh, and at the same time she, uh, uses her talents to improve our country."

"Thank you for the compliments," Pedro responded. "But how is she special to you?"

"The other girls I've, uh, possessed, as you say it, were pretty. And pretty eager. If they hadn't been eager, too, I wouldn't have done it. But there's something a lot more about Anya…" Leon hesitated.

"Well, go on," Pedro insisted.

"How can I put it?" Leon hesitated again. He was desperately trying to organize his feelings for Anya into thoughts he could express to her father. "I simply enjoy so much being with her, doing things with her. Far more than with any other woman, or even man, I've ever known. What I shared with the other women I've consorted with seems now to be very shallow. I'll put it in our gracious queen's own words. Queen Agatha instructed all the schools to teach how men and women couple. She has required us to memorize the textbook's opening sentences: 'The best carnal experience comes with someone you admire, respect, and trust, whose friendship you would treasure even if his or her body were unavailable to you. When he or she offers his or her body completely to you, then the coupling is truly wonderful.' I remember also a few sentences later, 'Come together naked and in dim light where you can see every beautiful part of your beloved without noticing the flaws in all of us.'"

Leon hesitated, and Pedro immediately challenged him again. "I can tell you're a bright young man who learned his lessons well. But what does this have to do with *my* daughter?"

Leon considered this and answered. "Queen Agatha's first sentence in that portion of our lessons describes perfectly what I have shared and experienced with Anya. I admire, respect, and trust Anya. I value her friendship far more than anyone else I ever knew. She and I share so much! We both desire to make schooling and caring teachers available to every child in Xana. I want to be one of those teachers." Seeing that Pedro was listening carefully, Leon continued. "Parliament doesn't need to meet often or have long sessions. All the members have regular jobs, and I can too. I want to be a teacher, to give other children the great gift of education and critical thinking. This has so much inspired my life, and Anya's life. Rearing children is hard work, but it's also joyful, and I want to share with Anya the raising of *our* children. And…" Leon hesitated, "Anya knows from Queen Agatha's inner circle that the queen approves of carnal relations before marriage. She even endorses the practice so long as it is with the right person. Everybody in Xana knows her own coupling with Olaf rescued us all from the Bad Times. But she strongly dislikes married people coupling with others. Wife and husband are supposed to completely fulfill each other. Let me assure you, Anya and I do, together. And please ask your daughter if she agrees."

"She does," Pedro replied knowingly.

Leon had stammered through his answers, but was entirely honest. He understood, quite correctly, that Pedro would have instantly recognized and pounced upon the tiniest speck of deceit.

Finally Pedro said, "I bless your marriage to Anya. May your love endure through happiness and sorrow, work and play."

Pedro continued, "Like many other older adults, I have chosen to remain unlettered to make room in school for my own children, and others. From what they have learned in school, my children have taught me a great deal about history, literature, and natural philosophy. I strongly support schooling. It has delighted me that all ten of my children have earned top grades in school. I accept as an apprentice every pupil who chooses glassblowing as his manual trade. Tell me, Leon. What are your ambitions for teaching children?"

Leon answered eagerly. "I'd like to teach the first year. That is the best time to promote the joy of learning Anya and I share. I'm sure we can pass this to all my pupils, and to our own children as well."

By now, seventeen years had passed since Agatha ascended to the throne. In the capital, though not yet in the provinces, every child entered school at the age of five. Though unlettered, Pedro's many years of service on Queen Agatha's council had given him an understanding of Xana's affairs second only to Queen Agatha's.

Betsy, with Lillian and Flora helping, was ready to serve the meal, and invited Leon to join them at the dinner table. Leon was pleased at how freely he was able to talk to everyone in Anya's family. At the end of the meal he said, "Thank you for all the good food and especially for your marvelous hospitality. You've really made me feel at home."

Pedro then invited Leon to return. "As our soon-to-be son-in-law, please come to dinner at our home again tomorrow night."

Without telling either Anya or Leon, Pedro went to the palace the next day to tell the queen about the young couple's engagement. He was one of very few people who had the privilege of being able to talk to Queen Agatha inside the palace without a prior appointment.

Pedro entered the palace through the public entrance in one of the side doors and said, "I request an audience with Queen Agatha. I will need only a minute."

"Yes, Mr. Mendez," came the reply. "I believe she is reviewing the budget, but I may be mistaken. If she is in conference with Hector Ramirez, we can save you some time if I take you there."

The courier knocked on the door and found Queen Agatha, as expected, engrossed with Hector and his deputies. "Your majesty," the courier interrupted, "Pedro Mendez requests prompt audience. He says he will only need one minute."

"Please excuse me," replied the queen, who walked through the door to be greeted by Pedro.

"Anya is engaged to Leon Levinsky, with my approval. He is the right man for her, a newly elected parliamentarian from Joslin. He also has an ambition to become a first-year teacher. Leon is a wonderful partner for Anya. He appreciates her many talents and will support her in all that she does. Like Anya, he wants a large family and I perceive he will be a good father. We invite you to dinner tonight and hope you will also endorse their marriage."

"Thank you for your invitation," the queen answered. "Olaf and I are delighted to come." Queen Agatha then returned to her budget conference and Pedro to his glass shop.

That night, Andre and Martin came with their father to his house. After they all cleaned up, Andre and Martin also embraced and caressed their wives, Chloe and Isabella, with the same fervor as Pedro and Betsy, oblivious as to whether others were watching.

Suddenly one of the younger children cried out, "Agatha and Olaf are here!" They all rushed to surround the royal couple.

Though he had seen her addressing parliament, Leon had never before been face to face with Queen Agatha. He could hardly believe the informal setting for this royal visit. "The queen," he asked Anya, "is a member of your family?"

"She's like a member of our family. I told you before that she comes to our house more often than we go to the palace, even though most of us are on her council. There are so many other homes where she's like family, but she can't visit any of them as often as we'd all like. Tonight Agatha and Olaf are having dinner here in honor of our engagement."

Leon noticed something he thought odd. "Why did Henri, Patrick, and Jerome all rush to Prince Olaf and Lillian, Flora, and the little girl—" He quickly corrected himself, saying, "I mean, dignified young lady—who is she?—go to Queen Agatha?"

"That dignified young lady is Nomi, Andre's daughter. She's five years old and sharp and creative as can be. Olaf understands boys much better than girls. He loves Agatha so dearly after seventeen years of marriage that he's uncomfortable with any other woman. But to boys and young men, he's a superb model—and a charmer. He strongly supports schooling, exercise, courtesy, hunting, and horseback riding, all by his own example. He's an especially good exemplar of a husband—absolutely faithful, comforting, and skilled in the marital bed."

"How do you know he is skilled in the marital bed? Does Queen Agatha broadcast her intimacies?"

"Of course not," Anya replied. "But women know these things." She smiled broadly. "And you'll be my wonderful husband, just like Olaf is our gracious Queen Agatha's wonderful husband."

Little Nomi ran to Queen Agatha and lifted high her arms, begging to be picked up. "Oof," the queen said as she lifted the girl. "You're growing so big. Soon you will be too heavy for me to carry."

"But you will keep on playing with me?" Nomi asked, a touch of anxiety in her voice.

"Always," Agatha assured her. A minute later, Agatha lowered Nomi gently to the floor. Nomi clasped her arm around Agatha's waist, and Agatha put her hand on Nomi's shoulder. To Leon, some distance away, it looked as if Queen Agatha was giving undivided attention to Lillian, Flora, and Nomi, all at the same time.

Before consenting to marry a new couple, Queen Agatha always consulted alone with each partner. She wished to assess whether they were truly right for each other. If she sensed the seeds of future strife and possible divorce, she declined to marry them. It is said that so perceptive was Queen Agatha of human character, that every couple she married remained happy together for the rest of their lives.

Leon was so frightened at having to confess everything to his queen that he was almost in tears. Understanding the necessity of being absolutely truthful, he confessed, "I've had several love affairs."

"I sympathize," Queen Agatha consoled him. "All young men crave the pleasures of the body, but too often, their first experience is with the wrong woman. And it is less satisfying than they imagined." Her sweet reply lifted a great burden from Leon.

"That happened to me," Leon continued. "But with Anya, our union was more wonderful than I could have dreamed. We share everything. I love her; I want to help her raise our children, and I wish to work with her. We can bring schooling to everybody, and make it inspiring, too. I also want to become a schoolteacher right here, in the capital, while I serve in parliament."

"I'm sure you can do all of these and more," the queen replied. She then asked a question he had not expected. "If you look ahead thirty years, how would you envision your life with Anya at that far future date?"

"May I take a minute to think about it?"

"Of course." Leon marveled at how the queen was putting him at ease.

Leon answered slowly and carefully, with pauses between sentences. "I think I'll still be teaching school—first-year pupils, I hope. We want a big family like Anya's, and our children should be mostly grown up by that time. But I'm not sure about serving in parliament. I probably won't seek another term. Anya is very interested in government, and I believe she will become a leader both in parliament and on your council of advisers. You are very fortunate to have at your service a person both so talented and devoted to your ideals. I truly believe she will become one of Xana's leading citizens. For my part, I promise to support her in all her many activities."

To Anya, the queen said, "You have always shown enthusiasm and vitality. This is rare indeed. I now sense in you an excitement that goes beyond even what I have seen before."

Fervently, Anya answered, "I know that Leon is the right man for me. He will be a wonderful partner for life. We talk so well together about every subject. It is so exciting just to be with him. I've seen how good he is with children. He will be a wonderful father for our children. I just know it. Please marry us. I promise you will be glad you did."

Around the dinner table, Prince Olaf sat with Henri, Patrick, and Jerome, charming them with exciting stories of real adventures. Some of the table talk was about family. Leon, knowing that most of these people would soon become his family, paid rapt attention. But Queen Agatha, Pedro, Andre, Charlotta, and Anya also spoke of sensitive state affairs, especially assessments of people being considered for important posts.

Leon said quietly to Anya, "I can see Queen Agatha trusts you and your father, uh, your whole family, with delicate matters. I promise I will keep absolute confidence with anything I may overhear."

Anya replied, equally softly, "I know we can trust you, dear. We are blessed that our queen values our advice and counsel."

Queen Agatha said, "Elias has been working hard to make our farmers more productive by selective breeding. He has developed a superior line of seeds." This was the same Elias who, sixteen years earlier, had been required to surrender his wealth and start over with nothing. "May you one day regain your honor through service, humility, frugality, and generosity to your people," Agatha had said on that occasion.

"Elias is a greedy son of a bitch," Andre declared.

Anya spoke softly in Leon's ear, "My brother is perceptive of character and pure of heart, but he is impulsive and lacks diplomacy. At the next election, this will probably cost him his seat in parliament." Then, even more quietly, she whispered, "Elias *is* a greedy son of a bitch."

"I can't believe you used such rough language," Leon replied aloud, shocked. "You are such a model of feminine tact, grace, elegance, and beauty. Why, if Elias is this bad, is he given any consideration at all?"

Wise Queen Agatha responded calmly. "Elias is interested only in Elias, true enough. He has no compassion for anyone else. Yet he is also hard working, intelligent, and creative. He has perfected the art of breeding in ways to greatly increase crop yields and produce greater wealth for all our people. I will go to his farm with several of the farmers I trust best. We will learn from him how to grow these better seeds. I understand that Elias has built a fine, large house with the honorable fruits of his labor. And he will demand a large payment from everyone who uses his seeds and copies his methods. This payment will not happen. He is quite prosperous without this robbery. I will tell him to be generous to our people. He, who is as weak of will as he is of morals, will freely give the seeds and the methods to select for the benefit of everyone." All of this transpired as Queen Agatha had predicted.

Five days after they had first exchanged glances in parliament, Anya and Leon were married by Queen Agatha. After the usual vows, Queen Agatha pronounced, "I declare you wife and husband. And now, like all newlyweds in all lands and at all times who choose each other freely instead of having the marriage arranged by others, you are eager to go to your marital bed. Go then, with my blessing, and celebrate your love all night long with the union of your bodies." From this night and into old age, Anya and Leon lived happily together. The union of their bodies was wild and passionate, and though likely not all night long, certainly occurred every night.

Queen Agatha finished all her weddings with these words. She intended the newly married couple to go immediately to their marital bed. By royal command, they were not to wait impatiently and interminably through post-wedding ceremonies before consummating their marriage.

Anya took nearly twenty years away from parliament to give birth to eight children and raise them following her queen's vision. For most of the rest of her life, she combined membership in parliament with her status in Queen Agatha's inner circle of most trusted and capable advisers. In both roles, she always worked toward the wealth and prosperity of Xana's people. And all the while, she stitched some of the most beautiful embroideries in the land.

As the years and decades passed, Xana's many artisans made goods desired by traders from all over the world. This trade enriched their land, which steadily grew wealthy. All the people prospered and, as Queen Agatha had decreed, the wealth was shared by all.

———

Despite the frequency and intensity of her coupling with Olaf, Queen Agatha remained childless. At the age of forty, twenty years after she became queen, her fairy godmother visited her once again, for the last time in Agatha's life.

"With love, you have prevailed over the mighty sorcerer Magi, and with equal love, you have made the land of Xana the most prosperous in all the world and in all time. Do not bemoan beheading Howell Granby. He was as evil as Magi, though without Magi's strength. You have seen not one beheading in the land of Xana in all the succeeding years. Yours is indeed the land of both peace and prosperity. You are blessed as no other monarch in all of time, but not all can be yours. Forever childless you will be. Be not sad. Godmother you are to hundreds of children throughout the land, with some now grown into productive maturity. To each of these you are revered as a second mother. No other mother in the land of Xana can ever call hundreds of beautiful children her own.

"But do not cease taking delight in your prince, for coupling in the marriage bed is surely the most noble and pleasurable pastime that a wife and husband can ever share. Whatever fluids his body can make during the day, drain them completely each night, and then go to sleep in his arms so he will feel you are truly his queen.

"And every time Olaf passes his seed into you, a new life begins, not in your body, but in the body of one of your land's humble and virtuous ladies. All their children are your children. Go forth gladly."

Prince Olaf was at her side. "I seem to have heard a voice," he said, "but I could not understand what it said."

"She said," Agatha replied, "that every time our bodies join in love, we make a new life. This is not in my body, but in the body of one of our people. All the children in Xana are our children. Come lie with me, my prince! And with our love, let us renew our land."

Two meanings have been suggested for the fairy godmother's message. Which one is correct, only Agatha's fairy godmother knows. In a land of one million people, a pregnancy—that is, the start of a new life—occurs in the usual way every night, and there are many reasons in nature why a loving couple with a rich and fulfilling intimate life may not have children. If Queen Agatha had to bear children in the usual way, she could have had, at most, but one child each year, with pregnancy and delivery causing great stress to her body. But if, each night, a new life began in her body with the entrance of Olaf's seed and was magically transferred to the body of one of the queen's humble and honorable subjects, then all the children of the land could indeed have been the queen's children. Queen Agatha herself could enjoy all the pleasure of her marital bed, and of playing with adorable children by the thousands, with none of the pain of delivery.

———

It was first suggested by the common people, when Anya was fifty-three and Agatha seventy, that Anya succeed Agatha as queen of Xana. Queen Agatha was now fifty years into her reign and as active and alert as ever. Her people were industrious and hard working in all their tasks, whether at their manual crafts; tending their gardens, orchards, vineyards, and farms; or serving the state in every way. Anyone prone to laziness was shamed into working by their neighbors.

———

Queen Agatha kept her coronation promise to govern with the consent of parliament. She included on her council some of the wisest minds in the entire land of Xana, and the council carefully prepared every proposal the queen sent to parliament. Thus, the people lost interest in governing and setting state policy. They had acquired unquestioning faith that their wise and compassionate Queen Agatha would always do what was right for the people of Xana, her people. Parliament gave consent to all that Queen Agatha asked. All candidates for parliament pledged to support their queen. Candidates won or lost elections on the basis of their personality traits instead of any conflicting views about government policy. Every day, Agatha talked with the common people as well as members of parliament and her council of advisers. She understood and supported both their material and emotional needs and was always receptive to new ideas. It is suggested that she once said, "I do not claim exclusive wisdom, only the ability to find the best policies inspired by my people and put them to work for the welfare of all." The suggestion by the fifth-year pupil Michael Gant to set up a tutoring system for the schools is but one of many examples. Queen Agatha had an authoritarian streak. Pleased with all the wealth and happiness her policies had created for the common people, she probably was not aware of their creeping dependence upon her.

Agatha should be forgiven for being authoritarian. As a youthful princess, she already had her vision of prosperity for all of her people. The aristocrats on Queen Julia's council had prevented her from taking the bold steps required to achieve it. Only on a very small scale, with covert gifts to individual artisans, did Agatha circumvent their obstinacy. As a strong queen, she naturally resolved to let no one stand in her way. Despite being authoritarian, her compassion for the common people was genuine. As the decades went by, everyone in the land perceived that she had successfully achieved her vision.

The reader may note that there is no mention of religious authority anywhere in the culture of Xana. The people did believe in a higher power, in God. They also believed in an afterlife that they called the Great Unknown. Although unknown, the people had an almost unconscious faith that it was better than their current life. But there were no clerics, religious authorities, or formal religious services. Families and neighbors *introduced to children the concepts of God and the Great Unknown. These concepts they blended into their daily activities, and were comforted by them, without special times of ceremony or group prayer.*

From their vast library all the kings and queens of Xana knew that in much of the world even monarchs were forced to submit to the power of religious authorities. Thus were they ever watchful against such a challenge. When from time to time a charismatic preacher arose among the people of Xana, whether aristocrat or commoner, the monarch exiled him before he could gather a large following.

———

Farsighted people were concerned about Xana's future after Queen Agatha was gone. Because she was childless, there were no obvious heirs to the throne. In such circumstances, claimants appeared, but their claims were weak, and their ability to rule was recognized as even weaker. Attention was called to Embroidery Anya. Her leadership in parliament was respected. After Sylvia Hartly had retired from the queen's council to enjoy a peaceful old age with her husband, Anya was said to have become Queen Agatha's most trusted adviser.

The suggestion that Anya succeed her as Xana's queen was repeated from time to time for the rest of Agatha's life. After Anya's parents had both died, a member of parliament introduced a bill specifying that Queen Agatha adopt Anya as her daughter. That, by primogeniture, made her heiress to the throne. "In the greatest of the ancient empires that came before us," he declared, "the chronicles show that three of their greatest emperors in turn adopted their successors as their sons. And thus the empire had its golden age." Each of those ancient emperors had identified a worthy and talented successor. Left unspoken was the fact that the last of these had his own natural children, and the one who succeeded him was a monster. Anya herself had eight children, several of whom had risen to hold high government posts. Had the member who proposed this adoption scheme chosen to remember only those parts of history that he himself liked?

Anya reacted vehemently. "To require one person to adopt another violates at least four articles in our Great Charter. If we, so visibly to all our people, violate our most cherished institution, sixty years of our glorious queen's achievements will be wiped out in an instant."

The author of the motion quickly withdrew it, but parliament did pass, on a split ballot, a gentler motion. This asked Queen Agatha to consider adopting Anya Levinsky.

Through the years, Anya had frequent private consultations with Queen Agatha, in addition to her regular service on the council of advisers. After reporting parliament's action, she asked the queen, "What are your feelings about this suggestion?"

"And what is your opinion?" Queen Agatha countered. "If I express my thoughts, they will become yours. I need your unbiased view."

"None of my children is like that monstrous emperor of old," Anya replied. "My firstborn, Eduard, is pure of heart and intelligent. He is a capable adviser, but leadership would overwhelm him. Cornelia is impetuous; she rushes to decisions without considering all their consequences; she is a poor judge of character. She would appoint unworthy persons to high positions." Anya continued to assess her children. All were well-meaning, honorable people, but none of a caliber even approaching that of Queen Agatha. "I recommend that upon your passing, the monarchy be abolished, and that the land of Xana become a republic. Thereafter, parliament, elected by the people and guided by the Great Charter, should be our land's sole government."

"You are very wise," replied Queen Agatha, "and I agree with you." The queen then addressed parliament: "All the people of Xana are my children. How can I rightfully adopt any one of you as somehow above all the rest? I respectfully decline your invitation and ask you, as worthy members of parliament, to select your own future leaders. Let the Great Charter always be your guide."

People have wondered whether Queen Agatha, though still revered by all her people and with a mind as sharp as ever right up to her death, looked at age ninety as one might expect: a haggard, wrinkled, and infirm old woman. While it is unlikely that her fairy godmother preserved her youthful beauty all her life, it is equally unlikely that she would have allowed such infirmity to develop. What is more likely is that at the end of her life, Queen Agatha retained the distinguished elegance of a most handsome lady of sixty.

Queen Agatha reigned for seventy years—happy years for herself and all her people. One day, as she was again outside her palace, connecting with her people, her fairy godmother called her away.

The people of Xana mourned their beloved queen as no monarch ever before or afterward. A simple platform was constructed in the middle of the public square, using the same timbers that had carefully been saved from her coronation and her marriage ceremony. Her Prince Olaf had preceded her in death by five years. The closed coffin was placed at the center of the platform. In keeping with the people's mood, the sky was somber and gray, but not raining.

There, the speaker of parliament gave a short but stirring funeral eulogy. That speaker was Anya, who shared with her father, the humble glassblower Pedro Mendez, deep insight into human character. The same Anya had wisely guided Queen Agatha for many years. Now seventy-three years old, her youthful beauty had been transformed, as had Queen Agatha's, into a dignified elegance.

As Anya spoke, the tens of thousands of people crowded into the square listened with the same rapt attention as they had listened to Queen Agatha. "Parliament has passed a resolution, which needed no discussion, and that carried with unanimous vote. This decrees that we will continue forever all the laws and customs that our dear queen gave to us. On this site, seventy years ago, I placed the crown on our queen's head. It was the happiest day of my life. My parents, and Queen Agatha herself, took great pains to ensure that, despite my young age, I would never forget the day. I remember crowning our queen as well as if it had happened yesterday. I remember how I, like so many of you here today, excelled in school because Queen Agatha wanted me to. Today, the saddest day of my life, we give honor to Queen Agatha, whose wisdom, courage, and compassion have brought to all now present the happiness and prosperity we enjoy. She gave to us our sense of self-worth, dignity, and self-confidence that we could take control of our own lives and give them to the service of our people. She taught us, and we have learned, that each of us flourishes best when all the people of our land flourish together."

Someone in the crowd shouted, "Anya, be our queen!" Chanting began, which grew louder, "Queen Anya! Queen Anya!"

Anya raised her arms and swung them back and forth, as she had seen Queen Agatha do so many times. The people of Xana, accustomed to their queen's signal, fell silent. Anya then answered, "No,

I cannot be another Queen Agatha. Though she is no longer with us, Agatha is still our queen, and she always will be. Perhaps not, one hundred years from now, when all who remember her are gone…

"We all know what Queen Agatha would have us do: continue our service to the land of Xana. Let us overcome our grief, go forth, and fulfill her wishes. Remember that Queen Agatha never called herself childless. She declared many times, 'You are all my children.'" After making this statement, Anya broke down completely. She had to be led away, sobbing, by her husband.

Others also gave respectful eulogies, recalling events in which Queen Agatha's nurturing had inspired them to great achievement. Unfortunately, all those words have been lost with the passage of time. Only Anya's eulogy survives.

The coffin was placed in a carriage and, as at her wedding seventy years prior, horses drew the carriage to the palace gate. The horses, descendants many generations removed of those that had driven the same carriage at the royal wedding, could sense the pervasive sadness. With their heads held low, they plodded more than trotted. The gate opened ever so briefly, the carriage passed through, and it closed. Seventy years earlier, Agatha had returned the next day. This time, she would never return.

Anya made an extraordinary journey. From a desperately poor three-year-old girl who nearly starved to death during the Bad Times, her achievements built her esteem so high among the common people that they invited her, even begged her, to succeed the childless Agatha as Xana's queen. It is a tribute to her greatness that she declined the offer.

Queen Agatha herself had been a terrible administrator. Hers was a vision for her people and a gift that perhaps only her fairy godmother could have granted, a gift for inspiring people and swiftly reading their character. Among all the common and ordinary people, women and men alike—of whom Pedro and all his family were a few out of many—Agatha could select those with extraordinary talent who could administer the land most capably and build it in accordance with her vision.

They say that no one is irreplaceable, but there will never be another Agatha. Though she declined the throne, Anya Levinsky was repeatedly reelected to parliament by the people and then, by her fellow members, as speaker. For the last nineteen years of her life, Anya was the *de facto* ruler of the former monarchy, and now republic, of Xana. She understood that she lacked the charisma by which Queen Agatha had earned the unwavering devotion and loyalty of her people. If Anya became queen, she would have to endure endless opposition. By appealing to the revered Queen Agatha's mystique, repeating the phrase, "We all know what our wise Queen Agatha would have us do," many times every day, she kept Xana on the course her queen had set for the remaining nineteen years of her life. And so, for nineteen years after Agatha's death, the people of Xana enjoyed their unprecedented prosperity. At age ninety-two, Anya was still spry and alert and could pass as several decades younger. And then came the morning that the housekeeper found that Anya and her beloved Leon had died together in their sleep.

Some sources suggest that upon Anya's demise, her oldest niece, Nomi, was elected speaker of parliament. Unlike all of Anya's children, Nomi had talent as a leader. Already seventy-seven years old and in poor health when elected to the top post, she lived only another five years. Nomi was faithful to all of Queen Agatha's ideals but less effective than Anya at promoting them. Nomi was the last member of Pedro Mendez's family to attain a high position in government. His descendants returned to the obscurity from which Pedro had come.

Younger people not infused with Queen Agatha's ideals achieved positions of prominence. As the years went by, corruption began to creep back into the government. One hundred years after Agatha left the world, the speaker of parliament, who had achieved that post through bribery and bullying rather than ability, declared himself king. The quality of school instruction on critical thinking, that Agatha had emphasized, had declined, and the speaker deceived many people with a corrosive disinformation campaign. He also enlisted the support of the descendants of Queen Julia's aristocrats, whom Agatha had removed from government at the start of her reign, most of whom had for several generations lived in obscurity. His first act as monarch was to disband parliament. His second act was to systematically destroy all monuments to Agatha, public and private, and remove her name and works from the history books. And thus her name was erased from the written record. But the common people passed her story on by word of mouth from generation to generation, never to be forgotten. To this day the people of that land, which is no longer called Xana, are industrious and thrifty.

As the centuries passed, the memory of Agatha faded into legend. Did there really once exist a queen who, through generosity and charisma, reigned over the happiest land there ever was? Did she really go everywhere naked before her people? Any certain answers to these questions are forever lost in the mists of time.

Agatha surely wore no jewelry. In some versions of the legend, she wore a simple dress—immaculately clean and neat but with no decoration. As her people grew more prosperous, large numbers of them could afford costly fabrics, jewelry, and decorations. Perhaps she was called naked due to the complete absence of the extravagant finery one as wealthy as she was expected to wear.

On the other hand, she may have shown her disdain for the public display of wealth by wearing nothing but her skin. She would not have been considered an object of lustful desire by her people, but rather an artistic masterpiece come to life—the beauty of her body complementing her wisdom, kindness, and compassion. A wise man once said, "Any woman who is truly beautiful should wear no clothes at all." Agatha must surely have been the most beautiful woman who ever lived.

Throughout all of history and in all lands, good times alternate with bad times. Rarely does any dynasty have more than one or two great rulers before a mediocre or poor one advances by heredity to the throne and the prosperity is lost. With their superb knowledge of world history, Agatha and Anya both understood clearly that as a monarchy Xana would decline. The ancient city-states that experimented with democracy survived in some form until they were overwhelmed and their lands absorbed by imperial conquerors. Agatha probably believed that in a parliamentary republic leaders both capable and honorable would arise indefinitely from among the common people. In retrospect, we can see this also was not achievable. Though the people lost their economic prosperity, they remained thrifty and industrious. That they retained their prosperity of character is, I suggest, the real legacy of Queen Agatha.

About the Author

F red Pilcher is a retired college physics teacher who knows from experience with his pupils that through nurturing, nearly all young people can become productive citizens. His great sadness is that in American society and in many other countries millions of underprivileged children are denied this nurturing. Both the children and their countries are poorer for losing what they could otherwise produce. As a scientist, Fred understands that critical thinking and following where the evidence leads are the only reliable ways to understand the real world.

Away from the real world of hard evidence, Fred reads science fiction and fantasy. His favorite childhood movie was the Walt Disney 1950 cartoon, *Cinderella,* and he greatly admires women who are both strong and compassionate. Fred brings together all of these ingredients in this story of a princess who becomes a wise and inspired queen with a personal mission to achieve productivity, prosperity, and happiness for all of her people. Fred says "In describing her means to achieve her glorious dream, I have, through a series of adventures, presented numerous viewpoints of moral, educational, and political philosophy with which readers may agree or disagree. If these viewpoints stimulate vigorous discussion and argumentation, pro and con analysis, and the like, then this book will have achieved a useful place in the world of literature."